PRAISE FOR THE ANDY HAYES MYSTERY SERIES

Fourth Down and Out (2014)

"Reporter Welsh-Huggins's . . . debut, the first in a series, introduces Andy Hayes, a Columbus, Ohio, PI, and—for reasons explained late in the story—perhaps the most reviled former football player in Ohio State history. . . . The author's use of iconic Columbus landmarks and lots of Buckeye lore will appeal to OSU fans."

—*Publishers Weekly*

"Columbus resident Welsh-Huggins has his scene down pat, from government buildings to trendy coffee shops, and he makes good use of his familiarity, such as knowing the best abandoned quarry to dump a body into. Similar to how James Lee Burke treats Cajun country or Sue Grafton the California coast, Welsh-Huggins is out to make Columbus a character."

—*Foreword Reviews*

"*Fourth Down and Out* is a tall, frosty stein of Middle-American noir, backed with a healthy shot of wry."

—Bill Osinski, author of *Guilty by Popular Demand* and *Ungodly*

"Andy (Hayes) is an agreeable narrator with a dry wit and a bit of a martyr's complex. His dark past under center for the Buckeyes plays into the satisfying conclusion of this solid debut thriller from an AP legal-affairs reporter based in Columbus."

—*Booklist*

Slow Burn (2015)

"Even more gripping than his debut novel, this second installment firmly establishes Welsh-Huggins as a rising star in the genre. Expect a late—and rewarding—night of addictive reading."

—Jay Strafford, *Richmond Times-Dispatch*

"Andy gets a lot wrong before getting it right, but his dogged digging is fun to follow."

—*Publishers Weekly*

"Brisk pacing and a convoluted plot make *Slow Burn* a juicy, satisfying thriller as Andy follows multiple improbable but increasingly convincing leads . . . a rousing read that will gratify the most jaded of mystery fans, with added interest for those familiar with Columbus."

—*Foreword Reviews*

"Great fun to read. . . . Grade: A."

—Jane Durrell, Cincinnati *CityBeat*

Capitol Punishment (2016)

"Ohio politics provide the backdrop for Welsh-Huggins's nicely plotted third mystery featuring disgraced former OSU quarterback Andy Hayes (after 2015's *Slow Burn*). . . . Andy must navigate a minefield of powerful personalities with few inhibitions in a cautionary tale that's a perfect read in an election year."

—*Publishers Weekly*

"*Capitol Punishment* is an entertaining private eye novel. . . . Andy is a likable, cynical, at times humorous, and always witty protagonist with a penchant for trouble."

—*Mystery Scene*

"Hayes's beer isn't the sole heady brew in this fine example of political noir, for which aficionados of smart crime fiction will vote with enthusiasm."

—Jay Strafford, *Richmond Times-Dispatch*

The Hunt (2017)

"The author has crafted a fine procedural based on human trafficking, and it's a pleasure to watch his PI, Columbus, Ohio–based

Andy Hayes, go to work. . . . Welsh-Huggins has a way with language. . . . [He] is an Associated Press reporter, and the urge to bring the news is an unkillable one."

—*Booklist*

"Welsh-Huggins's strong fourth Andy Hayes mystery finds the Columbus, Ohio, PI still struggling with personal relationships but a bit more confident as an investigator. . . . Welsh-Huggins handles equally well the complex motivations of politicians, social workers, cops—those who are supposed to help victims—and of those who prey on them, such as pimps and johns. This series gets better with each book."

—*Publishers Weekly*

"Intelligently plotted, with prose as tight as a garrote, a strong stamp of place and a multidimensional gallery of characters, *The Hunt* excavates the filthy underworld of major cities. Call it Rust Belt noir. Call it a hybrid of whodunit and thriller. But above all, call it splendid—and this talented author's best yet."

—Jay Strafford, *Richmond Times–Dispatch*

"With *The Hunt*, Andrew Welsh-Huggins proves himself a master of heartland noir. Seldom, if ever, has the dark side of the Buckeye State been so honestly examined."

—William Kent Krueger, author of the
Cork O'Connor mystery series

The Third Brother (2018)

"[Welsh-Huggins] excels at storytelling. With a reporter's eye and a novelist's flair, he raises the bar with each entry in his series. And his deepening development of Andy adds gravitas. *The Third Brother* gives frightening and poignant voice to the scourges of bigotry, whether from jihadists, white supremacists, zealots of any stripe—and even people who silently assume the worst of those who differ in appearance or background."

—Jay Strafford, *Richmond Times-Dispatch*

"An anti-immigrant attack propels Welsh-Huggins's timely fifth mystery featuring Columbus, Ohio, PI Andy Hayes. . . . Welsh-Huggins educates and entertains as he explores immigrant issues through his empathetic hero's investigation."

—*Publishers Weekly*

"Ohio PI Andy 'Woody' Hayes has ex-wives to support, a penchant for rubbing people the wrong way, and with a sideways code of honor that makes him a knight in tinfoil armor. In other words, Andy Hayes is a lot of fun. Andrew Welsh-Huggins spins a tale of intrigue and a human warmth surprising for the genre. He's a writer on the rise."

—W. L. Ripley, author of *Storme Warning*

Fatal Judgment (2019)

Finalist for the 2020 Nero Award

"Intriguing. . . . Fans of Robert B. Parker's Jesse Stone books will be pleased."

—*Publishers Weekly*

"Readers who love old-fashioned detective novels will be in hog heaven as they tear into Welsh-Huggins's latest adventure featuring Andy Hayes."

—*Booklist*

"*Fatal Judgment*—like its predecessors—offers multiple rewards and further evidence of its author's prowess."

—*Free Lance-Star* (Fredericksburg, VA)

AN EMPTY GRAVE

ANDY HAYES MYSTERIES

by Andrew Welsh-Huggins

Fourth Down and Out

Slow Burn

Capitol Punishment

The Hunt

The Third Brother

Fatal Judgment

An Empty Grave

AN EMPTY GRAVE

AN ANDY HAYES MYSTERY

ANDREW WELSH-HUGGINS

SWALLOW PRESS
OHIO UNIVERSITY PRESS
ATHENS

Swallow Press
An imprint of Ohio University Press, Athens, Ohio 45701
ohioswallow.com

Printed in the United States of America

Swallow Press / Ohio University Press books are printed on acid-free paper ♾ ™

Library of Congress Cataloging-in-Publication Data
Names: Welsh-Huggins, Andrew, author.
Title: An empty grave : an Andy Hayes mystery / Andrew Welsh-Huggins.
Description: Athens, OH : Swallow Press, [2021] | Series: Andy Hayes mysteries
Identifiers: LCCN 2020048496 (print) | LCCN 2020048497 (ebook) | ISBN 9780804012324 (paperback ; acid-free paper) | ISBN 9780804041003 (pdf)
Subjects: GSAFD: Mystery fiction.
Classification: LCC PS3623.E4824 E47 2021 (print) | LCC PS3623.E4824 (ebook) | DDC 813/.6—dc23
LC record available at https://lccn.loc.gov/2020048496
LC ebook record available at https://lccn.loc.gov/2020048497

For Gillian Berchowitz,

the best coach Andy Hayes ever had

Now the rest of the ghosts, the dead and gone
came swarming up around me—deep in sorrow there,
each asking about the grief that touched him most.

—*The Odyssey*, Robert Fagles translation

1

"WHAT ABOUT MURDER?"

Even in the crowded restaurant, conversation at high Saturday-night boil, the question turned heads at more than a few tables. I gestured for the stranger to sit, but he shook his head and repeated the query. Joe and Mike, despite how accustomed they were to such interruptions, stared in fascination at the ungainly man looming over us like that relative at Thanksgiving you'll do anything to avoid but secretly can't stop glancing at to see what happens next. I sighed, aware of the attention we were attracting and realizing there was no easy way around our predicament.

"Murder?" I said.

"You heard me. Do you investigate it?"

"I usually leave that to the police."

"But what if they won't?"

"Won't what?"

"What if the police won't investigate a murder?"

"That's not been my experience."

"Then maybe you haven't been paying attention to what's really going on."

"Listen, we're running late, and I don't have time to talk right at the moment."

"So you're just like all the rest? You won't help me. Is that it?"

"I can't help you because I don't know what you're talking about. I also can't help the fact I'm running late. Now if you'll excuse me—"

"Fine," he said, squeezing himself into the booth beside Joe before I could object. "I'll start from the beginning. My dad was a cop, and someone killed him. And I need help finding the bastard who did it."

LET THE record show this whole sorry mess started because, as usual, I bit off more than I could chew.

I'd taken an early-afternoon surveillance gig to shore up my moribund bank account, even though I knew my schedule was tight. In my defense, the job should have been a cinch—trailing a furnace repairman who was claiming workers' comp for a bad back through Home Depot while he loaded multiple four-by-four timbers onto a cart. Instead, as usual, things got complicated. It turned out he was also having an affair—the lumber was destined for the deck he was building for his girlfriend—which meant extra tracking time. As a result, I was late picking up my sons from the houses of my respective ex-wives, as usual, and my plans for dinner at home as part of my custody weekend went out the window.

Plan B was a couple of large pepperonis around the corner at Plank's on South Parsons. We ate quickly because we had only thirty minutes before movie time—one of the Marvel films, the name of which I'd already forgotten. Something to do with avenging and justice. I was mapping out the fastest route to the theater in my head, Mike was complaining we were going to miss the previews, and Joe was fiddling with his phone when the man approached our table.

"You're Woody Hayes."

I looked up. Just what I needed. Another Ohio State football fan eager to berate me for ancient sins I'd spent half my life trying to atone for—not that I'm counting. He was heavy, balding, with thick black-framed glasses just short of factory-floor protective wear. Intensity glowing in his eyes. I thought about making a dash for it. But as often happens to me, there was no place to hide.

"Once upon a time. I go by Andy now. Was there something—"

"I've seen you on the news. You're a private eye."

"That's right. An investigator, technically."

I checked the time on my phone. Twenty-five minutes before showtime. At this point, maybe faster to forget surface streets and head straight for the highway. Cutting it close but still doable, especially if the previews started a minute or two late.

"What kinds of things do you investigate?"

Mike sighed loudly. Joe, despite the sullen mood he'd been in recently, looked on with interest.

"Missing persons, missing money, very rarely missing pets." I dug for my wallet and retrieved a card. "Maybe you could give me a call?"

And that's when he asked the question.

"What about murder?"

I GLANCED up the aisle and saw a woman at a far table staring at us. The man followed my gaze. "It's just my sister. She's not too thrilled I walked over here."

That was an understatement. To judge by her expression she couldn't have been more mortified had the man sauntered up to us in his birthday suit.

I nodded at her. "Your father. When did he die?"

A pause. "Last month."

"Around here?" I hadn't heard of any cops being killed recently.

"Yeah. But it took him forty years to die."

That was just enough to pique my curiosity.

"Keep going," I said, ignoring Mike's groan. "But make it fast. We're in a hurry, like I said."

Without invitation, he picked up a piece of our pizza and started talking. He said his name was Preston Campbell. He lived nearby, in the house where he and his sister grew up. His father was Howard Campbell, but everyone called him Howie.

A beat cop in the late seventies who worked a bunch of precincts but eventually settled for the University District up by Ohio State.

"Lot of guys didn't like that rotation because of everything happening on campus in those days. The hippies and the music and the protests and everything. He didn't mind it so much. Plus, back in those days the neighborhood was still intact. Lot of professors lived around there. But fall of '79, cops started seeing a bunch of burglaries. Not random, either. Professional. They figured it was a team, knew what they were doing. Had a system for watching places, checking out people's movements, striking when residents weren't home. Some professors got cleaned out. University raised a stink and the city put on extra patrols. My dad was assigned a swing shift, 8 p.m. to 4 a.m., to keep an eye on things."

"We don't have much time here," I said.

He continued as if he hadn't heard me. "So, this one night, him and his partner were coming back from a dinner break. They're making a pass, up by Indianola and Chittenden, when they see this van that hadn't been there earlier. They drive by, going slow, my dad at the wheel. His partner notices a man in the driver's seat who slumps down real low when he sees the cruiser. They keep going, pull over half a block up, and get out. They start walking back toward the van when his partner—guy named Fitzy—spots someone in a yard with something in his arms. They both take off running after him. That's when it happened."

"What?"

"Dad," Mike said.

"My dad goes around back, to the left, OK? Fitzy cuts right. My dad's checking out the rear door, which is partly open, when he hears Fitzy yelling. He runs around and sees Fitzy on the ground, unconscious, and some guy hightailing it. He starts chasing and the guy turns and shoots my dad, three times." Jab, jab, jab, went the piece of pizza in his hand. "He goes down, but still manages to get two shots off."

"He get the guy?"

"Oh yeah," Campbell said. "Now they're both down, both bleeding out. My dad calls out to Fitzy, he wakes up long enough to call it in, and that's the beginning of the end."

"What do you mean?"

"I mean my dad survived, but his days as a cop were over."

"What about Fitzy? And what about the guy who shot your dad?"

"Fitzy was fine—he was back at work the next day. The guy who shot my dad? That's the problem. He disappeared."

"Disappeared? Like, ran off? After being shot?"

Campbell shook his head. "After they arrested him. But before he could be prosecuted."

"That doesn't make any sense."

"Tell me about it."

"Dad. We've got like *fifteen* minutes."

"Hang on," I said.

"But this is the thing," Campbell continued. "I just found out he's still alive."

"The guy who shot your dad?"

He said yes emphatically, pizza-flecked spittle flying from his mouth.

"After all these years?"

"You heard me."

"Where?"

"That's the problem. I don't know."

Our server appeared and inquired how everything was. I nodded blankly. Mike asked for the check.

I said, "You know he's alive but you don't know where?"

"That's right. Which is why I need you to find him." He retrieved a lumpy wallet and pulled out what looked like several twenties. "I'm not a charity case. I can pay."

"*Dad!*" Mike said.

"Just hang on," I said, eyeing the money. "We've got time."

Except that we really didn't. And sure enough, we missed the previews. As usual.

AT TEN THE NEXT morning I pulled up in front of Campbell's house, a one-story brick bungalow two blocks off Parsons and very much looking its age, which had to be pushing the century mark. Both boys still asleep back home. A note on the kitchen table explaining breakfast options and reminding them to at least start their homework. A one-in-three chance they'd even be awake by the time I returned, but a guy can dream. It's how we fathers of the year roll.

Campbell opened up after my second knock and led me into the living room, which was dark and stuffy. The furniture inside looked old and the house smelled of something fried too long. His sister, the woman from Plank's the night before, rose from a chair as I entered.

"This is Monica. She wanted to be here."

"Monica Mathers," she said, shaking my hand with an odd formality.

"Pleased to meet you."

"Same," she said, though her curt response and body language, stiff and withdrawn, suggested otherwise. Her trim figure and newish-looking jeans, blouse, and sweater contrasted sharply with Campbell's heft and the thrift-store vibe of his clothes. Beauty and the Beast, siblings edition? Campbell reclined on a couch and gestured for me to sit in a second chair opposite Monica.

"Here's the file," he said, lifting a thick manila folder from the coffee table.

"File?"

"Everything that happened with my dad."

"Our dad," Monica said.

I took the file from Preston, opened it, and read the headline from the top document, a photocopied clip from the old *Columbus Citizen-Journal*.

CITY COP GRAVELY WOUNDED IN SHOOTOUT WITH BUCKEYE BURGLAR

"Buckeye Burglar?"

"Ebersole's trademark," Campbell said. "He left a freshly shucked buckeye in plain view in the houses he took down. Thought he was being cute, I guess. Somebody leaked it, and that's the nickname they gave him."

I turned back to the article. The Buckeye Burglar turned out to be one John J. Ebersole. The story noted that Ebersole had also been wounded, as Preston had explained the night before, but with few details. I skimmed through a couple more *C-J* and *Dispatch* articles and saw further references to Ebersole, whose injuries left him hospitalized, but nothing about charges.

"So what happened? Was he convicted?"

"No." Campbell shook his head angrily. "I told you, he wasn't even charged."

"Why not?"

"At first, too badly wounded, supposedly. I guess they figured he wasn't going anywhere. But then the next thing anyone knew, he just walked out of the hospital one day and disappeared."

"Left town?"

"As far as anybody knows."

"But how could that have happened?" Maybe things were looser in the Columbus justice system four decades earlier, but I had a hard time believing that even then a cop shooter could just slip through the cracks.

Campbell leaned forward. "I'll tell you what happened. They let him go on purpose."

"On purpose?"

"Preston," Monica said.

"He had something on somebody," Campbell continued. "He knew things he shouldn't have. That's the only way a guy beats what should have been a twenty-four-hour guard."

The room went still. Though the day was cool, Campbell was sweating and his fleshy face was florid, as if he'd been walking in the hot sun instead of sitting on a couch in a darkened room looking at old newspaper clippings. From her chair Monica stared sadly at her brother.

"Preston," she repeated.

"Something like what?" I said.

"That's the question, isn't it?"

"I suppose," I said, trying not to sound impatient. "Any ideas?"

"Preston," Monica said again, voice barely above a whisper. "The fire?"

"I don't know what he had," Campbell said, ignoring her. "That's your job—to find out."

"And if I can't? I mean, it was forty years ago. I'm guessing a lot of the people who were involved then are retired, or . . ."

"Or dead. Tell me about it. We'll get to that part in a minute. I didn't say it was going to be easy."

I did my best to avoid the manic gleam in Campbell's eyes as I considered the hour of sleep I'd given up to be here on time. The third cup of coffee I could have lingered over. The extra five minutes I could have spent chatting with the attractive woman walking her collie at Schiller Park, who'd stopped to exchange pleasantries as her dog and Hopalong sniffed each other's hindquarters.

"Listen, Preston—"

"He did it in Rochester too."

"I'm sorry?"

"Just walked out of jail."

Monica was slowly shaking her head, her eyes meeting mine as if silently begging me to stop before things got any worse.

"Rochester? Like Minnesota?"

"New York State. Up by Buffalo."

"OK. Why there?" I knew Rochester by reputation—and by one incident connected to my days with the Cleveland Browns that I'd rather not revisit—but had never been.

"It's where he was from, originally. At least according to the articles from when he was arrested."

"What happened there?"

"He got arrested on a theft charge. But there was no hold on him or anything, so he just disappeared again."

"In that case, how do you know about it?"

"I have a Google alert on him and it popped up one day. Just a little brief in the daily paper. I called everybody as soon as I saw it—cops, prosecutor, FBI."

"And?"

"Preston," Monica said. "You're wasting the man's time. Either you tell him or I will."

"Tell me what?"

"We can't be sure," Preston mumbled.

"Sure about what?"

Before Monica could respond, Preston took the folder from me, flipped the documents over, pulled out a single sheet of paper from the back, and handed it to me. It was an obituary clipped from the *Dispatch* for someone named Wayne Stratton. He'd died two weeks earlier, a few days before Labor Day. The black-and-white photo showed a guy in his thirties with a thin beard and a wide smile, wearing a JEGS ball cap and giving the camera a thumbs-up. Thirty-four when he passed, according to the obit. "Died suddenly," it said.

"And the connection here is—"

"There," Campbell said, jabbing the paper with a fat forefinger. "Under 'survivors.'"

I read down the list, which included a mother, father, stepfather, brother, and sister, two grandparents, and a great-uncle. I stopped when I saw the name. **John J. Ebersole.**

"You think that's the same person?"

"Who else could it be?"

"Wayne Stratton's great-uncle?"

"That's what it says."

"Possible it's another Ebersole?"

"Oh, for God's sake."

Monica. We both looked at her. She rose from her chair, yanked the file from her brother's hands, leafed through it, stopped, and handed me another piece of paper.

"There. Read that."

"What is it?"

"It's the thing my brother's afraid to tell you about."

"Which is?"

"Ebersole died in a fire forty-eight hours after he got out of jail in Rochester. He's not gone because he disappeared. He's gone because he's dead."

3

THE PAPER SHE HANDED me was a photocopy of a ten-year-old online article from the Rochester *Democrat & Chronicle*. Maybe six paragraphs. Headline:

MAN FOUND DEAD AFTER HOUSE FIRE

The briefest of details, with the cause of the blaze indeterminate, but the identification of the body clear. John J. Ebersole, recently released from the city jail. Before I could ask the obvious—how did they know it was the same person—Monica handed me another piece of paper. An article from the *Dispatch* ten days later.

NOTORIOUS BURGLAR DIES IN NEW YORK STATE FIRE

Mostly a rerun of the Rochester paper's story, but with confirmation from authorities on the Buckeye Burglar's demise, background on the Howie Campbell shooting, a brief statement of regret from Columbus police, and a no comment from Campbell himself. I replaced the articles on top of the file folder.

"Seems pretty definitive."

"Then how do you explain this?" Preston said, waving the obituary.

"Coincidence? It's not that common a name, but still."

"It's him—I know it is."

"Preston," Monica said. Exhausted sounding, like a patient coming to after a long surgery.

"Your sister has a point," I said as diplomatically as possible.

"She always has a point. But listen to this," he said, ignoring her frown. "After the funeral home refused to tell me anything, I found the address for this guy's widow. I went over there but no one answered. A neighbor told me they weren't around, but I didn't believe him. There was a car right there in the driveway. I left a note about Ebersole, but they never called me back. Why do you think that is, unless they're scared of something?"

I could think of a million reasons why someone peeking through the curtains at the sight of Preston Campbell on their doorstep might not call him back, but I kept my mouth shut.

"After that I didn't know what else to do. Then last night I saw you at Plank's and it was like a prayer had been answered."

His comment hung in the air as I sat back in my chair and pondered how to proceed. The name was an odd coincidence, but one thing I'd learned over the years was the difference between coincidences and connections is a lot bigger than most people think. Most of the times the reason things don't add up is because the math is wrong, pure and simple.

I said, "Your dad."

"What about him?"

"He died last month?"

"That's right."

"How, if I may ask?"

Preston and his sister exchanged glances.

"He ate his gun," Campbell said.

"I'm sorry."

"Our mom died two years ago, and he was all alone. Not a lot of friends. He had cancer. And he still had a lot of pain from his injuries, all these years later. And . . . he just never really got over what happened. You can say whatever you want"—this comment directed not at me but at Monica—"but it's all related. Ebersole didn't kill him that day. But he lit the fuse."

"That's what you meant when you said he was killed forty years ago."

Campbell nodded, suddenly unable to speak.

"And you want me to find Ebersole—if it's the same guy."

"Yes."

"Jesus Christ, Ebersole is dead," Monica interjected. "It's right there, black and white. He died in a fire. Why won't you just admit it?"

"Then what about the obituary?" Campbell said, nearly shouting.

"Who cares about that? It's another John Ebersole, like I've already told you a million times. There's got to be more than one. You're just clutching at straws. There's nothing there, Preston. Nothing."

I watched Campbell struggle with his emotions. His already short breath grew raspy.

I said, "Have you shown the obituary to the police?"

"Of course."

"And?"

"They said they'd check it out."

"Did they?"

"I'm not sure. They're not returning my calls."

"Which doesn't necessarily mean they didn't do it."

"Maybe. Or maybe they just blew it off because they're scared."

"Of what?"

He leaned forward, eyes now bright as a flu patient in the final throes of a fever. "Because of all the people who died."

"Preston," Monica said.

"Like who?"

"Ebersole's accomplices, for starters. One got knifed in prison. The other got run over by a car, hit and run. Then there's the detective in charge of the shooting that night—crushed by his own car while he was working in his garage." He shook his head. "Guy was an experienced mechanic. Like those people who discovered King Tut's tomb. They all died, one by one—"

"Preston," Monica interrupted. "We've been over this so many times."

"Prosecutor's office too—nobody's talking," Preston said, charging ahead. "They're all scared as rabbits. Won't touch it."

"Not returning your calls isn't the same thing as being scared," Monica said. "I told you last night, we shouldn't be bothering him with this stuff."

"He's not bothered. It's what you do, right? Take on cases like this?"

"In a manner of speaking." I try to avoid lost causes whenever possible, though I didn't say that aloud. Also left unspoken, my recent drought of billable hours, leading to messes like the day before, tailing the furnace repairman when I should have been picking up Joe and Mike with plenty of time before the movie.

"So, will you do it?"

I stalled for time. The fact that both the police and the prosecutor's office were apparently giving Campbell the cold shoulder was telling, since you had to believe they'd pursue new evidence in such a case, despite the passage of time. On top of that, Campbell bore all the conspiracy theorist hallmarks—a person bound to see shadows in the sunlight at high noon and glimpses of light at midnight in the darkest forest. Just because you believe a preposterous hypothesis doesn't mean you're not batshit crazy. During our conversation I'd peeked at his bookshelves, and along with volumes about Kennedy's assassination, they were crammed with doorstops about extraterrestrials and the great pyramids and the lost continent of Atlantis. Putting all that aside, I was also bothered by the more prosaic feeling—despite his display of money the night before—that to judge by his house and his living situation, Campbell might not be able to afford my fees, as reasonable as I thought they were.

As if reading my mind, he said, "Like I said, I can pay, no problem. I'll hire you for a full week. Do whatever you have to."

"Preston," Monica said. "You need to think about—"

"Whatever you need," he continued. "I just want some answers. I'm not stupid. I get this could be a wild-goose chase. But here's the thing. I've been looking for Ebersole for thirty years, ever since I was old enough to know exactly what happened. Maybe he did die in that fire. But just in case, I don't want to lose the opportunity. I want justice for my dad, that's all." He looked at Monica. "For **our** dad." He pulled out his wallet and fanned several bills on the coffee table in front of me. "So will you help me? Please?"

4

"MR. HAYES!"

I turned and saw Monica skip down the steps of her brother's house as I walked up the sidewalk to my Honda Odyssey, Preston's twenties in my wallet, where I'd placed them a few moments after agreeing, somewhat against my better judgment, to take the job.

"Call me Andy," I said when she caught up.

"I just wanted to explain about my brother."

"Explain? Or dump on?"

She stood on the sidewalk and folded her arms. Glared at the flash drive in my hand that Preston had given me, containing all the scanned documents from the file folder.

"You have to understand. What happened to our father—it was terrible, obviously. It changed everything. We were never the same again. But Preston took it especially hard. I loved my dad, but he idolized him. When he was little, Preston always talked about becoming a police officer, 'just like Daddy.' He'd sit up front in the cruiser and our dad would drive him around the block. Probably against the rules, but nobody cared back then."

"But?"

"That all changed, afterward. Dad wasn't ever a real effusive guy. But after he was shot, he sort of shut down for good. They put him on desk duty, once he was out of the hospital, but he hated it. Called it the 'rubber gun squad.' Eventually he retired on disability. He worked for a couple security companies after that, checking people in at offices, that kind of thing, but he kept quitting because he couldn't stand the fact he wasn't doing real police work. He was also hard on Preston. Yelled at him if he ever talked about being a cop. Told him it was the dumbest thing he could ever do. Preston took it hard and, well, developed problems. You've just seen the tip of the iceberg. His bathroom cabinet's like a mini-pharmacy—I've lost track of everything he's on."

"I get what you're saying, believe me."

"Do you? Because Preston finally got his meds evened out, and then when Dad died, he had a big setback. And now—"

"And now he's corralling a private eye he only knows from the news and asking him to check a name from an obituary in exchange for a big wad of cash he probably can't afford to give up."

She relaxed for the first time that morning. "That's about it. I tried to get him to leave it alone last night, when he saw you."

"What's your brother do when he's not, you know, looking for Ebersole?"

"IT—works for the state. Department of Mental Disabilities. Helps keep their computers running."

I tucked the flash drive into the inner pocket of my sport coat. "You're not thrilled about me taking this job."

"Honestly, I wish you wouldn't."

"I understand you wanting to look out for your brother. But putting the fire aside for a second, aren't you just a little bit curious about the obituary?"

"Of course I'm curious. But I also have to look at the bigger picture because I'm the grown-up in the situation now. And that means making sure Preston doesn't go around the bend again. Maybe I can't stop him from chasing his theories, but at least I can stop other people helping him do it."

"I understand—"

"I don't think you do. I'm asking you as nicely as I know how—drop it. Hand me my brother's money and I'll take it from here. It'll be ugly, but I can work it out. He'll understand, in the end. You can't see it, but he's on the top side of his cycle right now. Once he smooths out, he'll be OK."

I looked down the street at Campbell's house. Thought about the patchy trousers and loose-fitting sweatshirt he'd been wearing, and contrasted that with Monica, the pretty picture of normalcy, whatever that meant these days. She had a point, and a good one. A lot of people who hire me are wedged into the fault lines of society, stuck there through self-fashioned demons. Oftentimes they're paying me to shovel them out of their own shit. But even homemade monsters need slaying sometimes, no matter if the knight in question is a washed-up ballplayer too stupid, and too cheap, to say no.

"Your brother's obviously not firing on all cylinders."

"That's what I've been trying to tell you."

"And if John Smith shot your father and then died in a fire, I'd happily hand you your brother's money and go on my way. Because despite what people say about me, I'm not a greedy guy. But—"

"I never said—"

"But John Smith didn't shoot your father. John Ebersole did. Not exactly the world's most common name. And a shot cop's a shot cop, no matter when it happened. So this is what I'm going to do. I'm going to keep the money, but not spend it, while I make a couple inquiries. If, as I suspect, nothing comes of it, I'll take a skosh off the top for gas money and kibble and return the rest as is. If I find evidence Ebersole might still be around, we'll figure it out from there. Fair?"

Her face hardened as if reacting to a cold wind. She took a step closer, defiant, squeezing her hands into fists.

"That's your answer? You're going to take my crazy brother's money for a fool's errand?"

"Like I said, I'm going to help if I can. And drop it if not."

"Don't you get it? You're not helping. You're making everything so much worse."

"Monica—"

But it was too late. She pivoted and strode down the sidewalk back to her brother's house, shoulders strained as if in the grasp of invisible hands, leaving me alone and wondering once again if I'd even come close to doing the right thing.

5

GINA STRATTON, THE WIDOW of the man in the obituary, lived less than ten minutes away from Preston in a tired neighborhood of sixties-era one-story houses. I parked and was about to get out of my van when my phone pinged with a text.

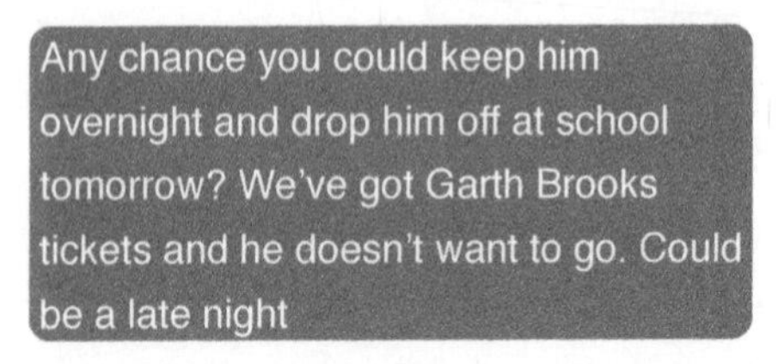

I clenched my teeth. Joe's mom. Crystal—Ex-Wife No. 2, if you're counting; girlfriend when I was still married to Ex-Wife No. 1, if I'm being honest about it.

What about Lyndsey?

She's staying at my sister's

So typical. First I'd heard of the concert. I texted back, explaining that Joe didn't have any of his school stuff. She asked if I might be able to run him up to collect it—she and Bob, her husband, Joe's stepdad, were in the middle of something. Of course they were.

Couldn't have told me this Friday when I picked him up?

Sorry!

I didn't respond. Crystal's suburban home wasn't all that far from where Mike lived with his mom and stepdad, and I had to drop him off anyway. It was just the principle of the thing. It also seemed a little odd Crystal didn't want Joe home alone, or joining his half-sister at their aunt's. He was fourteen, after all, and a mature kid at that. But there was just never any telling with Crystal and Bob. I texted Joe, explained the change in plans, said I wouldn't be much longer, got out, and approached Gina Stratton's door.

The woman who answered stared at me with suspicion in her eyes. She was maybe five feet, long gray hair tied back in a ponytail, wearing jeans and a faded brown button-down blouse.

"Gina?"

"She ain't here."

"Any idea when she'll be back?"

"Nope."

I showed her my private investigator's license, handed her my business card, and explained my reason for visiting. Closer up, I saw fatigue etched on a prematurely wrinkled face.

"I don't know this Ebersole guy."

"He was listed on—"

"On the obituary. I know. And I'm telling you the same thing I told the cops and the other guy. I don't know no John Ebersole."

"The police were here?"

"What I said." She scratched her left forearm and turned to look at something inside the house.

"When?"

"Few days ago."

"Do you remember who it was?"

"No idea. Said they were investigators."

"With Columbus police?"

She took a step back and made to close the door. "We done here?"

"Almost. What about Wayne Stratton? Did he live here?"

"On and off. Off, more recently."

"How'd he die, if I may ask?"

"Overdosed." Spoken without emotion, like a pronouncement of punishment.

"I'm sorry to hear that. He was your—?"

"He was nothing to me. Absolutely nothing."

"How about Ebersole?"

"I already told you, I don't know who that is."

"Was Gina the one who wrote the obituary?"

A sound in the house behind her. Someone moving around.

"I suppose."

"So she must have known him. Or known he was important to Wayne?"

A pause. "No idea. Now if you don't mind—"

"Hey."

A large man appeared in the doorframe behind the woman. Correction—a large man filled the doorframe. Mid-twenties maybe, tall and wide the way a freezer stood on end is tall and wide, with a shaved head and suspicious eyes narrow as slivers of flint.

"What's this about?"

I reintroduced myself and my mission.

"Beat it. We don't know anything about Ebersole. We've been through enough with Wayne already—we don't need more trouble."

"I understand that. Maybe I could just talk to Gina—"

He was out the door and in my face a second later. I stepped back, making room. "Easy now," I said. "I'm only—"

"You're only what?" He pushed me in the chest and I staggered backward; it was like a blow from a hydraulic press with size 14 sneakers.

"I'm only trying to get some answers."

"Answer this." He took another step forward and shoved me again, nearly felling me. I thought fleetingly of Monica's parting words outside Campbell's house. *You're making everything so much worse.* I took another step back and looked over his shoulder. The woman stood in the doorframe, all ninety-eight or so pounds of her, watching with the expression of a zoo visitor bored by a couple of Kodiaks wrestling in the sun. I looked at the young man, saw the pistons rising to deliver another blow to my chest, and backpedaled fast. I couldn't tell if the brightness in his flinty eyes was anger or sadness or psychic pain, and I didn't want to find out.

"Could you at least let Gina know I was hoping to talk to her?"

"Get the hell off our property," he said, planting himself in front of me.

Now there was no question: his eyes were bright with rage.

I tried a last time. "Somebody must know something about Ebersole, about why he was in that obituary."

"Nobody knows nothing." He stared at me for a full count of ten, flipped me off, and stumped back up the walk. I backed up, eyes on both of them, reached the street, gained safe harbor in my Odyssey, locked the doors, buckled up, and slowly drove off.

Another satisfied customer. Eat your heart out, Avon lady.

DRIVING UP SOUTH HIGH Street, I puzzled over my reception at Gina Stratton's house. The woman and the man—her son?—were obviously not fans of Wayne Stratton, which might be understandable given Stratton's fatal addiction. Many of my missing person cases in recent years involved tracking down people strung out on pain pills or heroin. When family members weren't distraught, they were pissed: at the thieving, the lying, the relapsing. Still, Mountain Man's reaction felt over the top, not to mention the real or feigned ignorance about anything to do with good ol' Great-Uncle John Ebersole. Could a visit from Preston Campbell and from a pair of detectives really have been all that taxing? And where exactly was Gina? Just not home at eleven o'clock on a Sunday morning? Or on extended leave? If so, why? And where?

As I pulled up outside my house my phone pinged with another message. I expected either Crystal or one of the boys. If only.

We still on for tonight? 6?

Oh shit, I thought. Could this day get any more complicated? In agreeing to keep Joe overnight, I'd blanked on my plans that evening. Dinner at the Refectory with Judge Laura Porter, followed by dessert—and not the confectionary type—back at her condo. Our normal practice, such as it was, involved brunch with benefits on Sunday mornings, usually the quietest time of the week for both of us, assuming I didn't have my boys. The rare night out a concession on the judge's part to the fact we hadn't seen each other in almost a month, thanks to several conflicts, most of them on me. Our irregular time together had begun to call our already unorthodox relationship into question. Were we dating? Friends with entitlements? Something in-between? Though Crystal bore the short-term blame for this latest screwup, it spoke to a deeper problem which I didn't want to admit to just then. Instead, knowing there was no way around it, I dialed Laura's number.

"Hi there," she said, sounding surprised. "Everything OK?"

"Not really."

I explained the reason for my call. Silence descended over the line.

"Really, Andy? We have reservations."

"I know. I'm sorry."

"Not that I'm counting, but this is the third time you've canceled this month."

"Not by choice, believe me."

"I wonder about that sometimes."

"Please don't. It's all coincidental, not that that makes it any better."

"No. It doesn't."

More silence. As I sat there weighing a response, the two Kevins strolled up the sidewalk, the pugs on leashes between them. Kevin M. spied me and waved. I nodded at my across-the-alley neighbors, mind elsewhere.

"As lame as this sounds," I said, "would a rain check until tomorrow night work?"

"Weeknights aren't great for me. As you know."

I knew. Laura often worked late in chambers, reviewing cases, and after that preferred a quiet evening and early bedtime. It's what made Sunday mornings work to begin with.

"Maybe next week, then—"

"But Mondays are the least bad of any day. Let's give it a try. But how about just takeout at my place? We can try a restaurant some other day."

"That would be great," I said, relieved. "What time?"

"Six o'clock. Sharp. And you're bringing dinner."

"I'll see you then. I'm really looking forward to it. I've got an interesting case to tell you about."

"Not as interesting as mine, I hope."

I flashed back to a patio overlooking Lake Erie. Gunfire. A scream . . .

"That would take some doing."

"Indeed. Enjoy your time with Joe."

I COULD tell right away something was wrong by the excessively hearty handshake and smile that Crystal's husband, Bob, bestowed on me when he answered the door of their McMansion on God's Little Quarter Acre later that afternoon. The faux-Tudor-Colonial-Mediterranean home sat at the rear of a cul-de-sac a mile or so north of Lewis Center, the tony address courtesy of Bob's successful plastic surgery practice. A tasteful autumn display of pumpkins and multicolored squash atop straw bales lined the walkway. Bundled cornstalks stood on either side of the heavy black door, which itself sported a fall wreath of red and yellow leaves and bright-red berries. I would have bet my lone pair of complimentary Browns tickets that Crystal hired out the whole setup.

"Thanks, guys. I really appreciate this," Crystal said, coming up behind her husband and touching Joe on the shoulder. He shrugged and pounded up the stairs to gather his things. I followed them into their den. The Bengals and Jets were on TV, the screen one of those you can practically see from space. Bob flopped down on the couch, casting a single nervous smile in my direction, before turning his attention to the game.

Crystal said, "Can I get you anything, Andy?" Without waiting for my response, she left the room and entered their kitchen, a gleaming expanse of brushed-aluminum appliances and a long marble-topped island.

"Water?"

"Too early for a beer?"

"Unfortunately, yes."

"For you, maybe," she said, helping herself to a Bud Light while pouring me a glass from the refrigerator door. "Listen." Her voice dropped to a whisper. "As long as you're here, there's something I need to talk to you about."

"OK," I said, immediately suspicious. The topics of most conversations with Crystal were like car crashes: you rarely saw them coming, and they almost always involved significant damage.

"Bob was wondering . . ."

"Yeah?"

She took a step closer. Her face was drawn and tired, and she was an appointment or two overdue at the hairdresser. Just as uncharacteristically, she'd gained more than a little weight recently, distancing her even further from her days as a red-hot looker so enticing I'd been willing to trash my short marriage with Kym in exchange for a few—OK, a lot of—rolls in the hay with her. Generally speaking, Crystal's well-being these days was of as much interest to me as the fortunes of the Michigan Wolverines, except in how it might affect Joe, and there was no question something was off.

She started over. "The thing is, Bob and Joe. They're . . . having some disagreements. The other day—"

"The other day what?"

She took a swig of her beer. "Bob says Joe took some money from his desk. In his office."

"What?"

"It's not that big a deal," she said hurriedly, deepening my suspicions. Crystal and money, whoever it belonged to, were parted with difficulty. "But Bob was wondering if maybe it was time to think about, you know, the custody arrangement. Giving Joe more time with you. Now that he's a teenager and all."

"Is that what tonight's about? The prelude to kicking our son out?"

"No, nothing like that. It's just that, you know, Joe's got his thing, which isn't exactly Bob's."

"What's that supposed to mean?"

"Well, like, sports. Joe doesn't seem that into them. And you know how Bob is."

"Joe runs cross-country, for Chrissake."

"You know what I mean. The *TV* sports. The ones people care about. You should know that better than anybody."

"Give me a break."

"Plus," Crystal continued, "Lyndsey's getting older, and maybe it's time—"

"Time for what?"

We both looked up as Joe entered the kitchen, duffel bag in his left hand. Slung over his right shoulder, a school backpack the size of something you'd take into the Rockies. He pushed a wing of brown hair out of his eyes and eyed us curiously.

"Time to go." I glanced at Crystal, who rewarded the look with a frown and another sip of beer. She trailed Joe and me through the kitchen and into the living room.

"See you, Bob," he said to his stepfather, and headed for the front door.

Interesting: normally Bob was "Dad," which never failed to drive me crazy.

"Have a good one," Bob said, dragging his eyes away from the TV. "Thanks, Andy. Good seeing you as always."

"Enjoy Garth Brooks. I hear his intonation is amazing."

"We will!" Bob said earnestly, as Crystal shut her eyes in dismay.

"What were you and Mom talking about?" Joe said as I fought my way out of their subdivision and its tangle of similarly named Courts and Drives and Boulevards. The Google map of the neighborhood looked like a plate of spaghetti thrown against a wall.

"Nothing. How're you feeling today?" I'd watched Joe run at Three Creeks Park the day before. He ran a personal best in a two-mile race, good enough to finish near the top of the bottom half of the pack.

"OK. I went for a little run this morning. Did Mom mention anything about me staying with you?"

I looked over at him. He was staring at me thoughtfully, brown eyes full and innocent.

"She said you and Bob were having some problems. Something about money, in his office?" I kept my voice as nonjudgmental as possible. I could hardly throw my own behavior as a teenager in either one of my sons' faces. My prowess on the football field and my mother's pull as my math teacher were all that kept me from permanent detention. "If you need money—"

"Mom told you about that?"

"She mentioned it."

"Anything else?"

"Like what?"

"Like nothing. I'm sorry I did that." His voice oddly detached as he looked out the window. "It won't happen again."

"That's good to hear. And really, if you need money—"

"I'm fine."

"More to the point, she said you and Bob weren't, you know, getting along?"

A long pause while civilizations rose in the Nile Valley, spread across the globe, and then fell a few thousand years later with the advent of social media.

Joe said, "It's not like I'm his kid. Not like Lyndsey."

I turned onto U.S. 23 and headed south. Carefully, I said, "I'm happy to consider it—you moving in, I mean. Unofficially, it's a possibility. Officially, I'm not sure the judge would go along with it."

"The judge?"

"In family court. He reads the headlines. He knows the situations I've gotten into recently. And you'd be so far from your friends."

"I wouldn't mind."

"I suppose we could give it a try. Sort of a trial basis. What's your mom think?"

"I think she wouldn't mind having me out of the house."

"I'm not sure that's really—"

"But she doesn't want to do anything to make you happy, either."

7

I SETTLED INTO A booth at Tim Horton's back up on 23 the next morning and opened my laptop. It was the crack of eight. Joe was safely ensconced at school. We'd spent what remained of yesterday walking Hopalong around Schiller Park, watching the Browns lose to Pittsburgh, and making spaghetti for dinner. While Joe did homework, I read a couple of chapters of *Tigerland* and then reviewed the case of Howard "Howie" Campbell at my kitchen table. I continued my research now.

Preston Campbell had done an admirable job amassing a file of articles and court documents about the shooting and about John Ebersole over the years. But what struck me both the night before and sipping coffee this morning was how thin the file really was.

Most of the articles dated from the first three days after the shooting. The most complete account came from the long-defunct *Citizen-Journal* two mornings after the November 1 incident.

OFFICER REMAINS IN SERIOUS CONDITION AFTER SHOOTING THAT ALSO WOUNDED ROBBERY SUSPECT

BY JEFF GRABMEIER

A Columbus police officer who helped apprehend the Buckeye Burglar remained hospitalized Wednesday with major injuries after a shootout that also wounded the alleged break-in artist, police said.

Patrol officer Howard Campbell was part of a special duty team investigating burglaries in the University District neighborhood north of campus when the shooting happened late Tuesday night, according to Police Chief Kenneth Oswald.

Campbell was shot in the abdomen, left arm and left thigh, and was in serious condition in Grant Hospital after undergoing surgery, Oswald said.

"Howie's a real fighter, and he's a real hero today, and we're hoping for the best," Oswald said outside police headquarters.

John J. Ebersole, 41, identified by the chief as the notorious Buckeye Burglar, was seriously wounded when Campbell returned fire, and was also hospitalized at Grant under police guard, according to the chief.

The chief said that after encountering Ebersole at the rear of the house at 624 E. Maynard Ave., Campbell shouted a command for the burglar to stop and raise his hands. Ebersole dropped a television in his arms, pulled out a .45 caliber revolver and began firing. Even though Campbell was hit and fell to the ground, he removed his own service weapon and shot the burglar, the chief said.

The owners of the house, James and Shirley Zimmerman, were not home at the time.

"We're very grateful to the police," Mr. Zimmerman told the *Citizen-Journal* Wednesday afternoon. "It looks like the burglars were in the process of cleaning us out when they were interrupted."

"Of course, we're very worried about the officer," Mrs. Zimmerman added.

The article went on to list the possible charges that Ebersole faced, including burglary, felonious assault, and attempted murder. The story also included a list of burglaries in the neighborhood that Ebersole and his gang were believed responsible for. It was an impressive rundown—an even dozen, according to police.

I read through the remaining follow-up stories, of which there were surprisingly few. An update on Campbell a week later, with the chief expressing relief that though still in the hospital and facing a long recovery, he was out of the woods for now. A similar update on Ebersole, with the burglar also expected to live, but with the timing of his prosecution uncertain. Another story two weeks later about Campbell's release from the hospital, including an awkwardly staged bedside photo of Campbell with his parents, his wife, and two children I realized after a second were Preston and Monica. Preston beamed as he looked at his hero father, while Monica stared straight into the camera, her face grim. A few weeks later, a couple more articles when the news broke that Ebersole had apparently left the hospital without permission, with Oswald expressing his outrage over the error and promising a full investigation. Next, the articles about Ebersole's death in the fire in Rochester ten years ago, and finally, copies of the Rochester fire department and medical examiner records of the death.

> Call time 2 a.m. Two-story wood-frame structure fully engulfed upon arrival. Cessation efforts hampered by freezing temperatures, recent snowfall and narrow street lined by cars. Badly burned body discovered on second floor, gender, age and race indeterminate because of extensive burns. Cause of fire undetermined at this time.

I scrolled over to the medical examiner's report, marveling at Preston's thoroughness in obtaining all these documents. Reading between the lines of the gruesome description—"leather consolidation," "presence of partly long splits," "pugilistic attitude resulting from shrinkage of tendons and muscles"—it was abundantly clear that Ebersole's body was burned beyond recognition. Fingerprint and dental matches were unavailable because of extensive damage to the body. In the end, Ebersole was identified as the victim solely on the basis of the driver's license found in the body's charred wallet and the fact the address corresponded with the one Ebersole gave upon his arrest a few days earlier. In other words, there was no way to tell, except why wouldn't it be him?

I reviewed the short obituary after Howard Campbell killed himself, with background on Ebersole and the 1979 shooting, and then turned to the items at the very end, scanned articles on the supposedly mysterious deaths that Preston flagged: Jerry Reade, the accomplice fatally shanked in the old Ohio State Pen shortly after he arrived in 1980; Harvey Heflin, the Columbus detective overseeing the pro forma investigation of Howard Campbell's shooting of Ebersole, killed in a freak accident in his garage shortly after the shooting; and the hit-skip that fatally injured the second Ebersole accomplice, Darrell Weidner, a decade ago. And that was about it. As conspiracy theories went, it was thin gruel indeed, in my opinion.

I sat back and weighed the information. The file and the clippings corroborated Preston's account of the shooting and its aftermath, and in their own veiled way provided a glimpse into a forgotten world—an old Columbus that seemed far removed from today's sprawling metropolis, where entire neighborhoods, including many around the University District, had been redeveloped and gentrified beyond recognition. The headlines and ads in the photocopies that Preston assembled spoke inevitably of a simpler, more transparent time. A lunchtime special at Marzetti's downtown. A new car dealership opening on the West Side. Workers added to shifts at Buckeye Steel on the South End. Events frozen in time forever, no more or less knowable now than museum artifacts glimpsed through glass. I lingered briefly over one headline, thinking of my two boys, headed so fast for adulthood: it involved a memorial vigil for a student at a local college who'd died in a freak fall. What memory did anyone have today of that tragedy?

And then there was Ebersole—or rather, there wasn't Ebersole, since he vanished from the file almost as completely as he vanished from the world before the fire. Was that kind of disappearing act really possible? And with that, I knew the time had come to see what the authorities Preston was so skeptical of really knew. I pulled out my phone and scrolled through the contacts for a number in the Columbus homicide division. He answered almost immediately.

"Stickdorn."

"It's Andy Hayes. Got a second?"

"Depends. I'm in the market for Michigan tickets. What are my prospects?"

"Nonexistent. Cockroaches with hemorrhoids are more popular with the university than me. And more likely to have tickets."

"A guy can dream. So what's up, Woody?"

There's a list shorter than confirmed cases of two-headed calves in Ohio of people allowed to call me by my former nickname, bestowed as a nod to Woody Hayes, the legendary Ohio State coach, when I was in my gridiron prime. Detective Bruce Stickdorn—"Dickstorm" to both friends and enemies, thanks to a string of marriages, affairs, and divorces that exceeded even my total—was not on it. I decided now was not the moment to remind him of that.

"I've got a question about Howie Campbell."

"Who?"

I gave him the short version of the story, from the 1979 shootout, to Ebersole's vanishing act, to the sighting in Rochester and the fatal fire, and finished with Howard Campbell's recent passing.

"Yeah, OK. I've heard of Campbell. What's your piece of the pie?"

I explained about Ebersole and the obituary and Preston's belief that his father's unindicted shooter was still alive. "I went to the house of the lady whose husband died, who supposedly wrote the obituary. Let's just say I've gotten more hospitable welcomes tailgating at Ohio Stadium. She said that in addition to Preston, a couple of investigators had come by to ask questions."

"She say who?"

"No. Like I said, our conversation was brief."

"This lady, she say anything to Campbell's son?"

"He couldn't get past the front door the day he came by."

"Not giving me much to work with here, Woody. The son really thinks the shooter is still alive?"

I confirmed it.

"Statute of limitations might be tricky either way. So, what's your question?"

"Preston, Campbell's son, doesn't think the division is going to treat it seriously, at least based on the fact that Ebersole was never indicted."

"That's on the prosecutor, not us, as you ought to know."

"No finger-pointing here. Just curious where this is on the division's radar. I'm 99 percent sure the guy died in a fire, but the name in the obituary got me thinking. I'm poking around, but I don't want to get in your way."

A belly laugh. "That'd be a first."

"I'm serious. Just looking for the lay of the land. I know things were a little different back then. But still—shoot a cop, win a get-out-of-jail-free card?"

"You're almost making sense, Woody. I'll make a couple calls."

"Thanks."

"Anything changes on the tickets, let me know. My girlfriend's a huge Buckeyes fan—gotta keep her happy, you know what I mean," Stickdorn said, and disconnected without bidding farewell. I knew from past experience that that was as close as he'd get to promising he'd be back in touch. I suspected he would. We both knew in this modern era that a suspect in custody for shooting a cop could no more disappear than receive comped tickets to the Policeman's Ball. The legal consequences would be as swift and profound as a barrage of cannon fire. And yet nothing close to that had happened to John J. Ebersole. The question was: Why not?

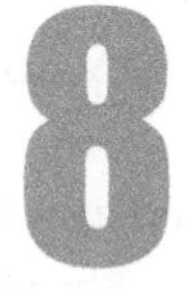

I CALLED PRESTON CAMPBELL'S cell phone, hoping to get more details about the day he dropped by Gina Stratton's house. He didn't pick up and I left a message, asking him to call. I finished my coffee, packed up my laptop, and headed back into Columbus. It was time to review the scene of the crime, such as it was.

The location of the decades-old shootout was a two-and-a-half-story stone pile on Maynard Avenue with a wide porch perched atop a scruffy, poorly tended yard. I sat in my van and compared it to the picture of the edifice the Zimmermans stood outside forty years ago, expressing their gratitude to a reporter for police saving their belongings and stopping the crime wave. Time had taken its toll on the house, the street, and the neighborhood as encroaching student rentals threatened longtime homeowners stubbornly digging in. At this point, the Zimmermans' old house was on the losing side. I wasn't sure what I hoped to accomplish by visiting the site, other than to orient myself to how everything played out that night. I was thinking of staying in the van to decide another course of action when movement in the window of the house caught my eye.

The young man who answered my knock a minute later was tall, thin, bearded, with a blond boy of about two perched on his hip. The kid could have been Joe's twin at that age, and with a pang I thought back to our conversation in the car the day before. *It's not like I'm his kid.*

"Can I help you?"

I produced my business card and handed it to him. I peered over his shoulder as he examined it. Cleaning buckets sat in a row in the hallway behind him, lining the edges of a painter's tarp covering the living room floor. At the end of the hallway a kitchen sink sat askew on the floor as if knocked there by a rare midwestern temblor. The smell of paint and spackle and bleach filled the air. I gave the young man a light-beer version of what I was working on and what brought me to the neighborhood. As I spoke, the boy squirmed in his arms. The man set him down and watched him toddle down the porch toward a pile of two-by-fours piled along the chipped stone railing.

"Careful, Zach." He looked at my card again. "This happened here? This shootout? Like, in the house?"

"Outside. In the rear, actually, according to the newspaper stories."

"Never heard of it. The cop died?"

"Not then. Just recently."

"I mean, you're welcome to look around. Probably not much evidence left—Zach," he said, cautioning the boy as he tried to pull a board free of the pile. "Outside, I mean. Inside's a mess, as you can see. We just moved in finally, and I'm pretty much gutting the place." He stood back a moment, gesturing, and despite the chaos it was hard not to notice the look of pride as he examined the house's interior. "Joel Benson, by the way." He stuck out his hand.

"Nice to meet you. Yeah, I agree, there can't be much. It might just help me understand what happened. I'll be quick."

"Take your time."

I walked down the porch and went around to the right. At the rear, a decent-sized patch of lawn stretched to a sagging wooden fence along an alley. The yard was in even worse shape than at the front. Grass close to calf-high in some places, with weeds sprouting higher. On the far side, a desiccated, out-of-control vine turned out to be the remains of a rose bush sprouting a couple of brick-red blooms. It was just possible, like an archeologist overseeing a dig site, to examine the weedy chaos and observe remnants of what once had been a pretty yard where flowers bloomed, children played, and dogs rolled in fresh-cut grass. How violated the Zimmermans must have felt, returning home that night to a carnival of squad cars and yellow police tape, their home ransacked. But yet how relieved, despite the shock of the events, that the neighborhood nightmare was over.

I walked back around to the front and called inside through the open door.

"Thanks," I said as Benson reappeared, a sanding block in his hand. "I really appreciate it. Good luck with all this. Looks like you've got a job on your hands. But I'm guessing it'll be great when you're finished."

"We hope so, whenever that is," he said with a smile. "And good luck with your case. I'm kind of glad you stopped by, honestly."

"Why's that?"

"Like I said, we never heard any of that stuff. Mrs. Zimmerman didn't say a thing about it."

"Sorry?" I said, not sure I'd heard correctly.

"Mrs. Zimmerman. The lady we bought the house from. She hadn't lived here in a while, as you can probably tell. Her son tried renting it, but . . ."

"Mrs. Zimmerman is still alive? She must be like—"

"Ninety-three a week ago. Oh, yeah. Alive and kicking. I e-mail her pictures of the work I'm doing every other day or so. She really enjoys them."

9

SHIRLEY ZIMMERMAN LIVED IN Thurber Glen, a twin-tower retirement center overlooking the banks of the Olentangy on the far north side of Clintonville, popular with retired Ohio State professors and their spouses, among others. It seemed a lucky break she was still around to interview, even though talking to her—like revisiting the scene of the crime—didn't make a lot of sense. She was a victim of Ebersole, after all, not a witness to his wrongdoing. While she might be curious to hear the full history of the case—just like her house's youthful new owner—she would hardly be in a position to know if the Buckeye Burglar was still around. But something told me to reach out to her, if only to establish another link to the past. Experience has taught me that the more anchors I pound into the sheer face of a mystery—the more rope lines I suspend from top to bottom—the more likely a route to answers may reveal itself.

I parked and made another call before I went in. I needed to pursue the not-so-subtle string Stickdorn had suggested, that the failure to press charges against Ebersole was on prosecutors, not police, who after all had done their job in apprehending him.

Reaching a homicide detective on the first call was one thing; reaching Gene Sprague, the county's elected prosecutor, was another. As expected, I had to leave a message with his secretary explaining the nature of my call. As expected, she paused as I gave my name, as if she'd spied a large bluebottle rubbing its forearms from its perch on the edge of her coffee cup. As expected, she promised not a return call, but "to let Mr. Sprague know you called." None of it surprised me. Sprague had threatened several times over the years to prosecute me. You could have filled a fifth-grade boy's valentine card with the love lost between us.

Thurber Glen's lobby was the usual senior-living combination of hotel lobby and funeral home parlor. An oak-paneled reception area sat off to the right. To the left, chairs and couches and lamps faced a fireplace where a gas flame the color of blue hospital gowns burned in an even, flickering band. A few residents, all women, sat in chairs or wheelchairs, reading, watching Drew Carey on *The Price Is Right*, or staring into space at sights, and memories, I could only guess at. At the sign-in desk I explained my mission to the woman at reception, calling myself an old friend of Mrs. Zimmerman while leaving out the whole private eye thing for now. There are times and places when identifying myself by profession has its uses, and times and places when it's as helpful as talking politics on a first date. I was instructed to wait in one of the unoccupied chairs before the fireplace.

I settled in, pulled out my phone, and checked my e-mail as I further pondered the idea of Joe coming to live with me. It would be a huge change for both of us, I knew. And talk about cramping my style—whatever it was—with Laura. I also wondered if I was missing something about the purported tension between Joe and Bob that Crystal raised. Could it have something to do with Joe's uncharacteristic moodiness the past few weeks? Something that Crystal was afraid to tell me about and just wanted to make go away?

"Do I know you?"

I looked up. The woman leaning on a cane before me was tiny, with short-cropped white hair, wearing blue pants and a beige pullover blouse and blue cardigan, with a wrinkle-lined face that nevertheless seemed more suited to a woman of seventy-three than ninety-plus. A pair of plastic-framed cheaters hung from a beaded lanyard around her neck, with an alert widget to press in case of emergency hanging below that. I wouldn't have minded one of those myself from time to time. I hastily shoved my phone into my pocket and stood up.

"I don't think so. I'm a friend of Joel Benson, the man who bought your house on Maynard?" A stretch, but I had to start someplace. "He told me you were living here. I wanted to introduce myself and ask you some questions, if I could."

"What kind of questions?" she said, suspicion clouding her eyes.

"Believe it or not, it has to do with something that happened a long time ago. The night your house was burglarized, and there was a shootout between police and—"

"Between police and John Ebersole. I remember, believe me. Only thing I blame the police for is not finishing the job that night. Would have served him right, and you can quote me. All right, whoever you are, if you know Joel, that's good enough for me. He's foolhardy, you ask me, moving in there the way things have changed, but I appreciate his initiative. Let's go to the library." She lowered her voice. "Too many ears around, with not enough to listen to."

The Thurber Glen library was empty except for a gaunt man, face dotted with liver spots, hunched in a wheelchair as he stared out the window. Maybe the same age as Ebersole had he survived the fire, and in about the same shape.

"OK there, Kenny?" Mrs. Zimmerman said.

Lips moved in response, but no sound. She patted him on the shoulder and moved to the far side of the room, where we settled into two upholstered chairs.

"You look familiar," Mrs. Zimmerman said. "Sure I don't know you?"

"Maybe you do." I pulled a business card from my wallet and handed it to her. Her eyes widened just a bit, as if examining an unexpectedly high restaurant check.

"A private investigator? Like on TV?"

"Just not as handsome. Or as smart."

That won a small smile. "What's all this about, then?"

"Well, I'm guessing you remember that Ebersole was never prosecuted. He just sort of disappeared." I reviewed Preston Campbell's belief that he was still around and explained the job I was doing for him. Trying to do.

"Oh yes. I remember how upset we were when that news broke. Ebersole really traumatized the neighborhood. Those burglaries were the beginning of the end, in Jim's opinion. Things weren't ever the same afterward."

"Jim, your husband?"

"That's right. He died ten years ago. Alzheimer's. Double killer." She peered across the room at the man in the wheelchair. "First your mind, then your body. It wasn't easy, the last couple of years, believe me."

I told her I understood. My grandfather, my father's father, had died of the disease. I worried about it in my dad, who occasionally struggled to find the right word, usually when arguing politics with me. I worried about it in myself, frankly, given the number of times that linebackers the size of the Hulk but with more muscles had bounced my head against Astroturf over the years.

"Your husband said that was the beginning of the end?"

"That's right," Mrs. Zimmerman said. "Ours was the thirteenth house Ebersole and his gang broke into. The whole neighborhood was on edge by then. The first few seemed random, since I don't think police found the buckeye he left every time. But people really took notice when they hit Gerhard's house. They just felt so bad, you know?"

"Gerhard? He was one of the victims?"

"Gerhard Schmidt. He lived three doors down. He was distraught, since that kind of thing was unheard of for him. Frankly, we were embarrassed. We felt like we had to apologize for our own country. You can imagine how hard that was for my husband—a Korean War vet and all."

"Schmidt—was he German?"

"*East* German," she corrected. "A visiting professor. Part of an exchange program of some kind. It was a big deal for him to be here, I remember that much."

"An East German professor at Ohio State? In 1979?"

"McCulloh College," she corrected. I nodded. The small liberal arts college on the northeast side of town was as far from Ohio State in demeanor and mission—not to mention the success of its tiny football squad—as you could get.

"I know what you're thinking, Mr. Hayes," Mrs. Zimmerman continued. "And we assumed it too, at first—Gerhard must have been a spy. Why wouldn't he be, with the way the world was then?"

"I didn't—"

"Don't deny it," she said, smiling. "I've told this story enough times to know what goes on in people's heads. Even Gerhard could laugh about it after a couple of glasses of wine. He used to joke that if he was a secret agent his government was in deep trouble, since he couldn't even spy on himself in a bathroom mirror. But deep down I know he was sensitive about it."

"And you said Ebersole broke into his house."

"Sadly, yes. About two weeks before us—before that awful night. Of course, he didn't have a lot of belongings, since he was only here on a twelve-month appointment. He rented the house from another faculty member who was off in the Amazon. Took his whole family—can you imagine?"

I told her I couldn't, and asked what was taken in the burglary.

"That's the funny thing. Nobody knew, as I recall, because Gerhard didn't even want it reported."

"What do you mean?"

"Gerhard wasn't home at the time. But a neighbor heard something, went outside, and saw a broken window in back. It stood out because it was a stained-glass block letter O—for the university. Do you know what I mean?"

"Of course." The octagonal representation of the O in Ohio State was omnipresent in Columbus. I'd been in more than one house where it was featured prominently on toilet seat covers.

"The neighbor didn't see Gerhard's car, got suspicious, and called police," Mrs. Zimmerman said. "It was natural, since we were all so nervous. Gerhard arrived home from campus shortly after. He was very upset to see the police when they got there, and at first blamed the neighbor for making a fuss over nothing."

"That seems an odd reaction."

"In hindsight I suppose it does. We assumed he was just scared, this being his first time in America. What a message to send to a visitor like that, especially from behind the Iron Curtain."

From down the hall came the sound of the TV, volume nearly all the way up. Farther off, the clink of dishes and silverware. Lunch setup underway. As I listened to the noises, something occurred to me.

"You said you were the thirteenth house broken into?"

"That's correct. The thirteenth and the last, thank goodness."

"The news stories all said twelve break-ins. You're sure it was thirteen? Is it possible one wasn't reported?"

Mrs. Zimmerman frowned. "I would doubt it. I mean, just for insurance purposes alone you needed the police report. Not to mention the fear we all felt."

"What about Schmidt? Could he have persuaded the police to drop the matter?"

"I don't think so, but to be honest I don't know. Like I said, he insisted it was nothing. But I do remember him talking to an officer who came."

I sat back. Was I was making too much of the discrepancy? Despite Mrs. Zimmerman's recollection of being the thirteenth and last break-in, it wasn't hard to believe that a rounding down had occurred in people's minds, that "about a dozen" break-ins became "a dozen" through natural shorthand.

"Is Mr. Schmidt still—are you in touch with him, by any chance?"

"I'm afraid not. He left not long afterward—cut his time here short. He was deeply affected by what happened, as far as we could tell, and we lost track of him after he was gone. I know he had a prestigious position back home that he was always worried about losing. It's quite possible he's dead. He was in his forties then and smoked like a chimney. All the Germans did." She peered at me, hands clasped in her lap. "I don't suppose any of this is much help?"

"Just the opposite. It gives me a picture of what it was like, when Ebersole was active. What it was like for all of you. How bold he was."

"You really think he's still alive?"

"I don't, to be honest. The evidence is pretty clear he died in a fire ten years ago. The only clue since then is a single reference to someone by the same name in an obituary, but no other context. No location or contact information or anything."

"So what are you doing?"

A fine question. "Double-checking things, I suppose." I thought back to the encounter at Gina Stratton's house, the deadeye I received from the woman at the threshold and the bum's rush from the freezer-sized man.

"I wish you luck." She studied her watch, a tiny, round clock face on a gold metal band. It hung loose on her thin, bony wrist. "If you'll excuse me, it's almost lunchtime." She paused hopefully. "Unless you'd care to join us?"

"I don't want to take up any more of your time," I said, trying to ignore the flicker of disappointment in her eyes. I glanced at the man in the wheelchair across the room; he'd been looking blankly at Mrs. Zimmerman while we talked, and now had dozed off. "But I'm hoping I could come back and visit again. If I have more questions."

"I'd enjoy that. The days get long here. Do you promise?"

"I do," I said.

10

BACK IN THE THURBER Glen parking lot I texted Preston Campbell a quick question:

12 Ebersole burglaries or 13?

I waited a few minutes, but no response. It was too soon to hear anything back from Bruce Stickdorn at Columbus homicide. There was no word from Gene Sprague, the prosecutor. I thought about reaching out to Laura, to see if she had thoughts on what it might take to persuade him to return my call, but dismissed the thought immediately. No point jeopardizing an already precarious situation, especially after last night's screwup and with the possibility of makeup sex on the horizon tonight. I was weighing my next move while regretting my decision to pass on Mrs. Zimmerman's lunch invitation when Twisted Sister's "We're Not Gonna Take It," my latest ringtone, signaled an incoming call.

"What's up?" I answered.

"God in her heaven, devil down below, shitstorm in between," Roy Roberts said. "Got a second?"

"One or two."

"Was wondering whether you were available this afternoon."

"Possibly. Why?"

"Theresa and I are doing a wellness check and I wouldn't mind some backup."

"I take it this involves more than Bible study?"

"You could surmise that."

Roy, an Episcopal priest, served a parish in Franklinton, a tough neighborhood just west of downtown. Theresa Sullivan, an outreach worker for the church, counseled prostitutes trying to break free of the life she'd once lived herself.

"I could probably squeeze you in, as long as I'm done by five or so. Got a hot date."

"Funny you should mention that."

"Why?"

"Tell you later. Meet me at three at the church. No need to come armed."

"Har har." Roy knew better than anyone that my long-ago plea bargain with the feds over my point-shaving arrest prevented me from carrying guns of any kind. Which mattered little because of Roy's own concealed carry permit. Not ordinary behavior for a minister, as far as I'd been able to tell, but for a former army chaplain, old habits died hard.

"Usual payment OK?" Roy said.

"As long as I'm finished by five."

"Hot date indeed."

"I just want to keep it that way," I said.

I SAT in my van for a few minutes, going back over my conversation with Mrs. Zimmerman. According to everything in Preston's files, the Buckeye Burglar struck "only" twelve times, and none of the articles that Preston compiled mentioned someone named Gerhard Schmidt. So, what to make of her story: the visiting professor standing outside his violated home talking to an officer? How much of that was accurate? Memory is a trickster, after all, dealing recollections like a card sharp, leading you to believe forthrightly in conversations that never happened, trips never taken, meals never consumed. I should know: who's better at selective remembrance than an aging ballplayer with a history of head injuries? Yet nothing in Mrs. Zimmerman's account rang false either, despite her age.

I thought about making a trip to the courthouse to look up the Ebersole indictment—surely that would list all the burglaries in order? Then I remembered the crux of the case. He hadn't been formally charged. No indictment existed. He'd been arrested and then through some fault in the system been allowed to disappear. Police reports and newspaper accounts constituted what passed for an official record. Pinning down the exact date of Schmidt's break-in wouldn't be that hard—assuming it actually happened—since Mrs. Zimmerman said it occurred about two weeks earlier than their own. But even if I ran that detail down, what should I expect to find that Preston Campbell hadn't, in his exhaustive search for the fate of Ebersole?

But of course, how could Campbell look for something he didn't know existed?

Frustrated, I tried the number again for Gene Sprague, the prosecutor, and hit a dead end once more. "He still has your previous message," the receptionist informed me in a frost-laden voice.

"Perhaps he could return it, in that case."

"Mr. Sprague is a busy man."

"It's an urgent matter."

"I'll let him know you called again."

I thanked her doubtfully, disconnected, and headed to the south end of downtown. When in doubt, feet to the street. There was more than one way to skin a prosecutor.

SPRAGUE'S OFFICE sat on the fourteenth floor of the Justice Center at High and Mound, a monument to the utility of poured concrete and lots of it. I parked around the corner, crossed the street, survived the wand-waving security gauntlet inside, rode the elevator up, and presented myself to the woman behind the counter in the front lobby. She examined my business card as if it had been used to spread bodily fluid samples on a forensic lab's microscope slide.

"Was Mr. Sprague expecting you?"

"We've been playing phone tag. I was in the neighborhood and decided to drop by."

"The neighborhood?" She raised an eyebrow.

"Had to pay a speeding ticket."

"That's muni court. An entirely different building."

"Sense of direction—one of my worst failings."

She shook her head. "One moment, please."

She made a call and informed someone of my intrusion. I fully expected Sprague's secretary, she of the frosty phone manners, to appear with a broom and whisk me away. But sometimes occupying space in waiting rooms, like using live bait over lures, is necessary to achieve results. To my surprise, when the door beside the receptionist opened, the person who emerged was Sprague himself.

I stood and extended a hand but he cut me off. "Office," he said, jerking his head as he held the door for me. We walked down a corridor of beige walls housing a series of small offices, half with doors open, half with doors closed, turned the corner, turned the corner again, and arrived at Sprague's inner sanctum. I stepped inside and took in an expansive view of the pretzel-like merging of Interstates 70 and 71 below us.

"Sit," he said, shutting the door and walking behind his desk.

I sat. It was hard not to follow orders from Sprague, who'd served in the marines between college and law school and still carried himself with the bearing of a military man, not to mention looking as fit and trim as if he'd stepped out of basic training yesterday. The county's first African American elected prosecutor, he exuded a sense of no nonsense the moment you entered his presence, which I tried to do as little as possible.

He said, "So what's your interest in John Ebersole?"

It took me a second to respond, so surprised was I that I'd won an audience. Recovering, I said, "The son of the cop he shot thinks he's still alive and wants him prosecuted."

"He died in a fire ten years ago."

"The son thinks differently."

"Preston Campbell? What proof does he have?"

I reached into my sport coat pocket, pulled out a photocopy of the obituary, and flattened it on Sprague's desk. He glanced at it without picking it up.

"A random name in a drug addict's obituary. Know how many John Ebersoles there are out there?"

"You know about the obituary?"

"At least 192. It's not Bill Jones, but it's not Dennis Kucinich, either. It's a relatively common name. It could be anybody."

"Ebersole lived on the South End. Just like Wayne Stratton."

"Who?"

"The drug addict in that obituary."

"Ebersole lived there forty years ago. You know how transient that area is now. Half the houses are rentals anymore."

"Since you know about the obituary, have you talked to Stratton's widow? Just in case? I mean, 192 names or not, the guy shot a cop and then disappeared."

"I'm not telling you what this office does or doesn't do. I'm just saying—"

"I tried," I interrupted.

"Tried what?"

"Talking to her. I received a rude welcome when I knocked on the door. I'm not talking a glare from a butler. It led me to believe that whoever lives there now is either worried or scared, particularly of strangers." I thought again of Preston's visit to the house, and what if anything he'd learned.

"So you didn't talk to the widow?"

Something in his voice caught my attention, but when I met his eyes his face was as inscrutable as a marine midsalute.

"I was informed she wasn't around."

"Too bad for you. And I'm supposed to be concerned that you received a rude welcome?"

"That would be sweet of you."

"Listen, Hayes—"

"Forget it. The only thing I'm interested in is what efforts this office may have made to run down a lead in an egregious cold case."

"Egregious?"

"Conspicuously bad, or flagrant—"

"I know what egregious means. I was just surprised to hear it coming out of your mouth. Why in the hell would I tell you anything about our involvement in a case?"

"Professional courtesy?"

"Good one. Join an accredited law enforcement agency and we'll talk. Oh, yeah, you can't—you're an ex-felon. In that case, I don't have anything to say to you." He leaned forward and straightened a pile of papers on his desk.

"You must have some interest if you know about the obituary, along with the fact there's 192 Ebersoles out there. And of course, there's the little matter of me sitting in your office after raising the subject. Everyone knows how full your dance card is."

Sprague's face tightened. "Seeing the name piqued our interest in between homicides and child-rape cases. That's all I can say."

"Really?"

He leaned forward. "Listen up. I've got kids on the East Side gunning each other down over Instagram posts. Dealers on the West Side handing out fentanyl like candy. Child abuse is through the roof, even in the suburbs. Had a guy spike his girlfriend's baby like a football last week—literally spike her—because she wouldn't stop crying. And this shit doesn't investigate itself. But despite all that, for your information we did take a look at Campbell's claim, because nobody likes the fact Ebersole skated. What I'm telling you is, we don't see enough **right now** to dedicate my already thin resources to a full-blown inquiry, especially given the fact he probably died in a fire anyway."

"Probably?"

"You know what I mean."

"Were those your investigators who stopped by the widow's house?"

"How did you—"

"The lady told me before I was sent packing. Look, that's fair, what you're saying about crime and resources." I didn't need a lecture to tell me how ugly things had gotten in parts of central Ohio. Two weeks ago I'd spent a day tracking a missing woman, a happily married new mom who vanished without a trace from her five-bedroom, two-and-a-half-bath home in suburban Westerville, only to turn up, stiff and cold, in a northside motel room with a needle in her arm. I got it.

I said, "Let me ask you one more thing and then I'll get out of your hair."

"One more thing like what?"

"It's probably nothing. But all the accounts I've seen, including Preston's file, say Ebersole and his gang were responsible for twelve burglaries."

"That's right, as far as I know."

"But supposedly there was a thirteenth break-in. A visiting professor from East Germany who rented a house on Maynard Ave. Taught at McCulloh College. There's no record of it, but one of his neighbors who's still around swears to it."

"Still around? He must be pretty old."

"She. Yes, she's ninety-three. But definitely all there."

"What's your point?"

"Assuming it did happen, the obvious question is whether he got some kind of special treatment. That it was, I don't know, not covered up. But handled differently."

Impatience crossed Sprague's face as if he were a teacher and I'd given the wrong answer to a long-division question. I caught him checking his watch.

"Handled differently how?"

"I don't know. Eastern Bloc professor gets broken into during a goodwill faculty exchange. Wouldn't have looked good, right? With the Cold War and everything?"

"There's not always a full report done when police show up, as you should know. There also could have been copycats, or people's imaginations running a little wild."

"Like he just **thought** a break-in happened?"

"You'd be surprised what goes through people's minds when they come home and see a lamp knocked over and the dog acting all innocent. And of course, there's always insurance fraud."

"Meaning?"

"We see it all the time with burglaries. A neighborhood gets hit and a bunch of reports come in. Meanwhile, one or two upstanding citizens see an opportunity and claim a missing TV or a laptop or diamond earrings worth a couple thousand that may or may not have existed in the first place."

"That's brazen."

"And too damn common," Sprague said. "Police report gets filed, the insurance company cuts a check, and presto chango, it's early Christmas for the Smiths."

"That would still require a report, though."

Sprague waved the objection away. "I'm just using that as an example. I'm not saying Schmidt did or didn't do something like that. I'm just saying things fall through the reporting cracks. Especially forty years ago. Maybe the papers got it wrong. Maybe paperwork got misfiled. What does it matter? We know Ebersole was the guy, and we know how it ended."

"Wait a second. You know about Schmidt?"

"What?"

"Gerhard Schmidt. You just said his name. Unsolicited," I added, perhaps inadvisably. But now I was curious.

"What about it?" Jaw set, as though he knew he'd screwed up but wasn't going to admit it.

"Just that he's a couple of layers down in this particular dig. I only stumbled on him by accident. Even more interesting, he didn't even want his own burglary reported. Which makes me wonder how much you really do know about this case. And about why Ebersole fell through the cracks."

Without speaking, Sprague moved a snow globe of Ohio Stadium from the left side of his desk to the right. He straightened a sheaf of papers. He moved the snow globe back across the desk. He said, "I know enough that we're done here."

"Are we?"

"Count on it, Hayes," Sprague said, rising from his desk and pointing at his door.

I WAS BOTH STARVING and a little pissed after I left Sprague's office, never a good combination for me. Something to do with several dates that ended the same way. I drove down West Broad and stopped by Tommy's for a burger to fill my stomach and kill time before meeting Roy for his afternoon expedition. I wasn't satisfied with what Sprague told me, especially after he revealed he knew about Gerhardt Schmidt, but what could I do? I saw his point about resources. The discrepancy involving the alleged break-in at Schmidt's home was puzzling, but it was hard to tell what it meant. It seemed more than plausible that an East German might be reluctant to interact with the police based on his experiences back home. Even if a report was filed, it was forty years ago, after all, in an era before the widespread use of computers in local policing, and it's conceivable it just fell through the cracks. As if to confirm all the confusion, I was no sooner seated than my phone buzzed with a text. Preston, returning my earlier query.

> Only a dozen burglaries.
> Believe me I know

So there you had it. Only twelve burglaries, yet Mrs. Zimmerman clearly recalled thirteen. Either way, the visiting professor was the weakest of three threads I had left to follow: that, the obituary, and the whereabouts of Gina Stratton. And "threads" was right: Were any of them, individually or even braided together, strong enough to justify any more time spent looking for Ebersole, assuming he was even alive at this point?

I was still turning everything over after leaving Tommy's and heading a few blocks over to Zion Episcopal Church. I skipped the bright red front door of the cottagey stone church and entered through a side door instead. I was headed to the office when I heard my name.

"Theresa," I said, turning around. "Where's the parson?"

"Nice to see you too, QB. Hey, I've got a good one. Want to hear it?"

"Not really."

Theresa Sullivan walked up to me and grinned. "Too bad. Know what a football player and a bottle of beer have in common?"

"I don't—"

"They're both empty from the neck up."

"You're in big trouble if I ever learn any social worker jokes. I hear we're taking a field trip?"

"Something like that."

"What's the deal?"

"The deal is we're late. Let's go." Roy, emerging from the office, dressed in black from head to toe as always, not counting his white dog collar. "By the way, we're taking your van."

"Do I look like an Uber driver?"

"Funnily enough, yes. Plus, more room to hide if the shit hits the fan."

We piled into my Odyssey and Roy gave me directions to an apartment complex off Sullivant.

"Can I get a sit-rep before the actual firefight breaks out?" I said, pulling into traffic.

"Theresa?" Roy said.

"Client of ours named Darlene Hunter," Theresa said. "Been off the streets and clean for six months or so. Working at McDonald's at the moment, but we're helping her look for something better."

"What about her?"

Theresa stared out the window at the same streets she'd sold herself on, once upon a time. She said, "She's missed a couple of appointments and she won't answer her phone. Something's going on, and we figured we might as well stop by."

"With me along for the ride."

"We didn't invite you for your looks, QB, that's for damn sure. Turn there."

I parked beside a green Dumpster outside a three-story red-brick apartment building. Plywood covered the windows of a couple units on the first and second floor. A child peered through another window, disappearing when I opened my door. Used needles and condoms lay beside cigarette butts in the parking lot. From inside a dog barked incessantly.

"Should I bring this?" I said, reaching for the Louisville Slugger I keep in the van in case of trouble, or in the event I'm finally called up to the majors.

"Let's rely on your sparkling personality for now," Roy said.

"Plus that bulge under your cassock?"

"Let's just say I'm happy to see you."

Darlene's unit was on the second floor. The stairwell on the way up reeked of urine, vomit, and fried food. A used diaper sat in a corner on the landing, and I was pretty sure a red stain on the wall wasn't an attempt at abstract art. As we arrived at the apartment, Roy stepped to the side and let Theresa knock on the door. She tried a second and then a third time. Finally, a male voice—deep and guttural—called out. "Who is it?"

"Looking for Darlene," Theresa said. "I'm a friend of hers."

"She ain't here."

"I told her I was coming."

"I said, she ain't here."

"What time will she be back?"

No answer. I stepped forward and whispered in Theresa's ear. She nodded.

Loudly, she said, "I've got her money. What am I supposed to do with it if she isn't here? I don't feel safe carrying this much around."

A long pause. A sound at the end of the hall distracted me. I looked over at something gray with a long tail scuttling into a hole in the wall.

A chain slid free of its track and someone shot the door bolt. A second later daylight appeared as the door opened a crack. I used my right shoulder to force it all the way open.

"The fuck?"

A man stumbled backward into the middle of a trash-strewn living room, gaping at me, then at Theresa and Roy as they followed me inside. Big, shaved head, gray hoodie, jeans, and the kinds of boots you see on construction sites worn by people who actually work for a living. Tattoos ran up and down his neck. Behind him, a thin woman half-sat, half-lay on a faded green couch as if she'd given up trying to right herself. Before Hoodie could say more Roy strode into the room as casually as if he were headed for the pulpit, stopped at a TV stand, lifted up the gun sitting there, and tucked it into the rear of his pants.

"The fuck?" the man repeated, moving toward Roy.

"Easy now," I said, planting myself between him and the parson. "Not looking for any trouble."

I saw the punch coming from a couple of kilometers away, which said less about my skills as a pugilist and more about Hoodie's hair-trigger temper. I blocked it with my left forearm, grabbed his right hand, bent his thumb back, and twisted his arm down as he gasped in pain. He fell to his knees. I released his hand, used both arms to flatten him onto his stomach, pinned both arms in mine, and knelt onto his back, ignoring the gasp of pain at the pressure from my weight.

"The hell is this?" he gasped.

"It's a game show," I said. "True or false—Isn't that Darlene sitting right there?"

He grunted a reply. I looked at Roy, who had joined Theresa on the couch. They sat Darlene between them, propping her up. Theresa offered her a sip from a bottle of water, which she refused at first. A moment later she took it from Theresa and nearly drained it. I made eye contact with Roy and nodded at the man beneath me. Roy gave me a thumbs up, and slowly I stood.

"Beat it."

"You're dead, all of you. Especially you, bitch," Hoodie said, slowly rising to his knees as he spat the words in the direction of the couch. It was unclear if he meant Darlene or Theresa, but the gist was clear.

"We're all going to die eventually," I said. "Let's enjoy each other's company while we can."

He stomped out, filling the air with a string of curses. I shut the door, drew the chain, and bolted the lock. I pulled up the room's only chair and sat a respectful distance from the couch.

"Leave me alone," Darlene said. "I'm fine."

"Is that your daddy?" Theresa said.

"He's nobody. Just go away."

"We're here to help you. Just like before. There's nothing to be afraid of."

Darlene made a sound that might have been a laugh and might have been a dry heave.

"Don't need any help. I'm just tired."

"Do we need to call the police?" Theresa said.

"No cops," Darlene said, voice inflected with energy for the first time since we entered the room.

I rose and wandered through the small apartment. The sink in the tiny kitchen was filled with dirty dishes. A cockroach sat atop a crusty bowl, waving its antennae at me. What looked like a package of bologna but smelled like something recovered from a landfill sat on the counter, crawling with ants. I lifted it and opened a cupboard and found the garbage. I dropped it in, went to set the bin back inside, then noticed something written on a greasy piece of paper beside the bologna. I lifted the paper up by one corner and read it. A notice of bond revocation for someone named Javon Martinez. The guy we'd just rousted from Darlene's apartment? Interesting. Carefully, I folded it in half, then in half again. I looked around until I spied an empty bread bag. I shook it free of crumbs, placed the paper in the bag, and tucked the bag into my back pocket. Finished, I found a half-filled bottle of dish detergent and a desiccated scrub pad. I turned on the water, rolled up my sleeves, and cleaned the mess in the sink as best I could while Roy and Theresa talked to Darlene.

A couple minutes later I walked back into the living room. Theresa was saying, "How about a place to stay, at least? Someplace different?"

"Just leave me alone."

"Just for the night."

She shook her head.

"Something to eat?"

Another shake of her head. Regardless, Theresa reached into her backpack. She retrieved a couple of Subway sandwiches, a package of granola bars, and two bottles of Gatorade. She placed them and a handful of White Castle coupons on the couch beside Darlene.

"You need anything, anything at all, you call me, OK? You still have that phone I gave you?"

No response. Theresa reached out and stroked the woman's hair, lifting it out of her eyes and back around her ears. After a second, the woman nodded.

"Anything you need, all right?"

Another nod.

Eyes peeled for Hoodie, we left the apartment, standing in the hall long enough for Theresa to persuade Darlene to lock up behind us. Outside, back in the van, I turned and explained what I'd found in the trash.

"Yeah, that was Javon," Theresa said. "Big surprise."

"Well, not to state the obvious," I said, "but how do we know he isn't going to come back and beat the living crap out of her?"

"We don't," Roy said, fiddling with his phone. "But we at least planted a question mark in his mind, tiny though it may be. Sent a message that someone's watching. Someone who could do some damage if he caught him off guard. Nice move, by the way, that wrist thing."

"Thanks. Otto taught me that. Said it was about time I learned some actual self-protection. Even though I think he just liked inflicting pain on me."

"Either way, it came in handy."

"Otto usually does." Otto Mulligan, bailbondsman and sometime drinking buddy—root beer and grape soda in his case—hired me for jobs now and then when his regulars, Moose, Buck, and Big Dog, weren't available. He liked to call me his JV squad, but the pay wasn't bad, so I let it go.

"I'm calling a guy I know in vice, let him know what went down," Roy said, lifting his phone to his ear. "Maybe they can send a cruiser through the lot a couple times tonight. Buy us a little time, figure out what to do."

"I feel bad for her. You said she was doing OK?"

"She was," Theresa said. She was back to staring out the window. She often did, seeing things on the streets that weren't visible to us, shadows of her past. She'd worked the same neighborhood nearly ten years, starting at fourteen, before Roy helped set her straight.

"Are you OK?" I said.

"Just drive, QB. Just drive."

12

A FEW MINUTES LATER Roy and I settled at a table at Land Grant up the street, two pints of beer between us. We clinked glass and I said, "What's a nice parson like you going to do with an absconded gun like that?"

"Got an artist friend who's a metalworker. Looks like Lucy's due for another decorative lawn ornament."

"Funny present for a wife."

"She's used to it by now. So, anyway, thanks for your help today."

"That's not going to end well, is it?"

"The forecast is cloudy," Roy said. "But you never know. Theresa doesn't give up easily."

"Thanks for the understatement of the year."

I took a drink of beer and proceeded to tell Roy about Joe, the money, and Crystal's assertion of trouble between him and Bob. For a priest and an atheist, a Bengals fan and a washed-up Cleveland Brown, we made a fairly compatible couple.

"Joe wouldn't be the first kid to lift loose change from his old man—or step–old man," I said. "I wasn't exactly a poster child for good behavior myself. But kicking him out? Seems like an overreaction."

"Sounds like it."

"Problem is, I don't really trust Crystal on the topic of Joe moving in with me as something that's better for him. It wouldn't be beyond her and Bob to just look for a way to get him out of the house and use the stolen money as an excuse."

"That's cold."

"Crystal's cold. Trust me. The hot sex was all a façade. It almost makes me feel bad for Bob. Almost."

"Would the courts go along with that? You're hardly a paragon of stability."

"I prefer 'differently time-managed,' but fair enough. I have no idea how I'd pull it off, truthfully, with school and Joe's extracurriculars and all that. It's the whole girlfriend problem—late-night stakeouts are just as bad for child-raising as they are for romance."

"Speaking of which, I saw Anne the other day."

"What?"

The parson's expression was pure innocence. "She gave a lecture. 'Beyond *The Handmaid's Tale.*' Lucy and I went."

"How nice."

Roy took a swallow of beer. "Lose the attitude. She's looking well. She's single again, I understand."

"Here," I said, pulling my shirt up out of my jeans. "Just stick the knife there, as long as you're performing unauthorized surgery on my love life."

"I'm just reporting the news," he said, unsuccessfully disguising a smile. "Lucy wanted to text you on the spot, but I talked her out of it."

"What happened to Ben—her boyfriend?"

"It didn't work out, I guess. Maybe something you're familiar with?"

Anne, my ex-girlfriend, was an English professor at Columbus State and an expert on women science fiction writers. Her first book, a survey of authors including Ursula K. Le Guin, Margaret Atwood, and others, had received rave reviews. I was smitten the moment I first saw her—a redhaired, green-eyed, brainiac beauty—in the midst of a case a few years back. But things just hadn't worked out. As usual.

"I'm surprised," I managed. "Ben seemed like a good guy."

"I think he is. But Lucy got the impression he was a good guy who wanted more from the relationship than Anne was ready for. You could imagine her being a little gun-shy."

This was another understatement, as we both knew. In addition to the complications I brought to her life, Anne was still processing her survival of a knife attack by her troubled husband, who then killed himself. She bore a scar on her face to this day.

"I'm not suggesting anything," Roy added. "Just making conversation."

"Yeah. And the Inquisition was a friendly Q&A."

"Don't lump me in with that crowd. Catholics were mean sons of bitches back then."

"And your team's hands are clean?"

"Episcopalians? We built churches with money from the slave trade. Totally different."

"If you say so."

"As the presiding judge here, I pronounce it to be true."

Presiding judge.

Oh shit.

"What time is it?" I reached for my phone.

"Five thirty. You want one more?"

Six o'clock. Sharp. And you're bringing dinner.

"Shit, shit, shit."

I looked through the window at the food truck parked outside. Two people in line. A twenty-minute drive to Laura's house under normal conditions. On the minus side, northbound traffic a bitch this time of day. On the plus side, I was extremely motivated not to be late. **Not that I'm counting, but this is the third time you've canceled this month.**

"Gotta run, sorry." I pulled out my wallet but he waved me away.

"On me, thanks to your derring-do at Darlene's. What's up?"

"Tell you later. Maybe say one of those prayer things for me?"

"I do every day."

"Supersize it, please."

And with that I was out the door and in line, saying my own prayer to the gods of commuter traffic.

"SINCE YOU know how much I like fish tacos, I'll take your penance as real," Laura said thirty-three minutes and fifteen seconds later, accepting the plastic bag of takeout as she let me in. We'll call it fashionably late and leave it at that.

"Lots of preplanning, as the morticians like to say."

"Ugh. I've always hated that expression. And what a morbid comment."

"Says the person who sends people to prison."

"Only the ones who deserve it."

She set the food bag down on her small dining room table. It was already set. Lights in the room on low. Flames flickered from a red candle. An uncorked bottle of white sat in the middle. I relaxed and took a deep breath, putting the race up the highway behind me. I hadn't made it easy on myself, calling Otto on the way, telling him, as I wove in and out of commuter traffic leaving downtown, about the bond revocation I'd found in the trash in Darlene's apartment.

"So what's this case you mentioned?" Laura said, filling our wine glasses as we sat.

I outlined the story so far, from Preston's collaring of me at Plank's while my boys and I ate pizza, to the story of Howie Campbell and the missing and presumed dead John Ebersole. I concluded with my conversations with Mrs. Zimmerman, the police, and the prosecutor.

"The guy just walked out of Grant Hospital? Wasn't he under police guard?"

"That was the idea. But obviously something went wrong."

"I would have thought there'd be hell to pay."

"I think there was. The chief at the time was pissed, according to the articles Preston has. But then somehow it all just faded away."

"Very strange." She took a bite of taco. "What are you going to do? I mean, if no one's talking and the guy's AWOL and/or dead. Go to Rochester?"

"I've thought about it. But it's a long trip without much to go on."

"Ever been?"

"Rochester? Not exactly."

"What's that supposed to mean?"

I again recalled my association with the city, and again tried to put it out of my mind. I finished a taco and reached for another.

"Nothing. To answer your question, I may go if I think there's something to get there. It's possible the cops may beat me to it. Just because they're not telling me what they're up to doesn't mean they're not interested."

"They have the manpower to chase something like that all these years later? From what I hear in my courtroom, they're barely keeping their heads above water as is."

"I guess we'll find out."

Laura had a good reputation with the law enforcement community, due largely to the long sentences she handed down for violent crime, a practice that led to her nickname. The Velvet Fist. Fair, but tough. Very tough, when she needed to be. Keeping that reputation intact was what brought us together, in fact, when she hired me years earlier as an unofficial bodyguard after a gang-banger threatened her in open court. She didn't want to run the risk of people in the gossipy courthouse knowing she felt vulnerable. Things had been bad enough after her divorce. Happy for the money, I took the gig, driving her from her condo off Dublin Road to the courthouse in the morning and reversing the pattern in the late afternoons. Our conversation was strictly business, mainly consisting of her talking about her cases while I occasionally offered a comment or posed a question. Then came a cold Friday night in January when she invited me inside, and twenty minutes later, slipping between her sheets, I was an ex-bodyguard and something else I was still struggling to come to terms with.

"What?" Laura said.

"Nothing," I said again, shaking the memory away.

"Nothing my foot. I know those eyes."

"Do you?"

Instead of a reply, she leaned over to me, took my face in her hands, and kissed me. I leaned in and kissed her back, reaching my right hand around the back of her neck.

"Mmm," she said. "You taste like fish tacos."

"You said it was your favorite."

"Yes, I did," she said, shifting herself onto my lap and kissing me again. I raised my hands and reached for the first button on her blouse. And then the second. And then I kissed her on the neck. And then a little lower, and then—

And then my phone went off.

"Shit," I said. "Sorry—"

"No need to apologize," she said, amusement in her eyes as she pulled away. "It's your turn, I guess."

Unspoken between us, a similar interruption—her phone on that occasion—had triggered the chain of events that led to her captivity, and near death, in a house overlooking Lake Erie. An escapade that ended a long estrangement between us, though it was hard to say exactly what our relationship had turned into since.

"This is Andy," I said impatiently, not recognizing the number.

"Mr. Hayes? It's Preston Campbell."

"Preston, right. Possible I could call you back in—"

"I'm sorry I missed your voice mail. I'm always doing that. I saw your text, about the burglaries, and figured that's what you'd been calling about, you know? And you got my text about that, right?"

"Yes, I—"

"I didn't check the phone message because I figured I'd answered it already. I mean, that there were only twelve, not thirteen. That's for sure."

Laura slid herself off my lap, picked up our plates, and took them into the kitchen.

"But then tonight I was going through my messages, because Monica called me a couple times, and she's always after me to listen to her messages *before* I call her back, in case she was looking for something specific I might be able to answer, so she doesn't have to repeat herself. I went ahead and listened to your voice mail, and realized I hadn't responded properly."

In the kitchen, Laura set the plates on the floor. Oliver materialized a moment later and began licking them clean.

"It's really all right."

"So I just wanted to call and clarify for you about Gina Stratton's house. You wanted to know what they told me. But like I said, no one answered the door. And they never called me back."

Finally he had my attention. "You never talked to them?" How had I misunderstood this?

He confirmed it. "I wish they had. Maybe they would have given me the answers and I wouldn't have had to hire you. How's it going, by the way."

I didn't respond. Instead, I thought back to my encounter outside the house. What was it the woman had said to me? *I'm telling you the same thing I told the cops and the other guy. I don't know no John Ebersole.*

If not Preston, then, who was this other guy?

"You're sure?"

"I'm positive, Mr. Hayes. Have you had any luck so far? Like I said, I really took it as a sign when I saw you in Plank's that night. I mean, the funny thing is, I hardly ever eat out like that. It's only because Monica wanted to see me that we even ended up there. She had to go over some things about our dad's estate. Isn't that funny?"

It took me another couple of minutes before he agreed to let me go on the promise that I would offer a fuller update soon. I disconnected and stepped into the living room, where Laura sat on her couch watching the news, feet tucked up under her, Oliver on her lap.

"That sounded interesting," she said, stroking the gray cat.

"Wrong number," I said, sitting beside her and kissing her on the neck. She turned to me and kissed me lightly on the lips. Then she pulled away.

"I'm sorry, Andy. I think the moment passed. Long day, and the wine made me a little sleepy."

"You're sure?" I tried again, lifting her hand and kissing her fingertips one by one.

"Yeah. My turn for a rain check. Maybe next Sunday? Or do you have the boys?"

"No. That's a free day."

"Let's plan on it. OK?"

"OK," I said, as enthusiastically as I could muster.

Which wasn't much, and we both knew it.

13

INSTEAD OF DRIVING STRAIGHT home, I headed back into the Franklinton neighborhood and the direction of Darlene's apartment. Night was falling and the autumn air was cool. Women stood on almost every street corner as I drove down Sullivant, most of them alone, sometimes in pairs. They stared at me as I slowed for stop signs, making eye contact, sometimes swaying as they did, before turning away as I pulled into the next block. I couldn't be sure, but one of them looked a lot like Darlene. I debated stopping to see if she was all right but realized that would likely confuse matters, and what exactly would I say? Besides, Roy and Theresa didn't know I was here, or what I was up to, and I wanted to keep it that way for now.

I planned to loop once through the apartment building's parking lot, then nixed the idea as I drove down the adjacent side street and spied a Columbus police cruiser idling between the main entrance and the Dumpster we'd parked by earlier. Leave it to Roy to light a fire downtown. So maybe Hoodie would leave Darlene alone for one night, assuming he wasn't back on the streets, lurking in the shadows just behind her. I kept driving, turned left at the next intersection, and headed for home.

Hopalong blinked at me from the couch when I let myself in. His days of energetic greetings had long gone the way of an evening walk, thanks to his arthritis and a couple other ailments that had me on a first-name basis with my veterinarian's receptionist. After a minute or two he eased his way down and walked stiff-legged to the back door. I let him out to water the Japanese maple at the rear of my postage stamp–sized backyard. Across the alley, I caught a glimpse of flames jumping from the two Kevins' firepit and heard the sound of laughter as they enjoyed a late dinner with friends. For my part, tonight more likely involved an episode or two of *Bosch* followed by a couple chapters of *Tigerland* before bed. For an extra shot of adrenaline, I might water the ficus drying out on a stand in the corner of my dining room, a long-ago gift from Anne. To stave off the lonely evening stretching before me, I fetched a Black Label from the refrigerator and settled at the kitchen table with my laptop. I opened Preston's file and scrolled through the pages without purpose. As my mind wandered, I found myself thinking not of what just happened with the judge, but instead what Roy had told me over beers at Land Grant about Anne Cooper. *She's looking well. She's single again, I understand.* What did I care about that? A lot, I realized, though it was a meaningless consideration. Beyond all expectations we'd stayed friends, in part because her daughter Amelia and Joe still hung out from time to time. But imagining myself back with her was like pondering a flying leap across the Grand Canyon. I could measure the distance all day long, but the trip was never going to happen, for the simple reason that it was impossible.

A scratching at the door. I rose and let the dog back inside. I drained my beer, tossed the can in the recycling, and grabbed another. I yawned. Not even eight o'clock and I was already exhausted. In my defense, it had been a long day, between dropping Joe at school early, picking Stickdorn's brain, visiting Maynard Avenue, meeting Mrs. Zimmerman, running into a dead end at the prosecutor's office, my pastoral counseling visit with Roy and Theresa, and of course the aborted date with Laura. Come to think of it, it had been a huge day. Any one of those appointments would have been enough activity to keep me plenty occupied. At least everyone—everyone not counting Hoodie—had been cordial, even Sprague, the prosecutor, despite his condescending tone as he related the concept of insurance fraud to me, as if I were a college criminal justice major interning in his office.

Once more, I thought about Sprague's slipup, revealing that he knew about Schmidt. That implied he was taking the possibility of Ebersole still being around seriously, even if he wasn't willing to spill the beans to me. That shouldn't come as any surprise: Sprague's blood ran as blue as any cop's in town. But an examination of a burglary that may or may not have been reported, and which led to an odd discrepancy in the total number of Ebersole's victims? That was something else altogether. It was also the second odd thing to emerge from the case today, after Preston's insistence that he hadn't spoken to anyone at Gina Stratton's house, leaving the identity of "that other guy" up in the air.

I opened my laptop and went online to search for Gerhard Schmidt and McCulloh College. Nothing through the college's own search engine, and a general search ran into the thousands, all random links with no apparent connection to him, the college, or Ohio. I sat back and recalled what Mrs. Zimmerman said about Schmidt. A visiting literature professor fighting the presumption he had to be a spy because otherwise, in 1979, what was he doing in the States, especially with a prestigious post back home? Goodwill couldn't possibly run that far at that point in the Cold War. Or did it? What did I know about that time in our history? Of course, if he was a spy, it raised an interesting question about what a burglar might have encountered during a break-in, which could provide an inkling of an explanation for Ebersole's special treatment. Even if Schmidt wasn't a Soviet agent, an event like that might have spooked him more than the average crime victim. Mrs. Zimmerman said he went home the following semester, cutting his visit short by months. Too rattled by what happened to him? Nervous about losing that prestigious post? Or for some other, more nefarious reason?

I located the address for the McCulloh College languages department and noted that it opened at eight. It might be nothing, or it might be a big deal, but either way it would pay to stop by there in the morning and see what kind of files they had on

Schmidt. I shut the computer down, took my beer into the living room, turned on the TV, turned it off, and picked up my book instead. I was three paragraphs into a new chapter when my phone buzzed with a text.

You were right Woody

Otto. The bailbondsman on the prowl for details of the revocation notice I'd pulled from the garbage can beneath the filthy sink in Darlene's apartment. Otto, legitimately on the short list of people allowed to use my nickname.

Meaning?

His name set off alarms. Give me a day to work out the details.

I told him thanks, set my phone on the coffee table, and returned to the book. An hour later I startled myself awake. I turned off the lights, instructed Hopalong to follow me into the bedroom, and went to bed. It really had been quite a long day.

14

SHORTLY AFTER EIGHT THIRTY the next morning I parked the van on Bennett Street on the northeast side of town and used my phone to locate the address I had for the McCulloh College languages building. Sleepy-looking students in jeans and sweatshirts lugged backpacks toward central campus, a mix of century-old Gothic buildings that brought to mind scenes from Harry Potter movies and less architecturally glamorous sixties and seventies–era brick halls. The quad was mostly empty this time of day, with only a few students and professors around, all on their way someplace. Even a young woman who stopped beside a sculpture to place something at its base seemed in a hurry.

The office I sought was halfway down a second-floor hallway in Weber Hall that gleamed from an overnight polishing job. To judge by the travel posters on the walls, it appeared the various language departments shared a common administrative space, which made sense in a school the size of McCulloh, whose enrollment usually hovered around twenty-five hundred students. Two students sat at a table on the far side sifting through piles of paper, the girl mechanically handing a sheaf to the boy, who stapled it to a second sheaf and placed it in a pile to his right. Their languid movements combined with the time of day suggested they'd drawn the shortest of the work-study straws.

"Excuse me?"

The pair stopped what they were doing. I asked if there was anyone available for a question.

"Frau Herschberger's here," the girl said. "She just stepped out for a moment. You could wait?"

I told her I would. I sat in a chair beside a coffee table piled with travel magazines, pulled my phone from my pocket, and checked for any new messages. I saw Crystal had texted me, asking if I could call. That wouldn't be good, whatever she needed, especially this early. I considered our conversation the other day. *Bob was just wondering if maybe it was time to think about, you know, the custody arrangement.* I shook my head and pored over my e-mail, seeing nothing of note other than an overdue notice for *Tigerland.* I was considering whether to text Otto when a woman in a high-collared beige dress entered the room, walked around the counter, and eyed me.

"May I help you?"

Solid figure, upswept silver hair, faint German accent. Frau Herschberger, I presume?

I stood and introduced myself, determined she was the languages department secretary, handed her a business card, and explained my interest in Gerhard Schmidt.

"What about him?"

"Do you know of him?"

She looked at my card. "It's a busy morning, Mr. Hayes. Was there something specific you needed?"

"It's possible he might have been the victim of a burglary that connects to a case I'm working on."

If that meant anything to her she didn't show it. Instead, she said with a frown, "Is your case from back then?"

"Not exactly. But I understand it affected him badly. That he cut his time here short as a result."

"Who told you that?"

"It doesn't matter. Is it true?"

"I'm sure I couldn't say."

Her eyes, a watery blue on their way to gray, never left mine.

"Are there any records I could look at?"

"Of what?"

"Of Professor Schmidt's time here."

In the hall outside, voices and the sound of feet filling the corridor as students arrived for class.

"What kind of records?"

Excellent question. "His personnel file, maybe? Details about his employment. Performance review. That kind of thing."

She looked again at my card, frowning, before setting it down beside her coffee cup on her desk. The coffee cup said, ***Mondays Will No Longer Be Tolerated.***

"We don't have any such records here, in this office. You could try at the registrar's, or perhaps the business office, although it's unlikely they'll hand anything over, even assuming they have anything after this many years. This is a private college, after all."

"I understand. Is there anyone around still who might have known him?" I hesitated. "You, perhaps?"

The look on her face told me the question had hit home. And it simultaneously made me wonder the obvious: had there been something between the two? She had to be in her mid- to late sixties now, if she'd been at McCulloh in 1979. Two German-speaking people marooned on a small Ohio college campus in a town much less sophisticated than today. He would have been older, more worldly. Even today, Herschberger was a handsome woman; it was easy to see the figure she would have struck forty years earlier. It wasn't hard to imagine the connection. As if reading my mind, she said, "I really didn't know him very well, Mr. Hayes. And now—"

"Does the name Howie Campbell mean anything to you?"

"It doesn't. Was he another student?"

I told her no, and explained his connection to Schmidt through the burglary at the Zimmermans, along with the shootout.

"I vaguely remember that case," Frau Herschberger said. "But I'm not aware of any connection with the college, or Herr Schmidt."

"You said 'another student' just now. What did you mean by that?"

She reddened slightly. "At this point, I think it's best you direct your questions to the business office. I have nothing more to tell you."

"Are you sure? Because—"

Before I could finish, a woman entered from the hallway and approached the counter. "Anything, Uschi?" A professor, by the looks of her business casual slacks, blouse, and scarf.

"If you'll excuse me now, Mr. Hayes," Frau Herschberger said, directing her attention to the woman.

Back outside, I stood at the edge of the quad, orienting myself as I digested the encounter. Trees as tall as Connecticut church steeples towered over the campus, the hint of reds and yellows in their leaves providing a picture-postcard contrast with the green expanse of the lawn and its intersecting brick walkways. Gargoyles jutted out from the upper corners of some of the older buildings, pop-eyed monsters coldly observing the comings and goings of students and faculty. In the distance, a clock struck the quarter hour with a series of deep chimes, as if calling pupils to a daily prayer for wisdom instead of faith. Cloistered and calm, the campus exuded a sense of higher purpose, of lofty ideals and purity of thought that bore as much in common with the hustle and bustle of a Big 10 campus as rural dirt roads did with four-lane expressways. I knew you could earn a business or communications degree here, but for the most part the college had stuck with a liberal arts curriculum, including foreign languages. The perfect place for a visiting scholar like Gerhard Schmidt, who might have found his own refuge here, far from the grinding suspicion and low-grade poverty of a Soviet Bloc country in the 1970s. Yet a refuge so contaminated by Ebersole's break-in that Schmidt had to flee home.

I checked my directions and continued toward the main administrative building and the business office. Halfway across the quad I stopped at the sculpture I'd seen earlier, where a student had dropped something on my way past. Bronze, perhaps eight or nine feet high, an impressionistic representation of an androgynous youth, his or her face gazing upwards with arms outstretched and fingers on both hands spread wide, the right leg slightly bent, the figure frozen as if caught just a moment before launching into a leap of joy. The sculpture stood atop a polished black marble base, which this morning was covered with a haphazard pile of flowers. I knelt to read words inscribed across the bottom of the base:

In honor of Paul Tigner, January 15, 1960–November 3, 1979

The earth has guilt, the earth has care
Unquiet are its graves;
But peaceful sleep is ever there,
Beneath the dark blue waves.
—Nathaniel Hawthorne

"It's sad, isn't it, Detective?"

I froze, heart pounding, recognizing the voice immediately.

"Haunting, in fact," I managed.

"I stop here often."

"I can see why," I said, standing and reaching out to shake Anne Cooper's hand.

WE STOOD AWKWARDLY, RELEASING our hands after a moment or two too long.

"What are you doing here?" she asked.

"I'm on a case. I was just on my way to the business office."

"What's it about—if I may ask."

I was happy to oblige, trying not to stare at her too hard as I went over the details. Her outfit, a dark green woolen sweater dress, jeans, and dress leather hiking boots, had always been one of my favorites.

"That's a handful," she said when I finished. "A Soviet spy hanging out in Columbus. You really think this burglar got the goods on him?"

"Alleged Soviet spy. And to be clear, that's pure speculation. There's also no evidence of this break-in other than the word of a ninety-three-year-old widow. And the fact the prosecutor mentioned him."

"Seems like something."

"Maybe. It's just one of those loose strings I can't let go."

She smiled. "I'm familiar with your need to pull loose strings."

There was nothing more to add. Anne broke it off between us for the same reason a lot of women parted ways with me—the unpredictability of my schedule, the dangers I brought down on myself, but above all, the tunnel vision that possessed me like the spiking fever of a seasonal flu when pursuing leads on seemingly impenetrable cases. Good for clients, bad for appointments with lovers. The same thing that had me worried about taking Joe into my house on a more regular basis.

"How about you? Why are you here?"

"I'm teaching a class on dystopias. It's a faculty exchange—I'm here this semester, and one of their profs is at Columbus State, teaching an upper-level course."

"Sounds interesting."

"I think so." After another awkward moment, she looked at the sculpture and its loose collection of flowers. "It really is sad, isn't it?"

"Do you know its story?"

"Just a little. Paul Tigner was a student here, a freshman, who committed suicide."

"That is sad."

"There's a backstory to it, though. He was gay, supposedly, but not out, and he killed himself because of that. It was Ohio in 1979, after all. Over the years the statue took on unofficial status as a campus rallying point to oppose homophobia."

"Thus the flowers?"

"Apparently whenever there's an act of hate someplace, students and staff spontaneously place them there."

I looked around, as if expecting to see a knot of antigay protesters. "Did something happen?"

"I'm not sure. I can check after class. The last time was when that student in Florida killed himself when his roommate posted the video of him kissing his secret boyfriend. It could be anything." She shook her head and frowned. "Andy? You OK?"

A memory, emerging from the muck. Stumbling out of the Varsity Club on Lane Avenue freshman or sophomore year with a couple buddies. Catching two boys kissing behind a Dumpster. Confronting them, hooting and hollering the usual. *Fags. Queers. Fairies.* I squeezed my eyes shut, thinking of the two Kevins.

"Andy?"

"Sorry. You were saying?"

"Just about the statue. Anyway, Amelia will be happy to hear I saw you. She's always asking about you. She has a scrapbook of articles about your exploits."

"Now there's a kid who needs another hobby." She laughed.

Encouraged, I said, "Roy said he saw you lecture recently. He and Lucy."

"That was nice of them to come. Even though it was just me reading from my book."

"A great book," I offered.

"Thanks, but this is a new one. It's about women writers of dystopian fiction. Still in manuscript form. Getting there."

"That's good."

Silence descended. Unspoken between us, the news that Roy shared. Anne was single again. But what was that to me? I was seeing the judge. Wasn't I?

"Need to go," she said. "Class in five minutes. It was good running into you. I hope things work out with your case."

"Where's your building? I can walk you partway."

"Over there." We strolled in the direction she pointed.

"You know, it's funny I saw you today," she said. "I've been meaning to call you."

"Why?"

"I was hoping we could get coffee."

"Sounds good," I said, shielding the eagerness behind my reply.

"Great. But probably not until Bonnie delivers."

"Ah, right."

Bonnie Deckard, my freelance IT consultant—"hacker for hire" in English—was pregnant with twins and due within a week or so. She and Anne had remained friends over the years, even after I was out of Anne's life. Bonnie and her boyfriend had asked Anne to be her doula on delivery day. Despite her pregnancy, Bonnie insisted on fulfilling the various jobs I sent her way over the past few weeks, though she drew the line at chasing suspects down mean streets.

"Soon, then."

"Perfect. And maybe we—"

"Excuse me!"

We turned. Behind us, a security guard lumbered in our direction across the quad. We stared, watching him approach.

"Excuse me!"

He was upon us a few seconds later. Heavy-set, pale face florid from the exertion of walking after us. Florid but hard-looking. Black pants, white shirt with a red McCulloh College Security badge on the shoulder, utility belt heavy-laden with the usual cop stuff—baton, stun gun, cuffs—but lacking a firearm, since the force here was not an official police department.

"I'm going to have to ask you to leave campus," he said, struggling to catch his breath.

I was about to respond when Anne said, "I beg your pardon?"

"You heard me, ma'am. This is private property."

"I'm a visiting professor with full rights to be wherever I want," Anne said in a raised voice that wouldn't have been out of place in obedience school. The guard hesitated, taken aback, which was just long enough for her to produce a McCulloh College ID from her purse and thrust it in his face.

"I'm sorry, ma'am . . . **Professor.** I didn't realize. You're OK, then. But he—" he said, glancing at me.

"He's my friend. What's the problem?"

For a moment I thought we were in the clear. I was guessing this wasn't the first time the guard had been dressed down by a professor, which also made me feel momentarily sorry for him, despite how impressed I was with Anne's reaction. It couldn't be an easy job working unarmed security on a private college campus brimming with egos, where it would be hard not to feel perpetually looked down upon. But then something in the man's face changed and he drew himself up.

"There's not a problem for you, Dr. Cooper," he said. Well played, I thought, seeing the twitch on Anne's face at his acknowledgment of her rank. "But I have to ask Mr. Hayes here to leave. He doesn't have permission to be conducting an investigation on campus."

"Who said I was investigating?"

"I'm sorry. Those are the rules."

"I was just going to the business office. As instructed." I explained what Frau Herschberger told me. Then it dawned on me: how had this guard known I was here? It's not as if he could have spied me from a distance, or even known who I was. Which meant only one thing: the languages secretary had tipped him to my presence. But why?

"Mrs. Herschberger was being polite, given that you walked in unannounced like that," the guard said. "But any questions have to be made in writing. You can send an e-mail. You can't just show up on campus without telling anyone."

"Come on."

"I can walk you to your car if you'd like."

I looked at Anne, who was still glaring at the guard, and then past her to the statue commemorating the short life of Paul Tigner. Flowers lying on the base like fragments of cloth haphazardly torn from a tapestry. I pondered how Gerhard Schmidt was increasingly a trigger point in this investigation, even though his connection to Ebersole was tenuous at best.

"I'm sorry, Andy," Anne said. "I really need to go."

"Me too," I said, but directed the comment at the guard. "I'm parked on Bennett Street. You can't miss it. It's one of those older-model Honda Odysseys."

"I'm familiar with them," the guard replied. "My sisters-in-law all drive those."

I could have been mistaken, but as I strode off, fuming, I might have heard Dr. Anne Cooper unsuccessfully suppress a laugh.

16

ANY GOOD FEELINGS FROM my encounter with Anne—and there were plenty—evaporated on my drive home as I heard Twisted Sister on my phone. Crystal was calling.

"What."

"Did you get my text?"

"Yes."

"Were you going to call?"

"Little busy—on a case right now. What's up?"

"I'm a little busy too." Her voice strained and nearly hoarse, as if she'd been shouting recently. "Maybe you could think of someone else for a change?"

"Don't start—"

"Forget it. Listen, I know it's out of cycle, but I was wondering if you could take Joe this weekend. Actually, starting after school Thursday."

"Why?" I said, immediately—and guiltily—thinking of my rescheduled date with the judge.

"Bob's got a conference in Orlando. I decided to go with. The flight's Friday morning."

"You've already booked the flight?"

"It was a good deal, Andy. I had to move fast."

"And Bob's known about this conference for how long?"

"What difference does that make?"

I didn't bite. Engaging Crystal at this point was futile, the warfare equivalent of employing redcoat tactics in the face of minuteman shoot-and-run maneuvers. The outcome was inevitable, and bloody.

"It's fine," I thought, wondering how many more missed opportunities Laura's and my relationship could weather. "What about Lyndsey?"

"She's staying with my sister." Bob and Crystal's daughter was two and a half years younger than Joe, her half-brother.

"Doesn't she have cheerleading?"

"Toni can take her. It's not like we haven't seen her cheer before."

"Nice."

"What we do with Lyndsey isn't any of your business, Andy. It's not like I'm asking **you** to take care of her."

"This time."

"That only happened once and you know it."

"Twice, not that I'm counting, because I like her. She's a good kid. Of course I'll take Joe. I'll pick him up after school Thursday. Assuming of course you've talked to him and he's OK with it?"

"Actually, I was hoping you could do that."

BACK IN German Village, I parked and walked down to the Brown Bag and ordered a turkey-and-Swiss to go. Sitting at my kitchen table, ignoring Hopalong's longing gaze at the sandwich, I put the mystery of Schmidt aside and went back to what I knew of John Ebersole and his whereabouts. Last sighting before his death, according to Preston, was the jail cell in Rochester about ten years ago. I was intrigued by the idea that he'd gone home after disappearing from a Columbus jail cell. It wasn't unusual: a lot of times criminals on the run, even the smartest ones, circle back to familiar territory, like flies drawn to dog crap. There was a reason why bounty hunters like Otto Mulligan started their searches at relatives' houses. Just because you're a badass doesn't mean you don't like coming home for the holidays. But Ebersole must have been confident he could hide there in plain sight, especially since he didn't even bother changing his name.

It took me ten minutes, including three transfers and two disconnections, but eventually I found myself speaking to a corrections officer named Andrea at the Monroe County Jail in Rochester who heard me out and agreed to see what she could find in the computer. After a period of silence over the phone that seemed to last nearly as long as one of Rochester's legendary winters, she came back on the line and asked me to again say and this time spell the name of the inmate I was looking for.

"Nothing," she said, a few seconds later.

"I beg your pardon?"

"Nothing comes up. No John Ebersole."

My heart sank. "You're sure?"

"I've got two Eberlys and three Eberts. But no Ebersoles. This old system's screwed up and cranky, but it's definitely complete. Was he homeless?"

"I don't think so. What difference does that make?"

"Not much, other than we had a lot of guys from the shelters in those days with the recession and everything. Lot of them didn't exactly have complete ID."

"I understand. In any case, I appreciate the effort."

"Got a middle initial?"

"I'm sorry?"

"On this perp. Middle name?"

I thought for a minute. "J," I said to the officer. "John J. Ebersole."

Instead of a reply, I heard the neutral trill of a ringing phone. A moment later the officer answered. There seemed to be a problem with a current inmate, to judge by the indistinct snatches of one-sided conversation I caught. "Oh-nine-hundred, I'm telling you . . . possession and receiving . . . only medications I got listed are Suboxone and aspirin . . . no, nothing like that . . . ain't my problem, sister, that one's for the judge, and you know he ain't gonna let that pass."

"Sorry about that." The officer came back on the line. "The shit some of these guys try to pull. You said G?"

"J, as in Jersey," I said, already figuring out the next item on my checklist. Maybe circle back with Preston, or take another run at the prosecutor. And of course, there was the little matter of Darlene Hunter and her good pal Hoodie to resolve.

"Got it. Yup, that's why. For some reason, the old system, you have to have the initial on some of these guys. Don't ask me why."

"So you—"

"I found him. John J. Ebersole. Had him two and a half days. Receiving stolen property. Got a recognizance bond and a court date. Guess he never made that, though."

"Did he give an address?" I said hopefully. She read it off. It was the house where he'd died. I explained that Ebersole was a suspect in the shooting of a cop many years earlier. That seemed to get her attention.

"Nothing like that in here. No record of a hold or anything. No warrants, nothing back from NCIC, far as I can tell." I knew departments regularly entered outstanding warrants into the FBI's National Crime Information Center database, one of the primary factors leading to the capture of felons on the run. Wouldn't an accused cop shooter be deemed worthy of submission? Or was this one more example of Ebersole, by luck or some other design, falling through the cracks?

"Anything that might explain why he got an OR bond?"

"You mean, besides the fact he was seventy-one years old? I'm guessing nobody thought he was going far. That plus the bag."

"The bag?"

"There's a note says he had a colostomy bag." Her voice went down a notch. "Just speculation, but an old man picked up on a nonviolent charge who's also got a medical condition? Not the kind of guy the county's looking to sign a long-term lease for, know what I'm saying?"

I told her I did and thanked her for her help. I left out the fact that if they'd hung on to Ebersole just a little bit longer, it was possible he might still be alive.

17

I SAT BACK AND considered the development. My excitement at independently confirming Ebersole's last-known arrest faded quickly with the realization that I'd learned only one new thing—the detail about the colostomy bag—after all that. Interesting, but hardly surprising given he'd been gut shot by Howie Campbell. It was a typical one step forward, two steps sideways moment. If you believe books and movies, the private-eye business compares favorably to big-game safari hunting, with all the accompanying adrenaline and danger. The reality is a lot closer to setting mousetraps in random corners all day long and judging success by how little cheese is stolen before you finally score a successful snap.

I decided to call Stickdorn to see if he'd learned anything more about a reopened investigation into Ebersole, but had to leave a message. Ditto for a call to the prosecutor for further explanation of what he actually knew about Schmidt. Back to scrolling through Preston's files on my computer screen. I glanced idly at the articles about the deaths of the various players over the years: the accomplice knifed to death in prison, the freak accident that killed the investigator of Howie Campbell's shooting of Ebersole, and the hit-skip involving the second suspect a decade ago. At the end I found a list of addresses and phone numbers, including one for Doug Fitzsimmons, Howie Campbell's partner.

With little else to go on, I called the number, but ended up leaving a message following a generic recording.

No sooner had I put my phone down than it buzzed with an incoming call. I didn't recognize the number.

"Andy Hayes?" A woman's voice.

"You've got him."

"Hillary Quinne here. Do you have a moment?" She said her name as if I should know it.

"Possibly. Pertaining to what?"

"You were on campus this morning. McCulloh College?"

"That's right. Until a security guard rousted me."

"Sorry to hear that. Wondered if we could meet. I might have some information that could be useful to you."

"Information about what?"

"Not what. Who. A man named Gerhard Schmidt."

SHE EXPLAINED she was a private investigator like me, working on a project for the college. She wouldn't say what or who it involved beyond Schmidt, preferring to meet in person. We agreed on five o'clock at Club 185 at the top of my street. I arrived before her and took a seat at the bar. I ordered a Heineken and declined a menu.

"Hi there."

"You," I said, turning around.

Standing before me was the woman who'd interrupted my conversation with Uschi Herschberger that morning in the languages office in Weber Hall, the one I'd mistaken for a professor.

She smiled. "Figured you'd make the connection." She stuck out her hand. "Hillary Quinne. Thanks for meeting me." She had a firm grip, professional and confident. She took a seat beside me and handed me her card. It said simply Hillary Quinne Investigations, accompanied by a phone number.

I traded her mine, and said, "You keep a low profile. I haven't come across your name before."

"Just the way I like it," she said, before adding with another smile: "Unlike some people I know."

Low profile indeed. My online search beforehand turned up a barebones website, a closed Facebook page, and a couple references to testimony she'd given in workers' comp fraud cases over the years. On the other hand, she was registered with the state and in good standing with no red flags. By contrast, my life as an investigator was practically an open book thanks to the messes I'd gotten myself and others into and out of over the years, messes which often ended up splashed across the front page or leading the six o'clock news. I wouldn't have minded a lower profile myself.

"So what can I do for you?"

The bartender arrived and she ordered a glass of chardonnay.

"Maybe what we can do for each other. I'm curious about your interest in Schmidt, for starters."

"Why?"

"I'll get to that, I promise. You first."

Just for a second I thought about bullshitting her, but then decided against it. If Quinne had a connection to the college, she would no doubt have already been filled in by Frau Herschberger. Plus, she came across like someone with little patience for deceit, regardless the reason. At this stage of my investigation, if that's what this still was, I could appreciate that attitude. I gave her the edited version of my interest in Schmidt, professional to professional, starting with Preston Campbell's discovery and finishing with the determination that there'd been a thirteenth, apparently unreported burglary at the East German professor's house.

"Mrs. Zimmerman sounds pretty sharp for ninety-three."

"She seems to know what she's talking about."

Our orders arrived before she could reply. We clinked glass and each took a drink. I took the opportunity to study her more closely. Late thirties to early forties, fit, with an ex-athlete vibe, collar-length brown hair, strong jaw, and just a touch of makeup. Under different circumstances, someone I wouldn't have minded getting to know socially.

"Your turn," I said. "What's your interest in Schmidt? And why now?"

"What do you mean?"

"Don't tell me it's a coincidence we're both looking into an East German professor who was briefly on campus four decades ago."

"Stranger things have happened."

"On TV, maybe. Answer the question."

She smiled and took a sip of wine. "Ever do any damage control, Andy?"

"That's 90 percent of the job, as I'm guessing you know."

She tipped her glass at me approvingly. "Name Grant Fulkerson ring a bell?"

"Should it?"

"Depends on your tolerance for pompousness. That was off the record, by the way. He's president of the board of trustees at McCulloh."

I processed the information and recalled something. "Isn't he running for U.S. Senate?"

"Score one for the dumb jock," she said, reaching out and touching my elbow with a smile. "He's hoping to knock off Dave Holley."

The normally popular incumbent had shown some vulnerability in recent months because of his support for trade deals hurting Ohio farmers. "Can he do it?"

"If the stars align properly and he stops putting his foot in his mouth. That was also off the record, not that I really care one way or the other. But as you guessed, our mutual interest in Schmidt isn't a coincidence. Preston Campbell isn't the only one who reads obituaries, it turns out. The name John Ebersole rang some bells in the Fulkerson household as well."

"Why?"

"Before I tell you, we've now reached the portion of tonight's program that really is off the record."

"Curiouser and curiouser."

"We—meaning Grant and me—know about the burglary at Schmidt's house."

"How?"

"Bear with me for a second. Because I was kidding about the dumb jock thing"—another light touch on my elbow—"I'm guessing you've wondered why it was never reported."

"Allegedly never reported," I corrected. "I just haven't found any evidence of it."

"And Preston Campbell hasn't found any either?"

"Apparently not. So what's the big secret?"

She looked around the bar. More than one man in the place, including a couple with their own dates, quickly looked away.

"Ever heard of something called DART?"

I told her I hadn't.

"It was a classified nuclear weapons program developed under President Ford. It stood for Dispersed Atmospheric Radiation Tactics. Basically, the idea was to ensure the maximum spread of radioactive isotopes upon detonation of hydrogen bombs to ensure the greatest possible civilian casualties. Part of the MAD approach to Cold War tactics."

"Mutually assured destruction."

"That's right. It was controversial inside the Department of Defense, for what I hope are obvious reasons."

"If it's classified, how do you know about it?"

"Wikipedia. It's all out there now."

"That's comforting, I guess. Putting two and two together, you think Schmidt—"

"Not think, unfortunately. Infer. No, more than that. Conclude. There's strong evidence that Gerhard Schmidt was here under false pretenses, and that someone was passing him secrets about DART."

I LEANED BACK IN my seat and took a drink of beer. She did the same with her wine. I looked around to be sure no one was eavesdropping.

"That's a big accusation."

"And not one made lightly. But Grant—Mr. Fulkerson—thinks it's realistic enough that he wants it nailed down."

"How?"

"By finding Ebersole, and seeing what exactly it was he took from Schmidt's house that night."

"If he took anything."

"We think there's a reason why Schmidt didn't want anyone to know about the burglary."

"Fair enough. Thing is, I'm assuming you know Ebersole died in a fire ten years ago."

"I've seen the articles. As has Grant."

"And?"

"And he's a no-stone-unturned kind of guy. Also, to be blunt, he pays well. He wants me to chase ghosts on his payroll for a while, I'm available."

"That's honest. So, assume for a second that that really is Ebersole in the obit. What do you do if he's found, and then assuming he'll talk, with any information he has?"

"Simple. Right a wrong."

"Meaning?"

"Fulkerson wants to know what the college knew about Schmidt's activities at the time. If it was in any way culpable, he thinks that should come out."

"An admirable sentiment."

"Admirable and expedient, obviously."

"Because of his campaign."

"The last thing Fulkerson needs or wants is evidence of a Cold War cover-up coming out connected to McCulloh. Since relations with the Russians are already so warm."

"Another admirable sentiment, but playing devil's advocate, who cares? It's not like he was on the board back then. I mean, how old is he?"

"In his sixties. You're right, he wasn't. But his stepfather was."

"His stepfather?"

"Jonathan Slagle. He was on the board when all this was going down."

"Different last name?"

"Grant's father died when he was young. His mother wanted him to keep the last name even after Slagle adopted him. The two were still quite close, though."

"Close enough for the sins of the father to rain down on the son?"

"Unfortunately, yes. At least according to Grant."

"Is Slagle still alive?"

She shook her head. "Heart attack at eighty. At his desk, if that counts for anything."

"What'd he do?"

"Slagle Construction. High-end homes. Built it from the ground up, pardon the pun, and passed it on to Grant."

I thought of Crystal and Bob's McMansion, and for the first time wondered if some of Crystal's stress might be related to whether they could hang on to such an expensive crib. Was that why Bob was so incensed at Joe for taking loose change? Every penny counted?

"If there's a story to be told here," Quinne continued, "Fulkerson wants to be the one in the driver's seat. In the interest of full disclosure, and also bald-faced political suitability."

"How cynical. Not a fan of your own boss?"

"My contractee," she corrected. "Don't tell me you've never questioned the motives of one of your clients at the same time you're cashing their checks."

"Big difference between a wife who wants to crush a cheating husband in a divorce and a Cold War espionage scandal."

"Is there?" she said with a grin.

My phone vibrated with an incoming text. Otto. I didn't reply.

"So what do you want me for?"

"A partnership of sorts."

"Of sorts?"

"Think of it as a way to share information. All Fulkerson wants is to find out exactly what the college knew at the time. In order to set the record straight and, yes, cover his own ass in his campaign. Line up the ducks, hold a news conference, get it all out there ahead of the media curve. Public Relations 101."

"And my role?"

"Just keep me in the loop. You find out anything more about Schmidt, or the burglary, or Ebersole, you let me know."

"In the interest of righting a wrong."

"Precisely."

"What do I get out of this partnership?"

She looked up and watched me watch her trace the tip of her third finger around the rim of her wine glass.

"You're privy to any information I gather, which helps you help Preston. Plus a retainer, obviously." She named a figure that would cover four months' rent plus an extended trip to the grocery store. I did my best to maintain my poker face. "So how about it?"

"I suppose I could carve out some time from my busy, busy schedule."

"Could that include lunch tomorrow? Take a meeting with Grant? Review our options?"

"Sounds good."

"Not to put you on the spot or anything, but are you OK doing that ex parte, so to speak? Or do you need to fill Preston in?"

"Like get his permission?"

"Or maybe his blessing. I assume you have a contract with him. Based on my own experience, clients also like to be kept in the loop."

"I'll work it out." I was trying to imagine Preston's reaction, given how high-strung he'd sounded over the phone. "What time tomorrow?"

"I'll text you when I figure out the details. Thanks, Andy. I appreciate you playing along. It makes my job a lot easier. Grant's not the most patient guy."

"In my experience, people in those positions usually aren't."

The bartender stopped by, raising his eyebrows at our glasses. Quinne shook her head, raised hers, and drained the last. I reached for my wallet but she beat me to it, placing a twenty on the counter.

"My treat, after dragging you out after hours like this."

I waited while she ordered an Uber, then walked her to the door.

"Working on anything else these days?" she said as we stood on the street.

I thought of Otto's text from a few minutes earlier.

Let's do this.

"This and that," I said. "You?"

"About the same. McCulloh's my main gig right now. Maybe we can get together after this is all over, talk shop."

"I'd like that."

"Me too," she said. "There's my ride." We shook hands. "Thanks again. See you tomorrow."

"Righto." I waited until she was safely inside the car and had given me a thumbs-up before walking back to my house at 837 Mohawk. I had my keys out and was reaching for the door when something occurred to me. I stopped and looked up the street.

For all her candor, Quinne hadn't said **how** she and Grant Fulkerson knew about a burglary that by all accounts either wasn't reported or disappeared once it was.

19

INSIDE, I LET THE dog out for the evening's final tour of the backyard. While I waited on him, I called Otto to confirm the details of our expedition. We agreed on nine o'clock. Next, I called Preston Campbell, hoping to ask him clandestinely about Schmidt and a secret nuclear weapons program called DART without breaking my promise to Quinne to keep the connection with Fulkerson quiet. I had to leave a message. I let the dog back in, refilled his water bowl, set the alarm on my phone, and lay down on the couch. I awoke two hours later feeling like I could have slept all night. Groggily I grabbed my keys, donned a jacket, and headed out the front door for my van.

We rendezvoused at Roy's church, which was simplest because of the parking and the proximity to our undertaking. It was also risky since he didn't know what we were up to, but I figured we'd deal with that problem later. Theresa was waiting for me when I arrived, pacing nervously beside her Honda Civic. Otto arrived a minute or two later in a minivan much nicer-looking than mine. A heavy-set man I knew only as Buck got out on the passenger side and without speaking reentered and disappeared all the way into the back.

"New wheels?"

"Something borrowed, something blue," Otto said. "And something that sends the right message."

"Which is?"

"Horny suburban dude looking for love in all the wrong places. That's you, by the way."

"I hadn't guessed."

Otto handed over the keys and we piled into the van. I reached for the string bag I'd brought along. I pulled out a pair of black-framed glasses with nothing but uncorrected plastic for lenses and put them on, tossed on my Clippers cap, started the engine, and headed over to Sullivant Avenue. Now came the hard part.

Over the next few minutes I drove through the neighborhood block by block, slowly enough to catch the dull, needy eyes of the women clustered at corners and beneath streetlights and standing around the entrance of mom-and-pop convenience stores, but not so slowly as to give any undercover cops probable cause to pull me over and ask me what I was doing so far from home in a neighborhood like this.

"Anything?" Theresa said.

"Not yet."

"You remember what she looks like?"

"Yes," I said impatiently.

I made it to the Town Street Bridge without luck. I turned, headed up to Broad, and circled back for another go-around. Still nothing, though not for any lack of women staring in my direction as I scanned the streets. Some of them hardly looked older than teenagers; others bore the weight of decades in their thin bodies and pinched faces. About as far from *Pretty Woman* as you could get. After my second unsuccessful loop I changed tactics and drove up and down a couple side streets, keeping an eye on figures trudging along crumbling sidewalks. Still nothing. I widened the circle by a few more blocks, to no avail. Half an hour passed. Behind me I caught a glimpse of the faint glow of lights as Otto and Theresa checked their phones. Otto and Theresa but not Buck. Buck was all business; his space in the van was as dark as the lonely corners of alleys I was driving past, craning my neck to spy our quarry. I headed back to Sullivant, driving the opposite direction now. I made it three blocks when I saw her.

"Bingo."

The phone lights winked out instantly as Otto and Theresa scrambled to join Buck in the back. Keeping an eye on my rear-view mirror, I pulled over so that the side passenger window was beside her. I dropped the window as I hit the unlock button on the door, leaned across the seat and stared. She spoke in a dry voice a moment later.

"Can you give me a ride?"

Darlene Hunter.

"Hop in."

Once she was inside, I let another car pass before slowly pulling away.

"What do you want?" she said.

"What do you got?" I said gruffly, praying she wouldn't recognize me.

She went over the list of things she'd do for me, or that I could do to her, for depressingly small amounts of money. As she talked, I turned left down another side street, feeling momentarily bad about the subterfuge.

"Where are we going?" she said, suddenly nervous. "The alley's up there."

Now a voice from behind us. "We're just taking a little ride."

Theresa, popping up from the back. Darlene whipped around, staring at her in panic.

"The fuck's going on?" She pulled at the door handle—*click, click, click*—but it was locked and wouldn't open.

"We're here to help," Theresa said, coming forward and handing her a water bottle. Darlene batted it away, then gasped as first Otto and then Buck also sat up.

"I don't want no help."

"How long until he notices you're late?"

"Who?"

"Your daddy," Theresa said. "What's his name—Javon."

"He ain't my daddy. You need to leave me alone. I'm fine."

"How long?"

"I said, leave me alone. I've got—"

"*How long?*"

Theresa's voice echoed in the silent van at drill sergeant decibel level.

Darlene mumbled something.

"What was that?"

"Thirty minutes, give or take."

"We'll make it forty, then," Theresa said. "You good with that, QB?"

I told her I was. I turned at the next corner and drove us up to Broad. A few minutes later I pulled into a United Dairy Farmer, busy even at this time of night. The steady stream of customers included a Columbus cop standing in line with a bottle of Gatorade. I slipped past him and went to the ice cream counter. As I waited on my order my phone buzzed with a text. Preston Campbell.

Give you a call tomorrow little
busy right now hope that's OK

His text as manic as his speech in person. I told him that would be fine. Ten minutes later I emerged with a large vanilla shake. I got back in the van and handed it to Darlene. She examined it as if I'd handed her a pipe wrench. But once I was back on Broad, I glanced over and saw her pulling hard on the straw.

We drove around for another couple of minutes to pass the time. I circled downtown, doing two trips around the Statehouse, lights in the cupola glowing in the dark, then headed west again, over the Broad Street bridge, past the new veterans memorial and the children's science center. In another minute or two I was approaching the intersection where I'd picked up Darlene Hunter nearly forty-five minutes earlier. At first I didn't see anyone. Then, as I slowly drove past the stop sign, he was there, agitated, moving in and out of the shadows like a crab scuttling through seaweed. Hoodie. Or, as the bail-revocation paper in Darlene's trash can put it, Javon Martinez, a.k.a. Hustle a.k.a.

Little J. Currently wanted for failing to appear on a domestic violence charge three months earlier. Not one of Otto's clients, but close enough since Otto was well-connected in the local bail bond community.

"Easy, Woody," Otto said from the seat behind me.

I waited until Martinez saw Darlene, who stiffened in her seat at the sight of him. Then I turned down a side street half a block past and parked. Nothing happened at first. Darlene looked around nervously, her breathing shallow. Then he materialized, no more than a mattress-length from the van, hands clasped tightly atop his hoodie in anger, or disbelief, rocking back and forth on the heels of his basketball shoes. I unlocked the van.

"Open the door," I said quietly.

"What?"

"Just do it," Theresa whispered. "It's OK."

The look of fear and uncertainty in her eyes might have been the worst thing I'd seen all night, and the bar was already pretty low. I stopped myself from reaching out to touch her, to let her know it would be all right. But would it? At last she tugged at the door handle. She pushed it open and stepped onto the cracked sidewalk as cool night air flooded the van.

"Where the hell—" Martinez said, but that was all he managed. The side door slid open and Otto and Buck were out in seconds. Otto was a fit enough fellow who could almost always hold his own, but Buck, despite his bulk, moved with the finesse of a ballet dancer as he bounded toward Martinez. It was over almost before it began. Less than a minute after I stopped the van, Martinez was in the rear seat, hands zip-tied behind his back, squeezed between Otto and Buck, cursing up a storm.

"Let's go, Woody," Otto said, steel in his voice.

I went. Theresa was in the middle seat now, arm around Darlene.

"You bitch. You fucking whore. I'm gonna fucking kill you," Martinez said.

"Shut up," Otto said.

"I swear to God, I'm gonna fucking cut your throat as soon as I'm out. I'm gonna—"

"Stop the van, Woody."

"Here?"

"Yes."

I stopped. We were halfway across the Rich Street Bridge, a minute or two from the jail entrance on Front. Across from us was one of downtown's better-known pieces of public art, a bronze deer standing upright, forelegs on the railing, as it contemplated the view. A popular place for selfies.

"Unlock the doors."

I did as I was told. A few seconds later, without a word spoken between them, Buck and Otto wrestled Martinez out of the van. They dragged him over to the deer, looking for all the world like a trio of buddies yukking it up with the sculpture. A moment later they lifted Martinez and tipped him halfway over the railing.

"The fuck," Martinez said, struggling to no avail.

"Water's cold this time of year," Otto said. "Takes your breath away. Makes it hard to swim, assuming you can. And assuming you've got hands free to paddle." They hoisted Martinez another few inches over.

"Don't—"

"Got some big catfish down there. River's a lot cleaner these days. Hungry sons of bitches—they don't leave much behind. Snappers too. Big ones. Beaks like branch trimmers—bite your dick off one two three." They pushed him even farther over, beyond the point where his center of balance would keep him from tipping. Now the only thing that prevented him going over the side was their hands on his waist and shoulders.

"Please—"

"You see how easy we picked you up on the street tonight? Like it was nothing, right?"

"Jesus—"

"Never saw us coming, did you?" Otto's voice as calm as a man reading ingredients off a cereal box.

Martinez, rigid as the deer, shook his head. I glanced behind me. Theresa was sitting straight up, eyes not on the scene playing out on the bridge but on the lights of downtown straight ahead of her. Darlene was rocking back and forth, hands in her lap, looking at I didn't know what. I didn't like what I was seeing, but it was too late to do anything about it now, something I'm guessing Otto was counting on when he conveniently forgot to mention this part of the night's playbook. As a bounty hunter picking up a guy with an active warrant, Otto was legally sanctioned to grab Martinez the way he did, and as his employee for the night I fit under that protective umbrella, if just barely.

"Otto," I called out, not sure what else to do. "We need to get going."

He didn't respond. I called his name again.

"Leave it, Woody," he said. "Everything's under control." He turned his attention back to Martinez. I had my doubts but kept my peace for now. I just hoped Otto knew what he was doing—not in regard to Martinez, but for the good of Darlene.

"Now listen closely," Otto said, directing his attention back to Martinez. "I hear one more word from you about that lady—one single word—you're gonna be in that river for good. I catch wind you've gone anywhere near her, that you've contacted her, spoken to her, **thought** about her, the last thing you're going to remember in this life is what it feels like ten feet under when you can't breathe and you're freezing to death and a snapper is biting off your itsy-bitsy little wiener. You hear me?"

Martinez nodded, shaking.

"I said, you hear me?"

"Yeah." Voice hoarse as if he'd just woken up.

"***You hear me?***"

"Yes!" Martinez screamed.

They were back in the van in a matter of seconds, Martinez again squeezed between Otto and Buck in the rear. This time he was silent, the only noise his labored breathing. I did my best to ignore the fact that he'd soiled himself as he'd been dangled over the bridge, the chilly ripples of the Scioto just a few dozen feet below.

"Drive, Woody," Otto said.

We were at the jail entrance a few minutes later. Otto and Buck wrestled Martinez out and dragged him through the main entrance. Behind me, Darlene Hunter started to cry.

20

AT FIVE MINUTES TO noon the next day I walked inside the Village Tavern in Dublin. The suburb close to eleven on the clock face of Columbus. Hillary Quinne was standing by a window, scrolling through messages on her phone. Seeing me approach, she tapped out a text, clicked the screen closed, and placed the phone in her purse.

"Thanks for agreeing to this, Andy. And coming all this way."

"My pleasure. Always good to see how the other half lives."

"Don't knock the other half until you see the invoices they're willing to pay. But really, Grant's a nice guy once you get past the persona thing."

"Persona?"

"College trustees are another breed, mainly because of the amount of money it takes to win the spot. Add in the campaign stuff—hoo boy."

"Having cold feet about the assignment?"

"Sometimes I wonder. How was your evening—what was left of it, I mean?"

"Uneventful."

"Good to hear."

After dropping Buck and Otto back at the church, Theresa and I had driven Darlene to the East Side, to a secure domestic violence shelter off Alum Creek Drive, where Theresa made arrangements for Darlene to stay for a few days while she figured out next steps. My head finally hit the pillow right before 1 a.m.

"Hillary—good to see you. Sorry I'm late."

I turned as Grant Fulkerson walked up, briefcase in hand.

"You must be Mr. Hayes," he said, extending a hand before Quinne could make introductions.

"Andy's fine. Nice to meet you."

"Nice to meet **you**. My stepfather was a huge fan, despite everything."

"I appreciate that."

"I mean it. Not sure he ever missed a home game, especially in your day. Shall we?"

We followed the hostess to a booth. Quinne and I exchanged glances as we walked. Already, the trustee wasn't quite what I'd expected, at least measured by Quinne's snide remarks earlier. For a so-called construction magnate, not to mention candidate for the U.S. Senate, Fulkerson had an easygoing way about him. A bit shorter than me, trim, with red hair that still maintained a bit of curl even at his age—sixty-five according to the internet search I'd done this morning. A nice suit but several notches below what you saw around Capitol Square every day. The fact he walked in unaccompanied another plus in my book.

"How's Madison?" Fulkerson said as we were seated.

"Good," Quinne said. "Starting to talk about colleges."

"Hard to imagine. Where's the time go. You have a son, isn't that right, Andy?"

"Two, actually." No surprise he already knew about Mike, whose budding prowess as a high school quarterback was regularly covered in the news, alongside the inevitable comparisons to his old man. He nodded with interest at my description of Joe. After a server arrived and took drink orders—iced teas all around—Fulkerson said, "Hillary's brought you up to speed, I take it."

"It sounds like a bad spy movie, honestly."

He laughed. "And it may be one someday. As long as the college isn't the bad guy in it."

"You have a lot riding on how this plays out."

"No question. This hits the wrong way, my campaign's in the toilet. I'd be lucky to win the nomination for dogcatcher."

"That's honest."

"It's practical. Anything to do with the Russians these days is toxic—who cares if it involves something that happened that long ago? The media would have a field day with it, especially because of Holley and the pipeline."

"Pipeline?"

"He's on a select committee considering further sanctions against Moscow for all their meddling with the Trans-European gas pipeline. Suffice to say it'd be one more headache for me. Like I said, practical. But practicality also carries a certain responsibility." He paused to wave at someone across the room.

"Such as?"

"To my stepfather, for starters. Not a lot of people know this, but McCulloh was on the brink of bankruptcy when he joined the board in the seventies. He not only helped save it, he made it into one of the top small schools in the country. I have no interest in squandering that legacy, his or the college's."

"Not to state the obvious, but you're aware there's strong evidence Ebersole died in a fire?"

He looked at Quinne. "We know all that. But you have to admit it's an odd coincidence. A name showing up like that."

"Absent the fire, I'd say yes. So let me ask you this. Who cares about Ebersole, dead or alive? Why not just hold a press conference and say what you know?"

Our drinks arrived. Fulkerson took a sip of tea, nodding in acknowledgment at my point.

"It may come to that. I'm just a person who hates surprises. I'm also anal retentive as hell. I like everything lined up, in a row, accounted for. Drives my wife crazy—people who work for me too. Hillary as well, I'm sure—don't deny it."

She laughed. "Only every other day."

"See? In any case, I've got a formal campaign launch coming in a couple weeks. Worst-kept secret in Ohio, but that's just how these things go. I've given us—meaning Hillary—until then to see what we can find out about Ebersole. If it's a coincidence and there's nothing there, we'll reevaluate."

"So how do I fit in?"

"You've got a good reputation around town. I value people who get things done. Did Hillary tell you how we met?"

"I don't believe so."

"God, Grant, don't bore him with that."

"It's not boring."

"It really is," she said, shaking her head.

"I assume you know I'm in construction." I told him I did. It was an understatement, as I'd learned in my research this morning. Slagle Construction was a midwestern business giant, with projects in half a dozen states at any one time. His office was headquartered in a gleaming new Dublin office building just up the street.

"I had this one job up in Union County. Lot of shrinkage—tools, supplies, you name it."

"Grant," Quinne tried, but he waved her off.

"My foreman was blaming the workers, who were all Mexican. Said they stole everything when his back was turned. I wasn't so sure. I brought Hillary on, had her stake the place out a couple nights. No instructions beyond that. Know what she did?"

I shook my head. Quinne sat, hands in lap, a small smile on her face, defeated in her attempts to silence her boss.

"She sat in a porta potty with a peephole drilled in the side. Four hours until she nailed them, and that particular unit was two days overdue for a cleanout. And it was July. Is that moxie or what? Sure enough, it was the foreman and his buddy."

"Very enterprising," I said.

"And . . . scene," Quinne said. "Back to the thing that matters. Basically, as I told Andy last night, I'm thinking two heads are better than one in this situation. As surprised as I was to see you on campus, it's nice to know someone else has this in their crosshairs. We could use your help."

"How far have you gotten?"

"I've been through the college files, what there are of them from the time."

"And?"

"There's not a lot there. On the surface, Schmidt was exactly as advertised. An East German professor on a cultural exchange."

"Those files—is that how you knew about the burglary?"

"That's right," Fulkerson said before Quinne could reply. "There's a brief report that ended up there, just because a professor was involved. But nothing about what was taken. That's what has us worried."

Turning to Quinne, I said, "Have you talked to the widow? The woman whose husband's obituary named Ebersole?"

"Not yet, and obviously she was first on the list. She won't return calls from the number I found for her, and I can't raise anybody at her house."

I recalled the mysterious "other guy" the older woman mentioned to me the day I was there, the man who, in addition to the police, had stopped by asking questions. I told Quinne what I was thinking.

"Any description?"

"I didn't get that far, sorry."

Quinne and Fulkerson looked at one another.

"What?"

"It could be nothing," Fulkerson said. "But it's what we've worried about. If someone from the other side found out about this somehow—don't ask me how—and they're digging up dirt, it's exactly the scenario we're trying to circumvent. The reason why we have to do this first, and the right way. Otherwise, I'm not going to Washington, and the reputation of an institution dear to my heart is tarnished, maybe irreparably."

"Your cause of concern is in that order?"

"Does it matter?" Fulkerson said. "A shitstorm's a shitstorm no matter what it hits first."

"I appreciate your honesty."

"Don't. Just help Hillary straighten this out. That's all that matters."

FULKERSON HAD meetings after lunch. He bid me goodbye with a businesslike handshake. Quinne accompanied me to my van.

"What'd you think?"

"Not quite what I expected."

"Meaning?"

"Nothing major," I said. "But with some guys like that the honesty seems fake, like they're trying to come off as no-bullshit types but they just end up sounding like, I don't know, parodies of themselves."

"He didn't?"

"He did a good impression of a guy looking out for number one who also happens to care about doing the right thing. I'll take him at his word, for what it's worth."

"That's good to hear. Is there anything else you need from me at this point?"

I was appraising the look that accompanied that last comment, at the same time admiring the sharp figure Quinne cut today in a pair of designer jeans and snug sweater, when my phone buzzed with an incoming call.

"Hang on," I said reluctantly. The number wasn't familiar. I answered anyway.

"I told you!" The voice of a woman, nearly hysterical.

"Hello?"

"*I warned you!*"

I raised a finger at Hillary and moved back a couple of steps. "Who is this?"

"Monica," she said, almost screaming. "Monica Mathers."

"What's wrong?"

"What's wrong is that Preston is dead!"

21

CONTROLLED CHAOS GREETED ME as I left my van and approached Preston Campbell's block twenty-five minutes later after breaking more than a few speeding limits rushing south on the outer belt. Half a dozen police cruisers lined the street, blocking anyone from driving up or down. Yellow crime-scene tape restricted further access, with a young uniformed cop standing by in case the tape didn't send a strong enough keep-out message. I didn't need to worry about penetrating the barrier. Monica broke away from a pair of officers as soon as I walked up.

"I warned you," she repeated, her voice weaker than on the phone.

"What happened?"

"His office called me looking for him. He hadn't come to work, which was unusual. Say what you will of Preston, he was habitual."

"They called you?"

"His agency's computer system went down midmorning. If they can't reach him there's a phone tree system. After they got me, I tried right away but it went straight to voice mail. It's not like him not to answer his phone. And then—he hadn't answered a couple of my texts last night. I got nervous and came over."

"How—"

"He'd been shot," she said quietly. Eyes red and face blotchy. "There was blood everywhere. It was so horrible."

In the distance, a knot of officers stood at the foot of Preston's porch steps. Past them, on the other side of the cordon, satellites sprouted from TV trucks.

"What are the police saying?"

"Nothing. They just asked me a few questions when they arrived."

"I'm so sorry."

"I asked you not to take this case." Voice newly charged again as she stared at me.

"Are you suggesting it's related? That this had something to do with your dad?"

"I don't know. I have no idea." She started to cry. "There've been break-ins. I told him to move out of here. It's not the neighborhood we grew up in. He wouldn't listen. The house meant so much to him, because of Mom and . . . Dad."

Not knowing what else to do, I put my arm around her and told her again how sorry I was. She tensed at first, sniffed, whispered her thanks, and for a moment leaned against me. A moment later she shrugged free as two detectives ducked under the tape and approached. One was Stickdorn, the other a woman I didn't recognize.

"Detective Herman is going to ask you a couple questions," Stickdorn said, eyeing me as he directed the statement at Monica. "Then you should probably get home, get some rest. It may be a long day."

She departed with the woman, but not before casting a baleful glance in my direction, equal parts exhaustion and anger.

"She called me just now," I said to Stickdorn. "That's the only reason I'm here."

"Better be. When's the last time you saw her brother?" The question straightforward but no-nonsense, like the man himself. A big guy, short-cropped hair, clean cut, waist thickening but his physique still reminiscent of his days playing high school football at Centennial High. A few years before my time, which accounted for the divorce or two he had on me.

"Sunday—the day I took the case."

"Talk to him since?"

I told him about his call Monday night while I was at Laura's condo, and showed him the text from last night.

> Give you a call tomorrow little busy right now hope that's OK

Stickdorn took out his phone and snapped a picture of my screen.

"That gives us a time frame, anyway, plus it's helpful because we can't find his phone. Probably one of the things on the shopping list. Huge black market for them right now. Halfway to China as we speak, I'm guessing."

"Since when do burglars shoot people, though? Unless it's a drug thing." But even as I said it, I recalled a remark Monica made, standing on the sidewalk after my Sunday meeting with them. *His bathroom cabinet's like a mini-pharmacy.* I repeated the comment to Stickdorn.

"Normally, most burglars don't carry," Stickdorn said. "They're just smart enough to know what a gun spec gets them if they're caught. But these aren't normal times. Opioids have everything turned upside down. The zombies are running the asylum and there's no saying what could happen. I'll let the crime scene guys know about the medications just in case."

"Neighbors?"

"Nobody heard anything, and there's no sign of forced entry up front. But the rear backs up to an alley, and it's pretty dark back there."

I reminded him of the rough greeting I'd received at Gina Stratton's house when I'd raised the issue of Ebersole.

"Believe it or not, I already thought of that. We'll check that guy out—the one who rolled you."

"He didn't roll me."

"Whatever you say."

I shoved my hands into my pockets and stared at the crime scene up the block. It had just occurred to me that Campbell was likely killed sometime between the moment Otto and Buck and I picked up Javon Martinez and drove him over the Rich Street

Bridge and when Theresa and I dropped Darlene off at the domestic violence shelter just after midnight. Was there something I could have done differently? What if I'd called him right after he sent his text? Would he be alive if I had?

"How's your case going?"

"What?"

"Your case," Stickdorn said. "Finding this guy who supposedly shot Howie Campbell."

"Not sure I have one at this point, since my client's no longer around. Plus, half of it's gone down a rabbit hole anyway."

"What's that supposed to mean?"

I told him about the work I was doing for Grant Fulkerson on behalf of McCulloh College, including the somewhat far-fetched allegation that Gerhard Schmidt had been a spy collecting Cold War nuclear secrets under the guise of teaching German literature and language.

"That sounds pretty loopy even for you, Woody," Stickdorn said. He looked up as someone called his name from across the street, and waved in acknowledgment. "My girlfriend might dig it, though. She loves all those spy novels. Gotta run. Not planning any out-of-town trips this week?"

"I'm around."

"Good man," he said, and walked away.

22

BACK HOME, I SAT at my kitchen table and fought the exhaustion that had settled over me like a hangover as soon as I drove away from Preston Campbell's neighborhood. Exhaustion and gloom. It was irrational to think I could have done anything to prevent Preston's death. Stickdorn was right; the ferocity of the opioid epidemic had ensured that all bets were off when it came to crime. I'd lost track of stories of parents overdosing with their kids in the car, at the park, in a McDonald's bathroom. Who's to say what anyone would do to find the next fix? One look at Darlene Hunter told you all you needed to know about the grip that addiction held people in. What I couldn't shake was something more elemental. Something thrown in my face by Monica in the street just now. *I warned you.* What if I hadn't taken the case at all? What if this wasn't drug related and someone out there didn't like the idea of old secrets being unearthed? What if I were the tipping point that brought Preston and his quixotic search into full view? What if Fulkerson and Quinne were right, as they said over lunch, and a campaign operative was sniffing at their heels? Given the toxic nature of politics today, was it a stretch to think extreme measures might be taken with a prime U.S. Senate seat in battleground Ohio up for grabs? Did it matter if Ebersole died in a fire if people mistakenly believed he was still alive? Less than zero evidence of the Ohio Grassman, our local version of Sasquatch, didn't keep Bigfoot hunters from trampling the fields of eastern Ohio year after year in search of a single sliver of evidence that their hunt wasn't in vain.

Another dark thought: Preston's murder underscored his own conspiracy theory that death stalked the principals involved in the shootout at the Zimmermans' house forty years earlier. But was that really true? For lack of anything better to do, I fired up my laptop and scrolled to the section in Preston's files on the three men who had died afterward. On the surface, based on the reports he'd compiled, it was hard to see something larger at work.

Jerry Reade, one of the two Ebersole accomplices, had been knifed in the state pen in Mansfield six months after his arrival. A dispute over commissary items that went down a few years before the state shuttered what had become a hellhole; today it was best known as the place where *The Shawshank Redemption* was filmed. No matter how I looked at it, it seemed like a run-of-the-mill prison shanking, as cold as that sounded.

Next was Harvey Heflin, the detective in charge of investigating the shootout, killed in a freak accident in his garage after a jack slipped on the car he was fixing. In the account in the paper his distraught widow said that she couldn't understand it, "because he was always so careful." That gave me pause. But you only had to screw up once working around machinery, as my father and uncle drummed into my head growing up in farm country. I scrolled further and realized, a bit to my surprise, that that was the only one of the three "mysterious" deaths not accompanied by an autopsy report, which seemed unlike Preston and his meticulous-bordering-on-obsessive research. And now he wasn't around to explain the discrepancy. Just to cover my tracks, I called a coroner's office investigator I knew to ask if the report was still around. I had to leave a message asking him to get back to me as soon as he could.

I was reading the reports on the most recent fatality, the death following the hit-skip of the second accomplice, a guy named Darrell Weidner, when Hillary Quinne called.

"Are you doing OK?"

The last thing I'd told her before sprinting to my van was that Preston had been killed.

"I'm fine," I lied.

"Any idea yet what happened?"

"Home invasion, as far as the police can tell. Sometime last night."

"Oh God, not while we were—"

"After that," I said, thinking of our conversation at Club 185. "Probably closer to midnight, based on a text he sent me."

"I hate to ask this . . ."

"Go ahead."

"Any suggestion it was related to, you know, Ebersole?"

"His sister certainly thinks so. And I've got some questions. But the police aren't looking in that direction. It's a tough neighborhood. Preston was the kind of vulnerable person that bad guys prey on. He had a lot of electronics in the house—if someone heard about that, or he let it slip, it made him a target. Plus all the pharmaceuticals he was on. I mentioned the rough handling I got at Gina Stratton's, and they're going to check it out. Probably another reason to avoid the place for now."

"Makes sense. And I hope you're right, about the electronics and all that."

"You hope I'm right he got killed by a burglar?"

"Sorry. That came out the wrong way."

"I understand. If I hear any differently I'll let you know. Same for anything else I turn up on Ebersole."

"After this, I appreciate it even more. Sure you're doing OK?"

I repeated my lie.

"All right then. Let me know if you need anything from me."

I told her I would, wondering again if I was reading too much into the tone of the question. I turned back to my computer, ready to shut it down and do something else to clear my head. Before I did, I looked again at the document still open on the screen. The report on the hit-skip that led to the death of the second accomplice. As suspicious as that sounded in the context of the other deaths, a closer inspection of the records told a different story. Weidner had been hit while walking along a dark South End street at two in the morning. Furthermore, the autopsy indicated he had a blood alcohol content of 0.17—in other words, he was drunker than hell—meaning he could easily have wandered into the path of a vehicle, which in fact was what both the police and the coroner concluded. I was about to close out the file when something occurred to me.

According to Preston's files, there was no immediate sign of any relatives of Jerry Reade, hardly a surprise given how long ago he died. As for Harvey Heflin, his widow passed away nearly twenty years ago.

But what about Weidner? He'd been the youngest of the three, mid-twenties at the time. Sure enough, obsessive as always, Preston had included Weidner's obituary in the collection. It named his widow as Carole. I plugged her name into a search engine and a few seconds later was staring at what appeared to be her current address, less than fifteen minutes away. I texted Quinne the information and told her what I was thinking. She responded shortly with a thumbs up. Other than Gina Stratton, Carole Weidner was the first person I'd come across who might have actually known Ebersole. Even if I was doing nothing more than honoring my commitment to Preston, it might be worth talking to her.

23

CAROLE WEIDNER LIVED IN a U-shaped single-street subdivision carved out of a pocket of property off South High, the kind of cramped development where the houses are perfectly new and adequate looking but sit just a little too close to one another, like boats bumping together at a small, low-rent dock. Since she hadn't answered her phone the first few times I tried, night was falling by the time I made it over. She invited me inside and served both of us decaf coffee.

"That was a long time ago," she said as we settled in her living room. "It seems like another lifetime."

"It must have been hard for you."

"It wasn't easy, that's for sure. After Darrell went to prison I had to find a full-time job. Fortunately, I landed something with the county. I made a good secretary, I guess."

"Is this where you lived when he got out?"

"Heavens, no." She lifted her cup and held it on her lap. Despite the short black hair that I assumed she colored, she seemed older than the sixty-plus years or so that I guessed. Age or arthritis had stooped her shoulders a little, and she moved slowly, as if warding off a little more than ordinary aches and pains. "We were still in a dump on the other side of High. It took a lot of effort to end up here."

Just for a moment the years fell away as she glanced in pride around the well-kept living room and its purchased-new furniture. A beribboned bichon frise napped on the opposite end of the couch from her. Fox News aired on the room's sizable TV, the sound muted while we talked.

"So you want to know about John Ebersole?"

"That's right." I explained briefly about the obituary, and Preston's belief, however foolhardy, that he might still be alive.

"Ebersole was a mean son of a bitch, I'll tell you that. I never wanted Darrell around him. But there was no telling him anything in those days."

"Mean how?"

"His manner, more than anything else. Demanding, dismissive, mouth like a pirate. I'll grant you Darrell was no angel, but the thing was, he was weak. He went along with Ebersole because he didn't know any better. Ebersole preyed on men like that. Recruited them and treated them like cannon fodder. Jerry Reade, same exact thing. He died in prison, did you know that?"

I told her that I did.

"That was on Ebersole, 100 percent."

I sat forward. "Are you saying he arranged it?"

"Not arranged, no. But Reade was a little simple, if you know what I mean. I'm not even sure he finished high school. He was putty in Ebersole's hands. Did what he told him, docile as a lamb. Kid like that was going to be eaten alive behind bars, and sure enough he was. And Ebersole knew that. Probably why he picked him for his jobs. No back talk. But also expendable, just like Darrell."

"You stuck by Darrell, though. That says something."

"What was I supposed to do? I was still married to him. Had one in diapers and another on the way when he went inside. Kids still needed a father, and it's not like other men were beating down my door. Prison wife with two rug rats and no money. Yeah, real catch I was."

"Darrell got out in 2000?"

"Two thousand one," she corrected. "Week after the towers fell. Great timing—that was always Darrell. Recession hit and whatever chance he had for a steady job was gone. He got by on menial labor, when he worked." She seemed about to say more but stopped.

"The hit-skip was later?"

"Just about ten years after that. He lasted a month before an infection took him."

"I've read the autopsy report," I said. "I know he was, well, under the influence that night."

A dry laugh. "That's putting it mildly. He was an alcoholic at that point, pure and simple. On his way back from the bar—walking because he'd lost his license."

As delicately as possible, I explained Preston's theory that people connected to Ebersole seemed to die under unusual circumstances.

"Course they did," she said.

"I'm sorry?"

"I already told you, Ebersole picked his boys carefully. He treated them good when they worked for him, but he didn't want anybody with a lot of gumption. Jerry Reade was simple. Darrell was weak-minded. People like that have a hard time making it in this world."

"You don't think Ebersole was involved in any way in your husband's death?"

"I didn't say that, did I?"

Something in her tone made me look more closely at her. She seemed nervous for the first time since I arrived.

"Mrs. Weidner?"

"I suppose it doesn't make any difference now. But the thing is, the worse Darrell's drinking got, the more he went on about Ebersole disappearing and him taking the fall and ending up in prison. He was always bitching about it. I told him the reason he went inside and Ebersole went free was because the guy was just smarter and meaner, both of which were true. He wouldn't listen. He told just about anybody who'd listen, especially down at the bars."

"Do you think he knew where Ebersole was?"

She shook her head. "He was just mad about it, is all. I let him talk. But then, a few weeks after the accident . . ."

I waited while she stared across the room, collecting her thoughts.

"Thing is, Ebersole sent me money, after Darrell died. With a note, saying he was sorry to hear it."

"You're kidding. When?"

"Whenever that was."

"You know Ebersole is supposed to have died in a fire, right? Could it have been after that?"

"Not likely. How could he, if he was dead?"

"Do you have any records of the money? A letter?"

"Nothing like that. It was cash. It helped a little, I was glad of it, even it being Ebersole."

"How much, if I may ask?"

"Enough," she said. She crossed her arms, forestalling further discussion of the amount. I recalled what she said earlier. *It took a lot of effort to end up here.*

"You suspected it was blood money? Is that it? That he was somehow responsible for what happened?"

"I'm not saying that. It just struck me as odd, given what a mean sonofabitch he was."

"Did you tell the police?"

"I thought about it. Wasn't sure they'd believe me, and didn't really want the aggravation, tell you the truth. They didn't exactly treat Darrell good, considering he was just working for Ebersole and not like the mastermind or something."

I tried not to let my disappointment show. Hearing of someone's recent contact with Ebersole—even if it was ten years ago—was like glimpsing the Grassman through a glade, only to find nothing there after dashing up to see. So close, but nothing to show for it in the end.

Carole interrupted my thoughts. "This fellow you know really thinks Ebersole is still alive?"

"He did." I explained what happened to Preston.

"That's awful. World's gone to hell in a handbasket, you ask me."

"But could there be any truth to it? About Ebersole, I mean?"

"He died in that fire, far as I know. And good riddance. Hope he burned alive."

"You feel that way even though he sent you money?"

"You never knew the man."

"Which means, like you said, you don't think he sent it out of the goodness of his heart."

She returned her cup to the coffee table in front of her and shifted in her seat. "Let me put it this way, all right? It came at a good time, and after the way he treated Darrell, I wasn't inclined to feel bad about taking it. As for his motives, you'll have to ask him—except you can't, I guess."

I took a sip of my own coffee, now lukewarm and flat. It was an intriguing tale, enough to imply that Darrell Weidner's death hadn't been accidental, but lacking any further substance to prove it definitively. To prove it, or even to say whether Weidner knew something about Ebersole's discovery the night of the Schmidt burglary or was just rightly pissed off at the shitty end of the stick he ended up holding.

I said, "I should probably go. I appreciate you taking the time."

"Not sure I've been much help. Like I said, I haven't thought about those days in a long while."

"I don't blame you."

"I wish . . ."

"Yes?"

A look on her face as if she'd spied a face in a crowd she thought she recognized.

"I wish I could help you more. It's just all jumbled together now."

"Don't worry about it. Call if you think of anything else."

I left my card, thanked her for the coffee, shook her hand—soft and frail, like something held loosely inside a felt bag—and headed home. As I drove, I pondered the irony that Preston might have been right all along, at least about Weidner, assuming Ebersole had had a way, puppet master–like, of manipulating events from whatever spider hole he was hiding in before his death. It also made me wonder more about the police detective's untimely demise in his garage while fixing his car, as far-fetched as linking that to Ebersole seemed. Of course, it was also possible there'd never be an answer either way.

I was still pondering these likelihoods and turning my conversation with Carole Weidner over in my head as I approached my door a few minutes later and unlocked it. And so it was that as I entered, a moment or two passed before I sensed that something felt wrong, as if I were on the verge of finding I'd left the window open on a day threatening rain and was about to pay the consequences. If only. Instead, I looked up and saw a man wearing a ski mask that didn't quite match the weather sitting at my dining room table, my laptop open before him.

"THE HELL ARE YOU?"

He didn't reply, but instead kept working, latex-gloved fingers tapping away at the keyboard.

I took a step closer, hand reaching for my phone. "I said—"

Without speaking, he lowered his right hand to his waist, produced a gun with a suppressor screwed onto the barrel, and set it on the table beside the laptop as nonchalantly as if he were laying out silverware in the proper order.

"Put the phone away."

"Make me."

Faster than I would have thought possible the gun was back in his hand and pointed between my eyes. Slowly, I pocketed the phone.

"Password."

"What?"

"I need the password to your computer."

"Why?"

"Because I'm going to shoot your dog if you don't give it to me." Hopalong lay on the couch, oblivious to the threat but within his sight line. The man's voice even and neutral; he might as well have been a bored schoolboy reading a poem.

I swallowed. I told him the password. To my surprise, he didn't enter it but instead continued staring at me through his mask's eyeholes.

"Say it again."

"What—"

"Again."

I repeated the password, an amalgam of Mike's and Joe's birthdays.

"Again."

Unbidden, an image popped into my head. A kind of sideways déjà vu. Not a vision I'd experienced before, not like that. But as if this scene had played out previously, and I had some knowledge of it. Played out, where else, but in Preston Campbell's living room. Preston kept paper files on his father's case, but he too had everything stored electronically. That's how he was able to hand me the flash drive so easily at the end of our interview, allowing me to transfer everything to my own laptop. Had the man at my dining room table, calm as an actual skier filling out an online rental form, performed the same scene with Preston? Requesting the password multiple times not just to obtain it, but to entrust it to memory because the person providing it wouldn't be around much longer?

I had one play. If my gut was right, the third repetition was all he would need to recall it permanently. But he also wasn't going to risk getting it wrong or the possibility I was bullshitting him. He would have to try it at that point. If I was right, his attention would be distracted for the tiniest amount of time while he tapped at the keyboard. That would be my sole opportunity: the stand-off equivalent of stealing home. If I was wrong, he'd shoot me on the spot, followed by Hopalong. Part of me knew it didn't matter either way. I repeated the password.

"You better hope you're telling the truth," he said, hunting and pecking.

"I hope so too," I said, charging him.

The gun was up and aimed at me faster than I would have thought possible. For no discernible reason, the image that came to mind as I hurled myself across the room—my last ever?—was Crystal's face from the other day, puffy and red, as she hoisted her Bud Light at one in the afternoon.

Bam bam bam!

25

BAM BAM BAM!

Someone was pounding on my front door.

Ski Mask looked up, startled.

Ark ark ark ark ark ark ark ark ark! went the dog.

"Guh," I said, making contact with the intruder a second later, sending us both tumbling to the floor.

Snick snick went his gun, shattering my dining room window.

Bam bam bam!

Ark ark ark ark ark ark ark ark ark!

Most of my weight landed on my adversary, and he was temporarily stunned. I used the moment to liberate his weapon with my right hand and send it skidding across the floor. With my left I pulled off the mask. A man I'd never seen before, with a surprisingly neat, reddish goatee, stared back at me. The moment I spent studying his face—hard, athletic, ambitious—cost me what little advantage I'd gained. He reared up and head-butted me, knocking me to the side. He wrestled free of my grip, and a moment later our positions were reversed. He hit me hard in the mouth with a solid right, and then both his gloved hands were around my neck and he was squeezing with the grip of a man accustomed to getting his way. I panicked as I couldn't catch my breath. I grabbed his hands and tried to break his grasp, but it was like trying to budge a pair of steel struts. Spots speckled my dimming vision. I tried arching my back, but his grip tightened further. The dog's barking and the pounding on the door became distant echoes within my oxygen-starved brain. As I slackened in defeat, he adjusted his position to bear down with even more strength, his composure finally cracking as he groaned slightly with the effort he was expending on crushing my larynx. Thorough is as thorough does. As I lost consciousness, my arms flailed above my head. My right hand brushed the plant stand in the corner of the living room. I closed my fingers around the stand's nearest wooden leg. I pulled, and felt the stand wobble. I pulled again, and then yanked with my remaining strength and a moment later twenty pounds of ceramic pot and soil and recently watered ficus tipped and crashed onto the head of the man atop me.

Stunned, he relaxed his grip for just a moment. I took a huge, shuddering breath and clapped both my hands on either side of his dirt-covered head as hard as I could. As he fell backward I kneed him in the groin and rolled free and used the seat of a chair to pull myself up. He rose to his knees and I kicked him in the head and his chin snapped back and bits of dirt and ficus root and ceramic dust floated to the floor.

Bam bam bam!

Ark ark ark ark ark ark ark ark ark!

I watched him warily as he slowly rose, blood streaming from his nose and a cut on his mouth. Eyes flicking back and forth, looking for the gun. A moment later he found it, in my hands, barrel dead centering on his chest. If he'd known what I knew about my facility with weapons he would have rushed me and we'd probably be talking game over. Good thing for me he wasn't a gambler. Instead, he rolled to his left, got to his feet, and limped into my dining room, heavy boots *clomp clomp clomping* along the way. He threw open the front door, turned, and said, "Lucky you." And then he was gone.

I took another breath, rubbed my aching mouth, rose with difficulty, and limped toward the door myself. I passed Hopalong, erect and still barking as though the long-dreaded invasion of the Squirrel People had begun, and peered outside.

"What the hell."

I stared at the man who'd spoken, and then at the person beside him. The last two people—the very last—I expected to run into that night. And possibly ever. Standing on my threshold, eyes wide, stood the hefty young man and the tiny older woman who'd given me such a warm welcome the first time I visited Gina Stratton's home, searching for whoever included the name John J. Ebersole in Wayne Stratton's obituary.

26

"JESUS, DUDE. YOU OK?"

"Don't think I'll be dancing the *Nutcracker* at the Ohio this year," I said. "Other than that, yes. Mostly."

"You gonna call the cops?" the man said nervously.

"Not just yet."

"Not that I'm complaining, but why not?"

"Just need a minute to process, is all."

We were sitting in the dining room. Or rather, they were sitting while I slowly cleaned up the mess that my encounter with Ski Mask made. I'd swept up as much of the potting soil as I could find and deposited it and the ficus and the large shards of the pot in the trash bin. My ill-advised charge as the intruder entered the password had knocked the laptop to the floor. I righted it on the kitchen table. The screen was blank, but it came to life again when I tapped the space bar. I paged idly through the electronic files Preston sent me, wondering if they'd been the man's ultimate target—obviously, all signs had to point to that—and if so, which of any of them were of the most interest. And was it just a coincidence the break-in happened while I was visiting with Carole Weidner, one of the last living links to the Buckeye Burglar's exploits and a possible Cold War scandal?

I flipped through a couple more documents, paused at one in particular, and took another pull of my Black Label, bringing it well below sea level. It was my second beer in the short time since my guests arrived. The beer lessened the discomfort of what appeared to be a tooth loosened when Ski Mask's fist hit home during our struggle. My visitors had declined a beer and were drinking Dr. Pepper from my fridge. His name was Jeremy. He was Gina's cousin. The lady was Mae, his aunt, sister to Gina's mother.

"OK." Setting aside the laptop and pulling up a chair. "Your turn. What are you doing here—not that I'm complaining. You saved my life, knocking like that."

"I should have tried to stop him," Jeremy said, apology etched on his face. "But I heard the gun and I just wasn't sure—"

"You did the right thing. He's not the kind of guy you want to get between. Which is why I'm so grateful to you."

"You know that guy?" Mae said.

Something about the way she asked the question, with more than an edge to her voice, made me study her face a moment. It was hard and unrevealing.

"Never saw him before. And hope I never do again. What makes you ask that?"

Ignoring the question, Mae asked another. "That day you came by the house. You wanted to talk to Gina?"

"Yes. Still do, actually."

Mae didn't respond. After a moment Jeremy cleared his throat.

"Gina's missing."

"Missing?"

"She left home. Her and Hailey. We thought maybe you might know where she was. Since you were poking around."

"Hailey?"

"Gina and Wayne's daughter."

"We looked you up," Mae said. "From the card you left. You're good at finding people."

"I didn't mean to push you like that, that day," Jeremy said apologetically. "We've gone through a lot recently."

I told him it was all right, that I understood.

"How about that guy?" Mae said, gesturing at the door.

Gingerly, I ran my left hand over my neck, tender and bruised from his iron fingers. "What about him?"

"Did he know where Gina is?"

"Why would he know?"

"Because he came by our house, asking about her."

I LOOKED at each in turn. Realized how downtrodden and defeated both appeared. Considered the effort it must have taken to come to my house after our first encounter. Mulled what it might have cost me if they hadn't made the effort.

"That's the same guy?"

"No question," Jeremy said.

"And he was looking for Gina?"

"That's right."

"Did he say who he was? Who he was working for?" I thought of Grant Fulkerson and his concern that Dave Holley, his Senate rival, was running a dirty tricks campaign.

They both shook their heads.

"Whoever he is, he's one determined guy," I said. "But back to Gina. How long has she been missing?"

"Since right after you showed up," Jeremy said.

"Was she there? That time you—"

"She weren't there, for real, that day," Mae interjected. "She'd gone to the grocery store. But we was real nervous, because of the cops coming by, asking about Ebersole. And then—"

"Yes?"

"We're pretty sure someone'd been watching the house. And following Gina. And parking outside Hailey's school."

"Who was it?"

"No idea. That guy just now? He's as good a guess as any."

I glanced again at the document I'd paused at on my laptop. A photocopy of a *Citizen-Journal* article.

"Ebersole," I said, forcing myself to focus on our conversation. "The one in the obituary. Do you know if we're talking about the same person as the Buckeye Burglar? That shot a cop, and got shot himself?"

If I'd been expecting a breakthrough in the case, Mae's response was deflating.

"We don't know, tell you the truth. Great-uncle to Wayne is all we heard. Gina said she'd never even heard of him until this summer."

I thought of something. "Do you know if Wayne had any connection to Rochester, New York?"

"I think that's where he was from, originally," Mae said. "Drifted to Ohio at some point. Sure they was glad to be rid of him. Wish he'd just stayed there, for Gina's sake."

"Meaning?"

"Thing is, Gina had it kind of rough," Jeremy said, almost as if apologizing.

"Rough how?"

"Rough like Wayne wasn't never much for work. Did odd jobs, fixed cars, occasionally got shifts as a warehouse picker, usually around Christmastime. That's how he got injured."

"What do you mean?"

"Threw his back out a couple of years ago, loading shit for Amazon. He already drank like a fish. Didn't take long and he was hooked on the percs he got at the emergency room. He went from that to heroin real fast. Barely worked from then on."

"Did Gina have a job?"

"Cashier at Giant Eagle. But she missed a lot of days, dealing with Wayne and watching Hailey. We helped when we could, but . . ."

"But we was scared of Wayne, is what he's trying to say," Mae said, eyes still in her lap, hands folding and unfolding over and over, as if she just couldn't clean them of dirt. "Him and his pill guy. He owed a lot of money, at the end. That might be . . ."

"Might be what?"

"That might be why that guy came by, looking for Gina," Jeremy said. "At least that's what we speculated." He paused. "Until tonight."

"What happened?"

"Things were getting pretty bad there," Jeremy said, glancing at his aunt. "Wayne was dope sick all the time. Almost any money Gina brought home he'd use to buy drugs. Even traded their groceries away. One day she was crying and screaming at him, telling him he had to stop, that Hailey was hungry, that the kids were making fun of her because she had holes in her clothes and she smelled because the shower didn't work and they didn't have any money to fix it. Wayne up and hit her, hard, left a bruise. And then he was crying too, begging forgiveness, talking bullshit about how sorry he was. He made a phone call that night, and a couple days later a bunch of money showed up."

"Money?"

"In the mail. Few hundred bucks."

"From where?" Immediately, I thought of Carole Weidner's story of Ebersole helping her out after Darrell's death.

"No idea."

"Return address?"

Mae shook her head. "Right after that Wayne left the house, said he was gonna make things right, and that's the last anyone saw of him. Cops came by three weeks later, said they'd found him up on the Hilltop. Overdose. Coroner said he'd been dead at least a week. It was a relief, tell you the truth. At least for a few days. Then Wayne's dealer came around, looking for Gina. Said he was still owed big time."

Mention of the coroner reminded me I still needed to find the results of the autopsy of Harvey Heflin—the detective assigned to investigate Howie Campbell's shooting of Ebersole, who'd died in the freak garage accident. But that seemed a low priority now. I asked them if they knew how much Wayne owed.

"Two thousand dollars, supposedly," Mae said. "Gina told the guy she barely had twenty day-to-day, but he didn't believe her. Said Wayne must have been holding out—he'd forked over that mystery money once, so there must be more. He threatened her. Gave her an ultimatum. The next day this other guy was there, looking for Gina and asking questions about Ebersole. We figured they were connected or something. Day after that Gina and Hailey were gone."

I said, "But still no idea why Gina put Ebersole in the obituary?"

"None," Jeremy said.

"Any chance the money that showed up came from Ebersole? And that she was, you know, grateful?"

"She knew more than we did, if so," Mae said. "He was supposed to have died in a fire, right?"

I acknowledged the point, even as I thought about the coincidence that money had shown up out of nowhere helping both Carole Weidner and Wayne Stratton, both people with connections to Ebersole.

Mae interrupted my thoughts. "So, can you help us?"

"Help you what?"

"Help us find Gina. Before he does."

"Who?"

"The dealer."

I finished my beer and leaned back. Eyed the article on my laptop. Thought about everything I'd been through so far with this case, which increasingly resembled a hall of mirrors, most of them cracked.

"Any idea who he is?"

"We never knew his name," Jeremy said.

"Just his nickname," Mae said dismissively.

"Which was?"

"Little J," they both said at once.

HOPALONG RAISED HIS HEAD, yawned, stretched, and went back to sleep at my feet. I fought the urge to reach for a third beer and instead flashed to the Rich Street Bridge a night earlier. *Got some big catfish down there these days*. I quizzed Jeremy and Mae further on the identity of Wayne's dealer. A minute later I had to acknowledge the truth. The man who might hold a clue to the mystery of the obit via the money Wayne had given him was Javon Martinez, the same person Otto and Buck dangled over the Scioto to protect the fortunes of Darlene Hunter.

"Something wrong?" Mae said.

"Not so much wrong as complicated."

"Complicated how?"

"Complicated in ways I can't go into."

"But can you help us?"

After this most recent revelation, I wondered if they'd really want my help. But I said, "Let me ask you this. Let's assume Gina's OK, but just hiding. If that's true, where would she go?"

Mae said, "Hard to say. My sister—her mom—is dead. Her father's out of the picture and good riddance. She was an only child. We were pretty much all she and Hailey had."

"What about Freddy?" Jeremy said. Mae uttered something under her breath.

"Who's Freddy?"

"Buddy of Wayne's," Mae said, the look on her face as if she was describing something rancid beneath the sink. "Came by from time to time. He was sweet on Gina."

"Any idea where this Freddy lives?"

They didn't know. Nor did they know his last name, or anything else about him, other than he drove a truck and was out of town a lot and didn't do nearly as many drugs as Wayne.

"That's not a lot."

"We tried not to pay him much mind," Mae said.

Rather than respond, I let my eyes settle on the headline of the picture on my laptop.

MCCULLOH COLLEGE MOURNS
STUDENT KILLED IN ACCIDENTAL FALL

I remembered the piece, one of several non–Buckeye Burglar articles running alongside updates on the shooting and Ebersole's arrest. But this time something else had jumped out at me.

"Everything OK?" Jeremy said, examining my face.

"Yeah," I said, turning the laptop away from me.

"So can you help us?" Mae repeated. "Help us find Gina and Hailey?"

Again, I wondered. Because how much help had I been to anyone so far? Counting those two, if you included Ebersole I now had three missing people to track down, without a clue where any of them were. It almost seemed easier at this point to turn the search for the missing burglar over to Quinne, not that there was much doubt about his demise. To Quinne and to the police, since Ski Mask and his attack—his attacks?—could hardly be ignored at this point.

"I'll see what I can do," I said at last. "That's about the best I can offer at this point."

"That's more than we've got now," Mae said. "And at least somebody besides us is willing to look out for her."

AFTER THEY left, I spent another fifteen minutes reorganizing my house. Finished, I treated myself to that third Black Label, took the laptop to the couch, and sank down beside a lightly snoring Hopalong. Despite the hour, I called Bruce Stickdorn's cell phone. He picked up after three rings. I explained my encounter, relieved at the background sound of light jazz, which meant at least I hadn't awakened the detective.

"Never a dull moment with you, is it? Are you OK?"

I told him about my tooth. "Other than that I'm fine, which is all that matters. Unlike Preston Campbell."

"You're saying there's a connection?"

"There has to be. Same guy shows up at Wayne Stratton's widow's house a few days before Preston's killed. And now this?" I explained how Mae had identified the man tonight.

Before Stickdorn could reply I heard the muffled sound of a woman's voice. He said something in reply, and I heard a feminine laugh.

"You called 911, right?" Stickdorn said a couple of seconds later.

"Called you first. Figured you'd want to know, since you caught Preston's case."

"Ass-kissing doesn't become you, but I'll take it anyway. I'll call it in now and then check with you in the morning, once I'm in."

I thanked him, disconnected, and checked the time. Pushing ten thirty. Despite the hour, I called Hillary Quinne, if nothing else to warn her to watch her back. I had to leave a message. I kept it brief and asked her to call me as soon as possible. After I disconnected, conscious of the time, I used my phone to look up the web page for McCulloh College security, then scrolled through the names and photos of the listed personnel. The officer who'd busted me earlier in the week turned out to be security investigator Corey Robertson. In five minutes, I dug up home and cell phone listings for an address on the far west side. It was a stretch reaching out to him like this, but something told me to do it. When he answered, I identified myself and reminded him of our encounter the day before.

"How'd you get my number?"

"It's not important. This is an off-the-record courtesy call."

"A what?"

"Listen carefully. I don't have a lot of time." I gave him a description of the man who'd nearly killed me this evening. "Anybody like that on campus recently?"

"Even if there was, why would I tell you?"

"You know who Hillary Quinne is?"

A pause. "What about her?"

"I'm working with her now. That's why you should tell me. I'm hoping we're all on the same page here."

Another pause, which made me think that after kowtowing to professors all day, the last thing Robertson wanted in life was to obey instructions from a private eye like Quinne, whose authority was unassailable because it came from the president of the trustee board. I sympathized with him, but only up to a point.

"I haven't seen anybody like that guy. Who is he?"

"He's not a Rhodes scholar, that's for sure. Just be careful, OK? Maybe let Uschi know too. Any sign of this guy, call 911 and ask questions later."

"You're telling me this even after I ran you off?"

"You were just doing your job. I don't have to like it to appreciate the position you were in."

A long stretch of silence. Then: "Thanks," he said abruptly, and hung up.

The last call was the one I least wanted to make. Otto's a night owl, so it wasn't a question of waking him. Plus, I knew that his mother, a jazz songstress, had a standing gig at Dick's Den each Wednesday, so there was a good chance he was either there or chauffeuring her home. Sure enough, he picked up right away, bar noises in the background.

"What the heck, Woody. This is way past your bedtime."

"Listen up—we've got a problem."

"What kind?"

"A big one."

HE HEARD me out. A couple of seconds passed when I was done explaining about my unwanted house guest earlier in the evening, the well-timed arrival of Jeremy and Mae, and what I'd learned from them about the unfortunate connection of Javon "Little J" Martinez to the late, great Wayne Stratton.

"Of all the sewer rats in the city, it had to be that guy threatening this lady and her kid?"

"Karma's a bitch, as they say."

"You think he knows where they are?"

"For their sake I'm hoping not. But he might know something about Wayne and a pocketful of money he forked over before he died. I'd like us to ask him about that."

"Us?"

"You know what I mean."

"I do, which is the problem. You telling the cops any of this?"

"Not yet."

"How come?"

"You want them talking to Martinez after the other night?"

"Good point, Woody. Why you're the brains of this operation."

"Spare me. How early do you think we can see him tomorrow?"

"Well, normally visiting hours don't start until noon. Maybe I can pull some strings. We made a lot of agencies happy bringing him back in. Let's just hope this doesn't ruin everything."

"How so?"

"We had him over a barrel last night. A bridge, actually, but who's counting? But now the tables are turned. After all that, he's gonna want something in return."

I was formulating my response when someone knocked at the door. I tensed, then relaxed as I peered out the window at a Columbus police cruiser sitting in front of my house. The cavalry, courtesy of Detective Dickstorm.

"Gotta run. I'll talk to you tomorrow."

"Bated breath, Woody."

I put the phone down, walked gingerly to the door, and opened it.

Hillary Quinne stood there, directly in front of a pair of patrol officers.

"Andy," she said. "I came as soon as I could."

28

THE OFFICERS, A MAN and a woman, parked me at my kitchen table while one took my statement and the other examined the gun and then the smashed window. Quinne disappeared into the kitchen, from which I heard the sounds of water running and china clinking. A few minutes into my interview she emerged with a full pot of coffee, cream and sugar, and mugs. She set everything on the table and without bothering to ask poured both officers a cup and pushed the condiments toward them. Then she retreated to the living room, where she sat beside Hopalong and pulled out her phone.

The interview lasted maybe half an hour. They bagged the gun and the shells and did a walk-through around the house and the perimeter outside. They asked a couple of times if I was sure the front door hadn't been forced, which they found puzzling. I assured them I found that puzzling too. Whoever he was, he was skilled enough to pick a lock. Because of the dog, I'd never bothered with an alarm system, which more than one person had told me was naïve. I had a feeling that was going to change after tonight. I took their cards and they said Stickdorn would contact me in the morning. They thanked Quinne for the coffee and went on their way. I suppressed a yawn as I shut the door behind them. It was now almost midnight.

"Don't suppose you have anything stronger?" Quinne said, picking up the coffee cups and taking them into the kitchen. "Stronger than Black Label, I mean. How can you drink that stuff?"

"To quote myself, 'It may be swill, but it's my swill.'"

"Didn't FDR say something like that?"

"Did he?"

"'Somoza may be a son of a bitch, but he's our son of a bitch'?"

"I think that quote was about Franco, not Somoza. Or maybe Mickey Mouse. Either way I stand by it. I think there's a bottle of Oyo someplace. Whiskey doesn't go bad, right?" A gift from Roy a few years back from a local distillery in an attempt to broaden my drinking horizons—unsuccessfully, I might add. I'd seen what the hard stuff had done to my dad before he went on the wagon and rarely touched it.

She laughed. "The older the better. Just point me to it."

A minute later we were both in the living room, jelly-jar glasses of brown liquid in our hands. I coughed at my first sip, to Quinne's amusement.

"Some hard-drinking PI you are."

"You should see the state of my fedora."

She laughed, then grew serious. "I'm so sorry about this. I feel responsible."

"For what?"

"For dragging you into something this dangerous."

"Unless that guy's working for you, I don't know how that makes sense."

"That's not even funny. He could have killed you."

"Sorry. But I'm not sorry I'm working on this. Shit happens in our respective businesses, as I'm guessing you know."

"Please," she said, tugging nervously at the sleeve of her sweater. "I do background checks and workers' comp fraud. I'm not used to this kind of stuff."

"Except for porta potty stakeouts?"

She flinched at the mention of Fulkerson's story. "Don't remind me. It paid the bills, but that's about it." She took another sip. I followed suit and coughed as it burned its way down my throat. She smiled again at my reaction. "So back to you. You think this guy was after your stuff on Ebersole?"

"There's no other explanation."

"Why not?"

I reminded her of the fatal break-in at Preston's and the fact Mae and Jeremy ID'd the man as the same guy who came by their house a few days before Preston buttonholed me at Plank's. I reviewed their story of Wayne receiving a surprise cash infusion. Then a separate thought occurred to me, so chilling that Quinne caught a change in my expression.

"What?"

"What if that was him who texted me, using Preston's phone, late that night after you and I met? 'Give you a call tomorrow little busy right now hope that's OK.' A way to throw off the time line of the killing."

"That's terrifying."

"Tell me about it."

"Did he see anything tonight? On your laptop, I mean?"

"He didn't get that far."

"It's too bad he didn't access it, in a way. I mean, it would have been nice to know exactly what he was looking for."

"Sorry I didn't give him a couple more minutes."

"Don't be an idiot. You know what I mean. He didn't ask you any questions?"

"Other than demanding my password, no. Thank God I pulled the flash drive earlier, after I transferred the files. If he'd seen that, he might not have bothered with the laptop at all."

"The flash drive from Preston?"

I acknowledged it.

"And it's safe now?"

"In my bedroom."

She nodded, satisfied. "Earlier. You texted me and said you went to see the widow of the accomplice. Cheryl?"

"Carole. Carole Weidner."

"Any chance he followed you from there or something?"

"I doubt it. Or if he did, he's got a hellava lead foot, since he would have beat me home by several minutes."

The thought unspoken between us: he could easily have been watching the house, waiting until he was sure I was gone. But how would he have known I was going out?

"And did she say anything?" Quinne said. "About Ebersole, I mean?"

I told her the story of the money. She raised her eyebrows. I said, "Problem is, it's a little hard to believe since she also said he was an asshole who used people. Not sure that's exactly breaking news. Takes a special person to shoot a cop in the first place."

"An asshole who looked after his own? Like FDR and Somoza?"

"Cute."

"You have to admit, that story of Wayne Stratton getting the money out of the blue is intriguing. Especially given what Carole Weidner said. Makes you think."

"I can't deny it. Except it doesn't necessarily mean it's Ebersole. Could be another relative, or just a massive coincidence."

"You really believe that?" she said.

"I'm not sure what to believe at this point." I tried another sip of the whiskey, with slightly better results. I rubbed my hand over my neck, which was sore to the touch and getting worse.

"Everything OK?"

"Other than the excruciating pain, sure."

"That bad?"

"I'll live, which is all that matters."

She scooted forward in her chair. "Let me take a look."

"Dr. Quinne, Medicine Woman?"

She flipped me the bird. "Never heard that one before."

"I hadn't guessed."

"How about, consider me a concerned partner?"

She moved to the couch and sat beside me. She examined my neck carefully, placing her hands lightly on either side like an actual doctor checking for swollen lymph nodes. I started at the touch of her cool fingers.

"Sorry. I took first aid in high school, which makes me an expert."

"I took typing. Does that count for anything?"

"Invoices, I suppose. Jesus, he must have had one hell of a grip."

"He was a man on a mission, that's for sure."

"I think you've got latex burns. Are you sure you don't want to see a doctor? There's an urgent care on East Livingston that I think's still open."

"I'm fine. Frankly, it feels good, what you're doing."

"Does it?" She placed her hands on my neck again. I shut my eyes and leaned my head against the back of the couch.

"You're easy."

"It's been a long day."

"I bet it has."

In the next moment I opened my eyes. Quinne was much closer now, looking at me intently. She moved her hands down my throat and onto my shoulders. She leaned in and kissed me. She was a good kisser, her lips warm and soft. I put my arms around her, pulled her close, and kissed her back. She pulled away a moment later.

"I'm sorry, I'm sorry," she said. "I think this violates every professional standard in the book. I just got a little overwhelmed, thinking about what could have happened. I didn't mean—"

"It's all right. Joint contractors are exempted from fraternization restrictions under section 5, paragraph C of the Administrative Rules."

She laughed softly, though I noticed she didn't make any effort to draw farther away. "I have to hand it to you, Andy. That's some platinum bullshit."

"Comes with the territory," I said, brushing my hand down her right cheek. "Don't tell me you've never had occasion to lay it on a little thick."

"I guess I have a lot to learn," she said, drawing close.

"Moving on to section 6," I said, wrapping my arms around her once more.

29

I JOLTED AWAKE. GRAY light filtered through the edges of my curtains, which meant it was late by my standards. I flopped my left arm over onto cold, exposed sheet. I propped myself up and encountered the light scent of Quinne's fragrance on her side of the empty bed. I called out, my voice scratchy. No answer.

I left the bedroom and walked slowly into the kitchen, realizing simultaneously that my tooth was indeed still loose, my neck ached even more than the night before, and the low-grade headache forming at the base of my brain was not going away anytime soon. Turbulence—of all sorts—has that effect on me. On the counter sat an overturned Columbia Gas envelope bearing a handwritten note in a precise, feminine script.

Hope you're feeling better. Call when you can to talk next steps.

I studied the note for nearly a full minute, thinking several thoughts, before undertaking the arduous journey to the sink to fill the coffee pot. Halfway through a sound stopped me. A beeping. I stumped through the house and followed it back into my bedroom. I found it a moment later, under the end of my bed, near my hastily removed jeans. A stamp-sized GPS tracker attached to an electronic fob. I lifted it, puzzled, and sat on the edge of the bed. It came to me a moment later when I spied "6C" on the fob. An electronic apartment key. The kind of thing that spills from pockets during hurried disrobing. I took a photo and texted it to Quinne.

Yours?

The response just a few seconds later.

There it is!

Her words accompanied by a blushing emoticon. I asked if she needed it. She said security let her in and she had a spare. I said I'd return it the next time I saw her.

Which would be when, exactly, I thought, setting the fob inside the top drawer of my dresser beside Preston's flash drive hidden inside an old sock.

IT WAS nearly nine o'clock by the time I returned from a slow jaunt to the park and back with Hopalong. He dawdled even more than usual, no doubt thanks to our late-night encounter with Ski Mask. I could empathize. I was also distracted by something that was bothering me, something I couldn't quite put my finger on. Something someone had said the night before, one of the officers or Quinne herself.

Quinne. That was another issue to reckon with, I thought, forcing myself to focus on what transpired between us. Not my smartest move, ever, though I suppose it took two to tango. I thought guiltily of the judge. Was it cheating when neither you nor your friend-with-benefits can get your acts together long enough to manage a rendezvous? That was cheap justification for an error in judgment, and I knew it. But the question was: how much did I care? I found myself pondering the flip side: was what happened with Quinne the kind of frying-pan-in-the-face moment I'd long been avoiding? Why date outside my gene pool—judges, professors, teachers—and endure all the complications my life brought to such relationships, when the answer was staring me in the face, or in this case, lying on top of me on the couch? A fellow private investigator might be the perfect mate, since "warts and all" meant the same to both parties.

I received a partial answer to my musings moments later when a push alert arrived on my phone from the *Dispatch*.

**JUDGE PORTER TO RENEW BID
FOR OHIO SUPREME COURT SEAT**

I stared at the headline almost as long as I had at the note Quinne left me, then hurriedly read the few paragraphs available so far. Sure enough, having shaken off the trauma of her kidnapping and near-death experience in Cleveland, Laura had decided to return to her quest for a seat on the high court. Without letting me know first. I couldn't decide whether to feel miffed at the exclusion or grateful she'd moved on enough to make the decision. Of course, after last night, I was hardly in a position to pass judgment.

After breakfast, I forced myself to stop dwelling on Quinne and the judge and instead returned to an outcome of the break-in that was still nagging at me. I pulled up the copy of the photo in Preston's files that had caught my attention the previous evening. The student who died in the fall from the parking garage was named Paul Tigner. It was his memorial I'd encountered on campus earlier that day while seeing Anne Cooper. The photo captured a scene from a vigil after Tigner's death, the news value of which was enhanced by the fact that the police chief, Kenneth Oswald, also had a son who attended McCulloh College. I recalled the significance of the memorial, which Anne explained to me on her way to class. The student whose death was not accidental, but a suicide by a young gay man struggling with his sexual orientation. A suicide two days after the arrest of John J. Ebersole for a string of burglaries, including the rental home of McCulloh College visiting professor Gerhard Schmidt. A name whose mention in the college's languages office had brought all kinds of unwelcome diversions into my life. Connecting these dots seemed silly on the surface, like pretending that random sidewalk cracks were the purposeful outline of a horse or a ship.

But after the past few days' events, ignoring any coincidence, no matter how small, seemed like a monumentally bad idea.

It took me a couple of minutes of Googling, but before long I determined that Paul Tigner's parents had both died a couple of years back. But Frank Tigner, Paul's older brother, was still around and living on the city's northwest side. He answered his cell phone after two rings. I told him my name and occupation and confirmed he was the man I was looking for.

"You said Andy Hayes?"

"That's right."

A couple of moments passed. "What's this about?"

"Actually, it's related to Paul." I paused, giving that a second to sink in. "I was wondering if maybe we could meet."

"Christ—don't tell me somebody vandalized the sculpture again. What the hell is it with these assholes?"

"It's not about the sculpture," I said, taken aback by his tone. "It's fine. I saw it a couple mornings ago. It's quite moving—"

"What then? What would Paul have to do with anything now?"

I explained how his brother's name had come up in a case I was working on.

"The thing is, I'm wondering if Paul happened to know a certain professor when he was in school. At McCulloh College."

"Who?"

"A German teacher. His name was Gerhard Schmidt."

"For God's sake. You're calling about this now? *Now?* After all the shit they put us through? Are you working for the school? Is that it?"

"What shit? What are you talking about?"

"Go to hell, why don't you. And don't ever call me again."

The line went dead. I stared at the phone, stunned, as if it had delivered an electric shock upon his disconnecting. That was the least expected outcome of all the ways I'd anticipated that call going. But one thing was certain. It seemed reasonable to assume that Paul Tigner had known Gerhard Schmidt, judging by his brother's reaction. But how to explain that reaction? Why the anger? And what had he meant? *All the shit they put us through.* Who?

I CALLED BACK, BUT Tigner's phone went straight to voice mail. I left a message, apologizing if I'd said something that upset him and asking him to call me back, since it seemed important for us to talk. Five minutes passed, then ten. When fifteen minutes had gone by the phone finally rang. But it was Otto on the line.

"Noon it is, Woody. Martinez is still downtown. Only one visitor at a time, and I'm thinking better you than me. Can you handle?"

"I'll be there."

"What are you going to tell him?"

"I'm going to burn that bridge when I come to it. I promise to keep you whole, though."

"Appreciate it. You OK? Your voice sounds like it's coming through a blender."

"Still recovering from last night. And by the way." I mentioned the strange call with Frank Tigner just now.

"That is strange. One more disturbance in the force, huh?"

"I guess so." His quip made me recall the epitaph from Hawthorne on Paul Tigner's sculpture. *The earth has guilt, the earth has care, unquiet are its graves.* I told Otto what I was thinking.

"Graves are noisier than you think, Woody. Especially the empty ones."

"Empty?"

"Like in the movies, when there's some mystery that can only be solved by exhuming a corpse, you know? And they go to dig it up, except when they do—cue the cellos—the grave is empty and the body's gone. That's when you know things are really bad."

"What do you mean?"

"Empty graves have the most secrets, Woody. The dead can't talk—it's the missing bodies you need to worry about."

After wrapping up on that comforting note, I made more coffee and settled back in front of my laptop just in time for a text to interrupt me.

All set for tomorrow?

Crystal. Orlando-bound with Bob.

Yes

After a moment, I added:

I'll pick him up right after XC practice.
Will drop him at school Monday

Thanks! You're the best!

I let that one go. The sentiment was debatable, for starters, and there was no point playing along with any pretense of camaraderie between the two of us, despite my feeling something was up with her and possibly off-kilter. Could Bob be having an affair? Or her? Neither option seemed out of the realm of possibility, though Crystal had hardly given off the vibe of a secret-keeping temptress the other day. More like a hard-living party girl whose chickens were finally coming home to roost. Either way, it wasn't my problem until it was Joe's problem. Or was it? After all, I'd been more than happy to indulge Crystal in her party-girl prime, and I also knew perfectly well our disastrous marriage and hellish divorce were squarely one-half my fault, if not more. I examined the hastily taped-up newspaper covering my shattered window and considered Joe's pending arrival. OK. Maybe it was my problem after all.

I shook the thought away and went back to work. I went down my to-do list related to Ebersole. I tried the number again for Doug Fitzsimmons—Howie Campbell's partner the night he was shot—with the same result. I left a second, shorter message and mentally crossed him off my list. Sometimes you just know a door has closed. I tried the coroner's office and also left another message.

Next, I went online and combined the names Paul Tigner and Gerhard Schmidt. The search produced the usual mishmash of random matchings, some in English, some in German, but nothing that looked remotely like a smoking gun, let alone an actual clue. No surprise, given that they would have known each other—if in fact they did—a good forty years ago. Same result for mixing and matching their names with John Ebersole and Wayne Stratton and Howie Campbell and Preston Campbell and even a secret nuclear weapons program code-named DART. Names I knew now were interconnected, though how and why remained unclear—they were like out-of-focus figures zigzagging a long way down a beach. I thought of Otto's explanation of my case. *Empty graves have the most secrets.* But whose grave were we talking about?

I wandered into the kitchen, opened cupboard doors and peered inside, ditto for the refrigerator, and frowned. Barely enough food for me and certainly not for a teenage boy, let alone one who ran cross-country. Time to stock up, not to mention that I was running low on Black Label.

I was dressed with keys in hand and headed for the front door and my appointment with Javon Martinez when my phone rang.

"I'm trying to reach Andy Hayes."

"You've got him."

"My name's Matt Tigner. I think you just called my dad. I was wondering if we could meet."

31

I WAS STILL PROCESSING my brief conversation with Matt Tigner—the nephew Paul never met—when Martinez shuffled into view in the downtown jail visiting room and sank heavily into an avocado green chair. A thick clear plastic partition, smudged with finger- and handprints, separated us. He looked wan in the fluorescent light, and tired, and pissed. We reached for our respective black phone receivers at the same time.

"What the fuck."

"Hello to you too. Thanks for seeing me."

"Go to hell. Where's Mulligan? I'm going to kick his Black ass."

"That's half-Black ass to you. It's Thursday, so he's probably getting ready for choir practice."

"What do you want?"

"I need your help."

He sat back, wiped his mouth, and tilted his head. "You have got to be fucking kidding me. After what those guys did to me? And just because you were driving, don't think that gets you off the hook."

"After they did what to you?"

"On the bridge?"

"What bridge?"

His hard stare made me extra thankful that nearly an inch of clear plastic separated us. He shook his head and stood.

"See you 'round, asshole."

"Wait."

"Why?"

"I told you, I need your help. And I'm not here empty-handed."

He stood for a moment, considering. Two seats away from me, a woman my age sobbed as she talked to a man opposite her who looked barely out of his teens. Next to her a visibly pregnant woman who also didn't look far out of her teens was swearing at a man who looked like he hadn't seen his teens in forever plus a fortnight or two. Out of sight, a guard yelled something about paperwork. A moment later, Martinez sat.

"What kind of help?"

I laid out the gist of what Jeremy and Mae told me about Wayne's addiction, the money he still owed Martinez, and their fear for Gina and Hailey's whereabouts. I concluded by saying I wanted any information he had about the source of the money Wayne paid him the final time.

"That bitch is lying."

"Which bitch would that be?"

"Gina. She had the money; she just didn't want to give it to me. But just because Wayne went and got himself killed doesn't mean I'm not still owed. Way the world works."

"From what I hear Gina had less than nothing to her name. How do you know she had the money at all?"

He leaned back, phone in his right hand, and rubbed his chin. What looked like barbershop floor clippings applied with Superglue jutted off his chin.

"You said you weren't empty-handed."

"I did."

"What are you offering?"

"Depends what you can tell me about Gina."

"Uh-uh. You first."

"What if I say no?"

"What if I say you can go fuck yourself and Gina too?"

"You'd prove your worth as a minor street poet. OK, here's the deal. You've got a bond-revocation hearing on Monday. Drug distribution, human trafficking, felonious assault. We can smooth over the first two. Leave 'em be, despite the fact you ran."

"What about the assault?"

"That one's out of our hands. You sent your girlfriend to the hospital."

"She ain't my girlfriend. She's my bottom girl. And she hit me first."

"The police report says otherwise." The woman was no angel; as Martinez's bottom girl she groomed women like Darlene Hunter. But a fractured jaw was a fractured jaw.

"I'm still inside, either way."

"But with more light at the end of the tunnel."

He leaned forward, grip tightening around the receiver. "Listen up, whatever the fuck your name is. When I said it's the way the world works, I wasn't kidding. You don't get to mess me up like that and then come begging for my help. I don't care what you're offering, which ain't shit, by the way."

"It's all we've got."

"In that case, this is all I've got." He shot me the finger. "Maybe should have thought harder before you picked me up the other night." He rose for the second time, a sneer on his face.

"Wait," I said again, feeling a drop of sweat slide down my right side.

"Screw you."

"I mean it. Just give me a second." I wiped my left palm on my pants. This had gone south much faster than I anticipated. The guilty exhilaration I'd felt the other night at seeing Darlene's tormentor humiliated on the bridge evaporated like steam rising from outdoors piss in the winter. It had been a cruelly cheap move, and Martinez knew I knew it.

"All right."

"All right what?" he said.

"We can't make the assault paper go away. It is what it is. But Otto can vouch for you. Tell the fugitive squad you came in willingly. Called him up, even, told him you were turning yourself in. Doing the right thing. That could go a long way, back in front of the judge."

Martinez sat down and stared at me without blinking until I gave up and dropped my gaze. We both knew it could go all the way to him being back on the street sooner rather than later. I knew Otto had a good relationship with the sheriff's office Warrants and Extraditions Unit. I just hoped it was that good.

"We have a deal?"

"Sure," he said. "Just prove it."

"You've got my word."

He laughed out loud. I couldn't blame him. The words sounded hollow to me too.

"You tell Mulligan to tell the COs what you just told me. That happens, I'll think about playing ball."

"I've got a schedule here. I can't wait for the next visiting hours—"

"Guess you don't have any choice, do you?"

"Fine," I said, almost shouting. "I'll try."

"Try?"

"I'll do it, OK? But now it's your turn. Prove you've got information that's worth us going out on a limb for you."

He smiled like a young pit bull cornering an old cat.

"How's this? I grabbed Gina's little girl after school one day and put her in my car and called Gina and told her to stop screwing around. She was real talkative at that point. I know stuff, trust me."

Without another word Martinez slammed the receiver down, signaled the guard, and a moment later disappeared through a steel door.

I stared blankly at his receding back through the door's small window. Three seats down, the pregnant woman slammed her own phone down so hard I thought she might break it, or her hand, stood up and stalked off, muttering "fuck, fuck, fuck" the whole way out.

A few minutes later, mouthing the same words to myself, I was standing outside by my van, on the phone to Otto.

32

OTTO MIGHT HAVE BEEN more polite than Martinez, and dropped fewer f-bombs, but I could tell he was just as angry about what transpired as Martinez was with my paltry attempt to pry information from him. He told me in a cool voice to stay tuned, and disconnected without saying goodbye. I didn't blame him. It was a colossal fuckup, letting a scumbag like Martinez turn the tables on us, and it was all on me, and we both knew it. Feeling sick to my stomach and light-headed, I walked up the street, crossed High, and walked into Dempsey's. I went to the far end of the bar, ordered a draft beer, and drained it in less than two minutes, wincing as the cold liquid hit my loose tooth. I ordered another one a little too loudly and the bartender asked me with a good-natured laugh if everything was OK. I lied and said it was and ordered a burger to prove it. My headache had grown from tropical depression to typhoon in the five minutes it had taken me to walk to the restaurant. Making matters worse, on top of what happened at the jail just now I couldn't stop puzzling over what was nagging at me about the night before—other than my tussle with Ski Mask and the ill-advised hookup with Quinne, that is.

My second beer arrived and I took it to half-staff. I was trying to decide what if anything I could do to redeem the situation when my phone buzzed. Stickdorn. I answered reluctantly.

"You gonna live, Woody? I hear this guy really worked you over."

"Have to see Dr. Hurtt about a loose tooth. Other than that, it's all good."

"Who?"

"Debra Hurtt. My dentist."

"Your dentist is named Hurtt?"

"Beats that guy from *Marathon Man*. What's up? Any news?"

"This explains so much about you, Woody. Well, let's see—your little visitor wiped the gun clean, so that's a drag. Plus you said he was wearing gloves? That's not gonna help in the prints department."

I confirmed the gloves, recalling them all too clearly protecting the hands slowly and inexorably tightening around my throat.

"So we're out of luck."

"Except for the stupidity of your average criminal, yes."

"Meaning?"

"Meaning this guy took a lot of precautions. And if he picked your lock, he's good. But he forgot one thing."

"Which is?"

"The tag on the inside of the mask."

"What about it?"

"Big ol' thumbprint, front and center. They're running it now."

"First good news I've had in a while. What about Preston Campbell?"

"What about him?"

I took a drink of beer. I said, "You're not telling me it's a coincidence this guy went for me two days after Preston Campbell was shot to death. You match any shells?"

A pause, uncharacteristic in conversations with Stickdorn. He had a talkative streak at the expense of his listeners that I sometimes figured explained all his ex-wives. But in that case, what was my excuse?

"No shells at Campbell's."

"Afraid you were going to say that." No shells also meant someone who knew what he was doing, at the very least, and argued against a home invasion gone wrong.

"Where are you, by the way?"

At the far side of the room the bartender wiped down the counter. "Just downtown. Why?"

"I ran by that house earlier today. Wayne Stratton's place. You said the guy last night stopped by there last week?"

"In that range," I said, carefully.

"Nobody around, is all. Just wondered if you knew where everybody was."

"Sorry."

"And tell me again why the two of them just happened to stop by last night? But weren't there when the officers arrived?"

"I left a card at their house," I said honestly. "I can't account for their timing, other than to be grateful for it. They left because they were kind of shook up, and I wasn't really in a position to stop them."

"Been better if they stuck around."

"I can see that now."

"I'll let you know about the print, OK? Good luck with Dr. Hurtt."

He disconnected and I hunched forward, elbows on the bar, and gulped the rest of my beer, tension from the encounter with Martinez finally starting to ease. Replacing it was a growing feeling of dread. With Ski Mask out there, it meant Gina and Hailey were still in danger. I considered the irony that they'd disappeared, perhaps just in time, because of Javon Martinez's threats over the money owed him by the late, great Wayne Stratton. But that didn't make them any safer. And how was I supposed to find them with nothing more to go on than the fact that a long-haul trucker named Freddy, a friend of Wayne's, was sweet on Gina and they might run to him?

My burger arrived. I stared at it. What was I thinking, with my tooth? I asked the bartender for a box. As he disappeared into the kitchen my phone rang again. Theresa Sullivan.

"I just went to see Darlene. Thought I'd let you know."

"How's she doing?"

"Better. Relieved Little J's inside. She's not saying it, but I think seeing that stunt the other night really proved to her that people are actually looking out for her."

I didn't say anything for a second, suppressing the desire to slam my head on the edge of the bar.

"QB?"

Without telling her about the deal I'd struck with Martinez, I mentioned my fear over Gina and Hailey's disappearance. As I talked, my phone beeped with an incoming call. Hillary Quinne. I sent it to voice mail.

Theresa said, "How about I check that one out?"

"Check what out?"

"That trucker named Freddy."

"Don't tell me you know him." Theresa's knowledge of the streets was extensive thanks to her own time on them, plus the work she did with women like Darlene Hunter. But even this seemed a stretch.

"Oh yeah, we're best buddies. Of course I don't know him. But I might know people who do."

"I accept your offer, as long as you let me pay you for your time."

"How about I do this one for free. Not for you, though. For Gina and her little girl."

"That's kind of you."

"Damn straight it is," she said. "I'll call you when I've got something."

She too disconnected before I could say goodbye. I listened to Quinne's voice mail, which was nothing more than a request to call combined with a hope I was doing OK. I didn't call back. I had more thinking to do about the night before, including trying to decide what it was that was still bothering me. Something Stickdorn said on the phone just now had threatened to shake it loose, but now it was gone. As I strained to conjure up the missing puzzle piece, the bartender returned with my boxed-up burger. I handed him a twenty and was on my way out the door when my phone buzzed with a text.

> Please call when you can. Wanted to talk about what's in the news today

Laura Porter. Make that Ohio Supreme Court candidate Laura Porter. I studied the text a moment later, then locked my phone and put it back in my pocket. If there was any way for this day to spiral more out of control, I didn't want to hear about it.

33

AFTER MY UNSCHEDULED TRIP to the dentist, I used the time before my meeting with Matt Tigner to return home and figure out what to do about the window shattered by Ski Mask's bullets. I dismissed out of hand contacting my landlord. He was more tolerant than most when it came to this kind of thing, since I'd earned my rent-controlled home in astronomically pricey German Village thanks to my rescue of his heroin-addicted daughter from the streets a few years back. But even his patience had its limits. The price that two repair shops quoted me was manageable, but only just, mainly because I didn't want to touch the money Preston gave me, and my liquidity was otherwise drying up fast. I gave in and texted Kevin H. He'd done much of the restoration of their two-story brick Dutch double himself, and had often offered his repair services if I ever needed. Without hesitation he promised to handle it and asked if Sunday morning would work. I said that it would. He said he'd see me then and gave me quick instructions on a handy temporary fix with cardboard and duct tape.

Thanks. Really appreciate it.

Pleasure's all mine. Life here's always more interesting thanks to you

I drank a glass of water and downed two ibuprofen with plans to rest for a bit. But I hadn't been asleep two minutes when the sounds of Twisted Sister filled my bedroom, signaling an incoming call.

"OK, Woody," Otto Mulligan said. "We're in business."

"Meaning?" I said warily.

"Meaning Little J just texted me. Said we're good."

"He texted you? How?"

"The how is easy: it's a jail, which means they've got contraband like cockroaches. The why is what matters."

"And?"

"It's his way of telling me—telling us—that he's connected. That he can call shots. And also, his way of daring us—you bust me on this phone, I'll bust you on what happened on the bridge."

"I'm sorry, Otto. I really screwed this up."

"Can it, Woody. This one's on me. I should have known better."

"Than what?"

"Than not finishing the job and dropping his sorry ass into the river when I had the chance. Anyway, here's what he said. Wayne's money was from New York."

"New York City?"

"He didn't know. But he didn't think so."

"Could it have been Rochester?"

"I don't know. I can ask him, but I'm not sure how much more we're getting out of this guy."

"You sure the information's legit."

"Yeah."

"Because?"

"Because don't ask me how, but he's got a picture on his burner phone of that little girl when he had her in his car. He texted it to me. He said it was his way of proving his story, but you know damn well he's just fucking with us. She's just an itty-bitty thing. Never seen anyone more scared. He said that's the picture he sent to her mom. No way she was in a position to lie after that."

AS PROMISED, Matt Tigner was waiting for me in the lobby at Otie's in downtown Hilliard out on the west side when I walked in a couple hours later. Late twenties, give or take, dressed in jeans and a golf shirt with an American Electric Power logo. He had short black hair and a de rigueur goatee. Nice-looking kid. Firm handshake, expression curious and not unfriendly, but not exactly welcoming, either. He worked seven to three, he explained, and this was the best time. I told him it was fine since I had to pick up my son later. The hostess showed us to a booth and placed menus before us. I did my best to stop thinking about the information Otto procured from Martinez, sparse as it was. And potentially worthless: even if "New York" translated to Rochester, it was still a mighty big haystack.

Tigner said, "Thanks again for meeting me like this."

"Believe me, not a problem."

"I asked my dad if he wanted to come, but . . ."

"I could tell I touched a nerve when I called. I'm sorry if I upset him."

"You just took him by surprise, bringing it up after all this time. After everything he went through. Him and my grandparents."

The server came and we each asked for a beer.

When she left, I said, "Bringing 'it' up. What do you mean?"

He studied his hands. "How much do you know about my uncle? What happened to him?"

"Not a whole lot, to tell the truth. I know his death was reported as an accident, but it's believed he killed himself."

"He did," Matt said sharply. "There's no 'believed.'"

"Of course. I'm sorry." Carefully, I added: "And I know it's because he was gay, and he suffered over it, given the times." I recalled Anne's explanation as we stood on the McCulloh College green, and my own misdeed, long regretted, taunting the gay couple outside the Varsity Club.

"What about Schmidt? What do you know about him?"

"Again, not much." I related the little I'd gathered about his time as a visiting East German professor at McCulloh, including the tenuous connection with John Ebersole and the string of burglaries. I left out the fact he had a more nefarious reason for being here, at least according to Grant Fulkerson, the college trustee.

"Schmidt was broken into by this guy, but it was never reported?" For some reason I had his full attention now.

"Correct, as far as I can tell." When he didn't respond, I said, "Did your uncle know Schmidt? Have him for class or something?"

He stared at me, brown eyes wary, and just for a moment looked much older than his three decades or so.

"He knew him, all right. They were having an affair."

THE SERVER ARRIVED WITH our drinks. I centered my beer on the coaster and waited until she was gone.

"An affair?"

"If that's what you call a middle-aged professor sleeping with a nineteen-year-old college kid who didn't know up from down, then yes."

"What do you call it?"

"Me?" he said angrily. "We—my dad, and my aunt—we call it sexual assault."

I kept quiet, afraid to speak.

"I'm sorry—you have to understand what this did to our family. Paul's death tore them apart. Obviously, I'm too young to have known him, and even as a kid I was only vaguely aware of who he was. 'Uncle Paul, who died in the accident.' Nobody talked about it, which seemed understandable under the circumstances. I didn't think anything of it, other than how sad it was. But then things changed."

Picturing the commemorative sculpture on the McCulloh College green, I waited for him to continue.

"Right after 9/11 my grandparents decided to downsize. They got rid of a lot of stuff. Some of it was Paul's things. Most of his belongings they'd just thrown in boxes after he died and never looked at. In the midst of all that, my grandmother found a diary that my uncle kept. Nobody could remember seeing it from before but that kind of made sense, given how upset everyone was. She only read a few pages before she had to stop. That's when she called my dad."

"Let me guess. That's where you learned about Schmidt?"

"Where my dad did, yeah. And my aunt. He, I mean Paul, poured his heart out. Pages and pages. It's hard to read, really hard. I only finally finished it last year. My grandparents were both great people, but devout Catholics. My parents too, until . . . well, until all this went down. Anyway, Paul didn't dare tell anyone."

"He was that afraid?"

"Are you Catholic?"

I told him I wasn't, and spared him tales from my youth suffering through endless Assembly of God services.

"My dad and Paul had a cousin who's gay who was basically disowned. And at their school, Bishop Mahoney? They knew a kid who was supposedly gay who got harassed so bad he had to drop out. Nobody ever disciplined. Yeah, he was afraid."

I nodded, knowing there was nothing I could say.

"In the diary, you can see how it was tearing him apart. When you reach the point where he starts writing about Schmidt, he uses words like 'love' and 'relief' but also 'guilt' and 'shame.' He was also really scared."

"Of Schmidt?"

"Of exposure. Something Schmidt was afraid of happening."

"Did Paul say what?"

"I'm not sure. I'd have to go back and look. At times I skimmed—it was just too painful."

"Your uncle went through a lot."

"He saw himself as an evil person who couldn't help himself and was probably going to hell, despite his feelings for Schmidt."

I swallowed the shoulders off my beer. His sat untouched.

"Schmidt preyed on your uncle."

"No shit. It's hard to imagine consent in a situation like that, gay or straight. I mean, the age difference alone. Plus, Schmidt had my uncle in class. He had power over him. It wasn't right in any shape or form."

I leaned back, weighing the left turn the case had taken. In speculating that Schmidt might have been working as some kind of spy—a suspicion promoted by Quinne and Fulkerson—it never occurred to me the professor might have something else altogether to hide. Something that in 1979 might have been nearly as dangerous if exposed. What was it Mrs. Zimmerman said? *I know he had a prestigious position back home that he was always worried about losing.*

I said, "It sounds as if the discovery of the diary changed everything."

"We thought it did, yes."

"Thought?"

"Once my dad and my grandparents came to grips with what Paul went through, they tried to decide what to do. Starting with getting some answers."

"Did they?"

He took a tiny sip of beer before answering. "First thing, they tried to find Schmidt. A lot harder than you'd imagine, with a name like that, plus the internet wasn't what it is now. But eventually they figured out he'd died."

I told him that Mrs. Zimmerman had suspected as much. Confirming her suspicions, he said it was lung cancer.

"That was a tough day, because they realized they'd lost the chance to go after him. So they approached the college, and that's when the real trouble started."

"Like what?"

"They hit a stone wall. Nobody wanted to listen. Maybe they thought my grandparents were after money or something, which wasn't the case. It really wasn't. They just wanted information. But the college shut them down. I guess they thought about the liability, how giant a headache this could be. My grandparents even hired a lawyer. He's the one who dreamt up the statue deal." He shook his head sadly.

"The commemorative sculpture?"

"You'll never see this in writing, anywhere. But they asked, and the college agreed, to put up the statue in honor of Paul. In return, my grandparents would drop the inquiry into what Schmidt did."

"The college. Anybody in particular?"

"What do you mean?"

"Do you know who at the college negotiated with your family?"

"I'm not sure, tell you the truth. I was barely in high school at the time. I could ask my dad."

"I'd appreciate it, if you could. So back to this deal. It was a payoff, of sorts."

"That's exactly what it was. But it gets worse."

"How?"

"The college also agreed to provide the family with tuition waivers for any grandchildren. Again, you'll never see this written down, but it was understood that an exchange was being made. Our family's silence for a shot at a college education."

"Did you take them up on it? Your family, I mean?"

"My cousins, my aunt's kids, didn't want to. They wanted someplace big, so they went to Ohio State. But me and my sister both graduated from McCulloh. Thanks to what they put our uncle through."

"That must have been hard for you. Knowing the price that was paid."

"I didn't really get it at the time. It seemed like a pretty good deal for me and our family, because otherwise we would have been looking at a lot of loans. And it's a really good school—don't get me wrong. But now? In hindsight? I wish to God I hadn't done it. It feels like a deal with the devil."

I thought back to the morning I stood by the statue with Anne. Recalled the *Citizen Journal* photo of the vigil after Paul's death. I said, "Paul died in 1979. November something?"

"November 3. Why?"

"By my count, that was two days after police caught Ebersole—the burglar I told you about."

"Is that important?"

"It depends on whether that timing was a coincidence."

"What do you mean?"

"Hear me out. Ebersole knew something—he had to. There's no other way to explain why he slipped through the cracks the way he did. Until tonight, I assumed he found something in Schmidt's house that set alarm bells ringing way far away from Columbus."

"Like what?"

I explained the theory that he could have been a spy of some sort. "My guess, at least before what you just told me, was that Schmidt's first call that night, when he discovered the break-in, wasn't to local police."

"That makes sense, I guess, if he really was a spy."

"But what if it was something else? What if Ebersole found evidence of Schmidt's affair with your uncle?"

"Evidence like what?"

"Who knows? Pictures? Letters? Something incriminating. Something that your uncle couldn't bear—"

I stopped. The color had drained from Tigner's face.

"And Paul found out."

"Again, it's speculation," I said quickly. "But it sounds like Schmidt had as much to lose as Paul if the affair was discovered. Screwing up an overseas posting to the Cold War enemy wouldn't have gone over well in East Berlin, I'm thinking. He might have told Paul in a panic—or as a threat, to let him know they were in danger or something."

"But if that's the case, why didn't my uncle kill himself then? The day after the burglary?"

"Maybe Schmidt didn't tell him right away. Or maybe he did, but suggested they were fine as long as the burglar was on the loose. It was only when Ebersole was *caught* that the real possibility of exposure hit home." Something occurred to me. "It's possible Paul's diary might shed light on it. You still have it?"

He told me he did.

"As I recall, about two weeks passed between the Schmidt break-in and the shootout. The entries during those days—they might tell us a lot."

Tigner didn't say anything right away. He took another sip of beer instead. He set his glass down and said, "My dad didn't want me to meet with you."

"Understandable."

"He said you're a disgrace to Buckeye Nation."

"He's probably right."

"He told me one of the happiest days in his life was the Purdue game your senior year. Ohio State down by five with ten seconds to go. Third and long at the fifty-yard line. You took the snap, scrambled way, way out of the pocket, and somehow found Mitch Stacy for the winning touchdown just as time ran out."

I nodded. Not two weeks ago I'd caught my dad showing my son, Mike, a clip of that very play on Mike's iPad. The play that saved our undefeated season up to that point.

"Glory days," I said. Neither of us finished the story: three days later the feds arrested me for point shaving, our run for the national championship ended, and Michigan drubbed us the following Saturday.

"I'm not sure what he was more shocked by. That someone was calling about Paul and Professor Schmidt, or that that someone was you."

"It's a gift," I said, which won a small laugh.

He pulled out his phone. "I probably need to get going. My wife's going to wonder where I am."

"Does she know about all this?"

"She knows about Paul and Schmidt. She doesn't know about you, that you called my dad."

"Are you going to tell her?"

"It depends. Do you know what you're going to do with this stuff? We're not exactly looking for publicity, despite our feelings about what the college did. Or rather, didn't do."

I considered his question. I'm obliged to report crimes, but this seemed way past the statute of limitations. And was what Schmidt did with Paul even illegal? A professor seducing a student no longer passed the smell test of anything approaching a consensual act, regardless of the parties' sexual orientation. But forty years on, with both parties dead, what could be done about it? In truth, I had more important things to think about. Namely, did Grant Fulkerson know anything about this? If so, what did it have to do with the possibility that Schmidt was also a spy?

I said, "Let's keep this between us for now. If you have a chance to find out who negotiated the deal, I'd appreciate it. And maybe check out the diary—it might help explain some things. I'm going to see if there's any more to be learned about Ebersole. Once I do, I'll get back to your dad, or . . ."

"Me. Get back to me."

"Deal."

We stood and shook hands with a promise to be in touch. I watched him walk away from the booth and towards the restaurant entrance, shoulders slouched as if he'd just learned he'd passed a big test but not nearly by the margin he was hoping for. I sat down to finish my beer. Pulling out my phone, I saw a text message from Joe.

Where are you?

Working. Be there shortly

You were supposed to pick me up at 4

I was about to dispute the information when I remembered Crystal's instructions. Practice was going to be short that night. She'd told me not to forget.

Turns out there was a way for today to keep spiraling downward after all.

35

"I'M STARVING," JOE SAID, opening the passenger door after rising from the curb outside the school entrance forty-five minutes later.

"I'm sorry, I'm sorry."

"Where were you? Mom said this was all arranged."

"A meeting. But it doesn't matter. I got the time wrong."

He rolled his eyes and looked out the window. "What's for dinner?"

An excellent question, I thought, recalling my still-sparse larder. I handed him my phone and told him to order out from Katzinger's.

"What happened to your window?" he said, walking into the house shortly before six. I ignored him as I set the bags of food on the dining room table and went to the kitchen for plates and silverware. When I returned, Joe was already tearing into his sandwich. I went back to the kitchen and poured two glasses of water.

"Dad—the window?"

"Someone's gun went off," I said at last.

Joe's eyes grew wide as late-autumn chestnuts. "Really? Whose?"

The slightest pause. "A man who was trying to kill me."

"Are you OK?" he said, uncertainly, mouth full of sandwich.

"Doing better than the window. Kevin's going to help fix it this weekend."

"Which one?"

"The one that's broken."

"I mean which Kevin?"

"Oh. Kevin H. He's the handy one."

Without replying, he swallowed and tore off another bite.

"Hey Dad?"

"Yeah."

"Would it still be OK if I lived with you?"

"What?"

"You know. Like we talked about. Me living here for a while."

I glanced at the cardboard covering a window shattered by gunfire. "Of course. Except—"

"Except what?"

"Well, where would you go to school? This is way out of your district."

"Aren't there schools down here?"

I realized that after nearly a decade in German Village I still had no idea where kids around here, the few you saw, went to school.

"Maybe. Probably not as good as yours, though."

"You mean not as White?"

"Joe."

"That's just what Bob says. He's always saying schools in the city aren't as good because they're 'economically challenged.'" Air quotes with his left hand as he chewed. "Like I don't know what that means."

"There's Black kids in your school and he knows it."

"He says that's different."

"Different how?"

"He says they're clean Black kids."

"That's absurd."

"I know. Like everything else he says."

I couldn't help myself. "That's an understatement—"

"I don't really care where I go to school and I don't really care who I go to school with. I mean, I could still see my friends, right?"

"Right," I thought, contemplating the nearly ninety-minute round trip I'd just made.

"So what do you think?"

"I think we'll have to think about it," I said, digging into a bag for my Reuben.

"That sounds like no."

"Normally you'd be right. But this time I'm being honest. Life here can get complicated." Another look at the window. "And my schedule isn't the most regular."

"At least it wouldn't be boring."

"Is that really fair? I mean—"

"And at least you'd want me here," Joe said.

That evening, as Joe sat on the couch doing homework surrounded by his tablet, a couple of textbooks, and several folders, I reviewed my messages. Somewhat to my surprise, Anne had texted me a link to another lecture she was giving on dystopian science fiction novels.

Hope you can make it!

Thanks

It was a noncommittal reply, though I put it on the calendar a minute later.

Crystal also texted, asking if everything had gone all right picking up Joe. It was past eight by now, and I knew she'd been in Orlando for hours, with more than enough time for checking in, a dip in whatever kind of luxury pool the hotel had, and a no doubt expensive dinner someplace. I told her everything was fine and passed the news on to Joe. He looked thoughtful.

"Hey, Dad?"

"Yeah."

"You know how Bob got mad at me. For going into his office?"

"And taking the change? I thought we worked that out."

Not making eye contact, he reached over and lifted Hopalong's ears. He raised them high up like a bat's, then lowered them over the dog's eyes, one at a time, like pirate's patches, then pulled them sideways like canine ailerons, before releasing them. A game he'd played for years. The dog barely stirred.

"We did, I guess."

"You sure?"

"Yeah. Is there anything to eat?"

I could tell something was on his mind. I was about to pursue it further when my phone went off. Hillary Quinne. I stepped into the kitchen and answered.

"There you are. Everything OK?"

"It's fine. I've just been running around."

"I was worried. Any news from the police?"

I recalled my conversation with Stickdorn earlier. *Big ol' thumbprint, front and center.*

"Nothing so far."

"Well, keep me in the loop. Listen, I tried calling earlier to tell you this. I went to see Carole Weidner."

"What?"

"I was hoping we could go together. But I was getting antsy, especially after what happened to you. Grant's on my ass to get some answers. He's worried the whole thing's going to blow up soon."

"But why go see Carole? I was already there."

"Please don't be mad. I'm sorry I went without you. I just wanted to meet her myself. It's a control thing, I know. But I'm glad I did, because she told me something really interesting."

"Like what?"

"Remember how you said she talked about what an asshole Ebersole was?"

"She was pretty clear on that."

"But also, how he sent her money."

"Supposedly. She only surmised it was Ebersole, right?"

"Something jogged her memory. And here's the thing, Andy. It's when the money was sent that matters."

"When?"

"Ebersole sent the money after he supposedly died in the fire."

I WALKED back into the living room. Joe was bent over his iPad. I approached to make sure he wasn't on a game. I saw he was typing out an essay of some kind and retreated to the kitchen.

"She's sure about that?"

"Positive."

"Does she have any evidence?"

"I asked her that, of course. She doesn't. But she's sure because she remembered seeing the story in the paper about the fire, and it happening after that, which surprised her."

"Any idea where the money was sent from?"

"None."

"I take it she didn't tell the police about the discrepancy."

"I don't think being a good citizen was at the top of her priority list right then."

I thought of Javon Martinez, smiling at me through the jail interview room window as he pulled the rug out from beneath me. Good citizenry seemed to be in short supply these days.

"Andy?"

"This is really interesting." I was being honest, despite how unprofessional it seemed that Quinne had gone around me to re-interview Carole Weidner.

"No shit. It's the first proof we've had that Ebersole is still alive."

"Could be alive," I corrected. "He'd be in his early eighties by now. And of course, it begs the question, if he didn't die in that fire, who did?"

"We need to get those records."

"We've got them. They're in Preston's file. I'll send over what I have in a bit."

"Thanks. I'm kind of juiced about this. I'm sorry I went over there without you. But to your credit, you talking to her the other day sparked her memory, as far as I can tell. You loosened the jar lid, you know? I just unscrewed it the rest of the way."

"Happy to oblige." I knew I should tell her about Matt Tigner as a quid pro quo. Colleagues trading information and all. But it rankled me more than I cared to admit that she'd big-footed me.

"You OK?"

"Yeah."

"Listen. About last night. How are you feeling about it? Be honest."

I paused before replying. "I'm having some regrets that have absolutely nothing to do with you. Or with our working together."

"I understand that," she said quickly. "That makes sense."

"How about you?"

She didn't answer for a moment.

"Hillary?"

"I have some regrets too. About how it happened. And when, I guess. But—"

I waited.

"But not *that* it happened. I don't regret that. I've been waiting a long time to meet someone like you. I mean, obviously, I'd heard of you. 'The famous Andy Hayes.'" She laughed nervously. "But in person? It was good to make the connection. Really good."

"That's definitely honest."

"Too honest?"

"Is there such a thing?"

"Sometimes I wonder. Let me ask you this. What would you think if I came over? I could take a look at that fire file and we could maybe talk this out. All of it."

I thought of the lingering scent of her fragrance in my bed this morning. Of the notion I'd had earlier, that maybe I'd finally met the person whose life was just crazy enough, and similar enough, to match mine.

I said, "I'd say yes, but I've got my son here tonight. For the weekend, actually. It's not the best time."

"I see."

"Tonight's not the best night, is all I'm saying."

"Roger that. I appreciate you being up front. Not to be that girl, but could you still send me that file, on the fire?"

"Consider it done."

But the first thing I did after we disconnected was to call Carole Weidner myself. I reminded her who I was, and that I was working with Quinne. She confirmed the details about the money.

"And no idea where it came from?"

"From Ebersole. Like I told the lady."

"I mean, where geographically."

"No. It was a long time ago now. I'm sorry I didn't remember everything when you were by. I've tried to put a lot of those days behind me."

"It's no problem. Thanks for helping us. We really appreciate it."

But did we? I thought as I hung up. Was it a joint investigation when your partner, who also happens to be a potential love interest, goes around your back? In the meantime, I now had two crucial pieces of information about Ebersole from separate sources. From Carole Weidner, if you could believe her, the fact that Ebersole wasn't the person who died in that fire. From Javon Martinez, if you could believe him, the fact that Wayne Stratton had received money recently from someone somewhere in New York State.

The question was, what to do with this knowledge. And more importantly, I thought, thinking of Quinne, who to tell?

I DROPPED JOE OFF at school early the next morning with a promise to pick him up on time that afternoon. I returned to my favored Tim Horton's down the road, ordered coffee and a bear claw, and opened the laptop to figure out what, if anything, to do next. I was just scanning my e-mail when Stickdorn called.

"Name Ray Lambert mean anything to you?"

"Should it?"

"That's his print on the ski mask."

"OK. Who is he? Sloppy Target employee?"

"He's a mope, is who he is. OHLEG lit up when we entered his vitals. In and out of the system for years. Paroled three years back and nothing since. Until this week."

"In the system for what?"

"Assault, robbery, attempted murder. All the fun stuff."

"That fits. Are you liking him for Preston's murder?"

"We'd like to find him first."

"OHLEG can't help with that?" The Ohio Law Enforcement Gateway tracked details on numerous felons, including current addresses.

"He's gone to ground someplace, just not his usual hangouts."

"He have any connection to Ebersole?"

"Not that we can find. But you're assuming he had something to do with Preston. We still don't have any proof of that."

As frustrating as that was, I had to concede the point. If Ski Mask—now known as Ray Lambert—had killed Preston, he'd been careful to hide his tracks. Picking up shells, no doubt wearing latex gloves—as careful as he would have been with me, I thought, had Jeremy and Mae not come knocking.

"We'll let you know what we find," Stickdorn said. "In the meantime, be careful out there."

"Always am."

"Keep telling yourself that, Woody."

After I hung up, I used one of my proprietary databases to run a background check on Lambert. I don't have access to OHLEG, but the database I paid for came close in terms of publicly available records on charges and convictions and time served. The results confirmed what Stickdorn told me. Lambert was a frequent flyer of the worst kind, with arrests in and around central Ohio—here in Franklin County, down in Pickaway County, over in Union, back down in Licking. No connection to anyplace in New York, as far as I could tell. A spotty employment record, to say the least. I thought about asking Bonnie Deckard, my IT expert, to do a deeper dive on him, but then remembered she was due almost any day with her twins. I figured I was good for now. I had enough to know that Lambert was a danger to society, not to mention me, and the sooner they picked him up, the better. In any case, I wouldn't have had the chance to call Bonnie, as my phone rang at that moment with an unexpected caller.

"It's Corey Robertson. From McCulloh College?"

The security guard who escorted me off campus. Not someone I was expecting to hear from.

"You have time to talk?"

"I guess. What's up?"

"In person's probably better."

I told him I could come to the college, but he said that wasn't a good idea. He gave me an address and we agreed on noon. A few minutes before twelve I pulled up to a two-story white house in Eastmoor off East Livingston. I rang the bell and received my second surprise of the morning when the door opened. Uschi

Herschberger, the McCulloh College languages department secretary, stood before me, beckoning me inside.

THE THREE of us sat in Herschberger's living room, coffee cups in hand and freshly baked streusel set out on a plate on a wooden coffee table. I looked between them both.

"Mind telling me what's going on?"

"First of all, I owe you an apology," Herschberger said.

"For what?"

"For calling security"—she nodded nervously at Roberston—"that day you were on campus."

"Don't worry about it. You were just doing your job."

"No, I wasn't. I panicked, because of her, and made the call without thinking. Things are in such an uproar at the college, all these questions about Gerhard . . . But what I should have done was follow you myself and tell you what was really going on."

"Her who?"

Robertson interrupted. "Hillary Quinne. The private investigator? Didn't you tell me you were working with her? That night you called me?"

I acknowledged it, then directed a question at Herschberger. "So are you saying you knew Gerhard Schmidt?"

She unconsciously smoothed out her slacks, resting her hands on her knees. "He arrived my second year. I was very young. But I remember him well. He was such an Ossi."

"Sorry?"

"So East German, I mean. All of them with chips on their shoulders. But secretly jealous of everything about the West."

"And Quinne's been asking you about him?"

"Several times. That's why she was in the office the day you showed up."

Something came back to me. Uschi's response when I'd mentioned Ebersole in the office that same day. *Was he another student?* I said, "Did she also ask about Schmidt and a student named Paul Tigner?"

She froze for a moment. "What about them?"

I explained my meeting with Matt Tigner, triggered by my call to his father after realizing Paul's suicide came just two days after John Ebersole's arrest. "He told me Schmidt had an affair with Paul—if that's what you could call it."

"Well, that's partly true," Herschberger said.

"What do you mean? Matt was very clear about it. There's a diary."

"What I mean is, Paul wasn't the only one. Gerhard had affairs with many students."

My stomach dropped. "Many?"

As she nodded, a stricken look on her face, Robertson produced a piece of paper and handed it to me.

"What's this?"

"It's the list of all the students."

I looked at the names. The first was *Paul Tigner, '81*. Then: *Warren Smith, '81. Jon Jarvis, '82.*

"Years are graduation years?"

Robertson nodded.

Aaron Gipson, '82. Carl Oswald, '81. Jason Byrd, '81.

"Six in total?"

"Six that I knew of," Herschberger said.

"You knew of these affairs?"

"Some of them. It wasn't hard to tell what was going on in a couple of cases. But after Paul died, I looked a little harder."

"Why?"

The room grew still except for the ticking of a wall clock encased behind glass in a polished walnut cabinet.

"You know of Grant Fulkerson?"

Carefully, I said, "The trustee board president. Yes."

"You know his stepfather was also a trustee? At the time I was there. Myself and Gerhard."

I told her I also knew about Jonathan Slagle, Fulkerson's stepfather.

"After what happened to Paul, Mr. Slagle demanded a list of all Gerhard's students. Well, not him personally. But through the department chair. It wasn't hard to figure out why. Along the way, I compiled my own, private list of the students I thought had been with Gerhard. The others." She pointed at the paper in my hand.

"Did you tell anyone your suspicions?"

She shook her head. "The department chair made it clear I wasn't to pursue it. Nobody, including the police, was interested."

"So why compile your own list?"

"Because I thought there should be some record, somewhere," she said, her eyes suddenly bright.

How could I not have anticipated this, I thought, reaching out to touch her shoulder in consolation. If Schmidt had one so-called affair with a student, why not more? Is that why he was so panicked about the break-in? Why he insisted nothing had happened? Because of the fear of what police might find inside—evidence of multiple male undergraduate sex partners? And the accompanying terror of what had been taken, making him liable to exposure? I told Uschi what I was thinking.

"That may be true," she said. "But unfortunately, he wouldn't have been the first professor to sleep with a student, gay or straight. The very next year we had a French professor get a student pregnant. No, what Gerhard really feared was word getting back to authorities in East Germany. He would have been ruined. Lost his university post—no small thing in that economy. What else would he have done?"

Thus his fear, passed onto Paul, about the Pandora's box that Ebersole's break-in threatened to open.

I said, "Fulkerson, Slagle's stepson?"

"What about him?" Herschberger said.

"He believes Schmidt was a spy, and the college was covering it up. That he was being passed information about a secret nuclear weapons protocol." I explained about DART.

To my surprise, Herschberger burst out laughing. Robertson and I both stared at her.

"What's so funny?"

"Even if such a thing were possible in Columbus, Ohio, at the time, which I highly doubt, Gerhard was the last person you'd want doing espionage. His imperious ways"—she fluttered her right hand in a mock-regal salute—"drew far too much attention. And can you imagine how exposed he would have been, because of those boys?" She looked at the list again, but now she wasn't laughing. "Perhaps his activities involved cameras, but not the kind you're thinking."

"So not a spy?"

"Hardly. Only because these were college students could you not call him a pedophile. But he was certainly the next-worst thing."

AS THE IMPACT OF her words hit home my resistance finally broke. I took a piece of streusel. It was the right decision. I needed to taste something sweet right about then.

Gerhard Schmidt—not a spy. Something far grubbier and sadly mundane, regardless of sexual orientation: a professor who abused his power to carry on multiple affairs with students. Students who, like Paul Tigner, were probably barely forming their own sense of identity at the time. Forced into lopsided relationships at the worst possible moment in their lives. Raped, for all I knew. Worse, to judge by my conversation with Matt Tigner, unknown to one another. The irony: at the time, a spy would have been considered a far worse crime than a man, even a gay one, having some fun on the side with impressionable students.

"Mrs. Herschberger?"

The secretary's eyes had grown bright again. She wiped a tear off her cheek and looked around as if she'd forgotten where she was. Robertson lifted a napkin and handed it to her.

"I was very young," she said quietly. "I was new to this country. I had many dreams. My husband was a graduate student at Ohio State—that's what brought us here. The job at McCulloh seemed a perfect opportunity."

I waited, afraid to rush her.

"But then my husband decided a secretary was not good enough for him and that was that. He left me and married an assistant professor. Suddenly, I needed a job, not just something to do. I was afraid of what might happen if I told anyone about Gerhard. And time passed, and life went on . . ."

I filled in the gap. "Let me guess. Until the day Hillary Quinne walked into your office."

"How did you know?"

"I'm starting to figure a lot of things out. Let me ask you this—did your office have Schmidt's file, with the report of the burglary? Or someone else?"

"I don't follow."

I told her Fulkerson's story of how Schmidt's file had contained a short report of the break-in at his house, the one he'd tried to dismiss. To my surprise, she shook her head.

"There was no such report in his college file."

"There wasn't?"

"I'm sure of it. However Grant Fulkerson knew about that burglary, it wasn't from the college."

Robertson walked me to my car a few minutes later, after I'd said goodbye and thanked Uschi profusely.

"Not that I'm sorry one bit, but why did you call me?"

"I hit the tipping point, I suppose," Robertson said. "She wasn't kidding—things have been in an uproar. Quinne's been up my ass for days. They want to know everything about everything from back then. I had no idea about this Ebersole guy until you told me, but it makes perfect sense now." He looked up and down the street warily. "Fulkerson must have thought everything was buttoned down from the old days. That his stepfather had handled it all."

"Except nobody knew what Uschi did—the complete list she compiled."

"That's right."

"Do they know now?"

"They know there was more than one student, if that's what you mean. But the fact Uschi has her own list? I don't think so."

"What about the statue? They know about that?" I explained the deal brokered by the college that Matt Tigner related to me.

"That had to be Fulkerson. He was on the board then."

"Meaning he knows everything that went on."

"He would have to," Robertson said.

"Any thoughts on how Fulkerson knew about the burglary?"

"His stepfather must have found out somehow. That's my only assumption."

I thought of the tale Fulkerson spun me over lunch. *Anything to do with the Russians these days is toxic—who cares if it involves something that happened that long ago?* Pure malarkey. The only grain of truth in any of it was the fear that Ebersole was still alive and had secrets to spill. Secrets that in today's enlightened #MeToo age would prove far more damning to a Senate campaign than four-decade-old revelations about nuclear espionage. As a motive for murder, though? That seemed more problematic. The more pressing question for me, though, was how much Quinne knew. Was she a dupe, like myself, just following orders? Or was she in on the subterfuge?

I looked back at Uschi's house. "Is she alone there?"

"As far as I know. She remarried, but they never had children. He died of a heart attack shoveling snow a couple winters ago."

"How about you?"

"Me?"

"Married?"

"Divorced—started way too young. I have a fiancée now. She's got two kids. We're saving up to get married."

"Any chance I could talk you into staying with Uschi a couple of nights?" I reminded him of Preston's murder and my run-in with Ray Lambert.

"Jesus, that's some serious shit."

"I know it is. And I have no reason to think Uschi's in any danger. It would just make me feel better."

"It would make me feel better too, now that you've told me. She's got a bit of a brusque exterior, but she's one of the nicest ladies you'll ever meet. Treats me better than almost anybody on campus."

"Got a gun, by any chance?"

He told me he did, along with a concealed weapons permit. "I just never bring one anywhere near the college. Wish we had a bona fide force on campus—makes you nervous, all the active shooters now. But the college is still opposed. Kid-glove approach, you know?"

"That's gotta be Fulkerson too, right, making that decision? I mean, board president?"

"Him and the others. It's a big board—thirty-five members or so."

"Fingers crossed it's never an issue. Thanks for agreeing to look after Uschi. Hopefully they'll bring this guy in soon."

"Thanks for letting me know. And for coming out like this."

We shook hands and I watched him walk back up to Uschi's door. I got in my van and started the engine but didn't drive off right away. Instead, I leaned my head back against the seat rest and shut my eyes. Thanks to Robertson, I had finally remembered what had been bothering me about the aftermath of Lambert's attack.

The casual remark he made just now. *Kid-glove approach, you know?* It got me to thinking of the gloves Lambert wore that night in my house to eliminate the chance of leaving fingerprints. The stink of the latex as he wrapped his hands around my neck and squeezed. I fast-forwarded an hour or more later, as Quinne sat beside me on my couch, running her hands down my neck. *I think you've got latex burns. Are you sure you don't want to see a doctor?*

I'd talked to a lot of people that night, from Mae and Jeremy to Stickdorn to the responding officers, and of course to Quinne. Things were jumbled up. But I was pretty sure of one thing: in my mounting fatigue, I hadn't mentioned that detail of the attack to her. So how had she known Lambert was wearing latex gloves?

38

AS IF ON CUE, a text from Quinne popped up.

I didn't respond. Instead I drove home, taking Livingston all the way. I tried to decide if I was overthinking things. Maybe latex burns were more common than I thought. Maybe she'd seen it in some aspect of her professional career. Maybe she was allergic herself. Taken as a lone bit of information, I might have convinced myself it was nothing, a meaningless coincidence. But Uschi's revelation about Gerhard Schmidt's multiple affairs had me on edge. Fulkerson had clearly been lying, and it's possible Quinne was too.

Back home I pulled up the files on Ebersole's death. They seemed as straightforward as the first time I reviewed them. Carole Weidner's recollection aside, they were definitive on the fate of Ebersole. What else was there to disprove that at this point? My phone buzzed with a call. Quinne, again. I sent it to voice mail. But I knew I had to make a decision and soon.

To buy time, I texted Theresa to see if she'd had any luck with a long-distance trucker named Freddy. I went down my to-do list and saw I was still owed a call-back from George Huntington, my friend at the coroner's office, about the accidental death of

Harvey Heflin, the detective who investigated the shooting of Ebersole. To my relief, Huntington picked up. At least someone was around.

"Sorry I haven't gotten back to you. I had to dig kind of deep on this one."

"Figured as much. How about I make it two growlers instead of one this time? Sideswipe's got some pretty good stuff these days."

"Might not be warranted. We don't have it. The autopsy report, I mean."

"You don't?"

"Nope. File's gone. All paper, back in those days so nothing on the computer."

"That's strange."

"I would agree. But there's something stranger."

"I'm listening."

"There used to be a checkout log, so you'd know who had the file—track the comings and goings. I pulled that to see what I could find."

"And?"

"And it turns out the file on Heflin is gone because the last person who took it didn't return it."

"Who was it?"

"Kenneth Oswald."

"Who?"

"The police chief at the time."

"The chief himself? That's odd."

"What I thought. I asked around, but nobody seemed to know much about it."

"Is Oswald even alive?"

"Beats me."

"I appreciate you checking. Sorry it was a wild goose chase. I still owe you a beer either way."

"Understatement, Hayes."

I was about to hang up when something came back to me about Ebersole. The tidbit from Andrea, the CO at the Rochester jail, that he had a colostomy bag thanks to his injuries from the shootout. I quickly reread the Rochester coroner's report. Sure enough, no mention of it.

"Hayes?"

"Sorry. Listen. I have another favor."

"Oh goodie."

I explained about Ebersole's autopsy and the incongruence of no mention of a colostomy bag on the corpse. "Any chance you could check with the ME in Rochester? Colleague to colleague? You might have better luck than me."

"On whose authority am I doing this?"

"Gene Sprague's interested in Ebersole for some reason. You could check with him?"

"The prosecutor? Like there's an open investigation?"

"I didn't say that."

"I gathered as much. Let me see what I can do. I'm sort of interested myself, at least because of this Heflin file. It's unorthodox."

I thanked him and promised him three growlers. He hung up without acknowledging the offer. Figuring his inquiries would take time, I spent the next few minutes searching online for records for Kenneth Oswald, for a possible address, or an obituary, but came up empty on both counts. I flipped through the documents in my Ebersole file until I found the photo of the vigil for Paul Tigner. Read the caption, including this line:

> Police Chief Kenneth Oswald, whose son attends the college, expressed his regrets to the family.

Whose son attends the college. I had read that days earlier, looking at the file, and found it unremarkable. But now something was bothering me. I thought back to what Uschi told me earlier in the day, eyes bright. *The department chair made it clear I wasn't to pursue it. Nobody, including the police, was interested.* But why wouldn't the police be interested in something like that, especially with the chief's connection to the college? And why would the same chief pull a coroner's report after the investigator's accidental death? It seemed as odd a coincidence as Quinne being worried about latex burns.

Corey Robertson picked up as soon as I called him. Yes, he said, he was still at Uschi's house, helping calm her down. I told him about Oswald and the autopsy.

He said, "His son—Carl Oswald."

"What about him? Other than he went to McCulloh too."

"He's on the list. Remember?"

"Which list?"

"Uschi's. Class of '81."

"Hold on. You're saying—"

"He must have been one of Schmidt's boyfriends. Or victims, if you prefer."

39

OSWALD'S SON, ALSO PREYED on by Schmidt? Another piece of the puzzle snapped into place. A boy's secret exposed by a predator's dalliances. A secret that the chief of police forty years ago had no interest in seeing spilled into the public eye. The need to keep it all under wraps. Unreported. Everything hush-hush—until Ebersole crossed paths with Howie Campbell two weeks later.

Had Harvey Heflin, the shooting investigator, stumbled on all this? Was his accidental death no accident? Was Oswald responsible? That beggared the imagination, not to mention seeming like an unbelievable overreaction. Kill a fellow police officer to keep quiet the fact your son is gay? But then why was the autopsy report pulled? Feeling uneasy, I called Stickdorn. Without revealing my sources, I explained what I'd learned about the former chief and his son, and the missing report.

"Jesus Christ, Hayes. You're accusing Oswald of *murder?*" His usual hearty skepticism was gone, replaced by something uglier and more rigid.

"No, I'm not. But he knew something about what was going on. And maybe Heflin did too—I mean, why'd Oswald pull that report otherwise?"

"If he pulled it."

"Let's say he did. Is there any reason other than a cover-up that he'd do that?"

"I have no idea. They didn't get along, I know that much. What the old-timers say, anyway."

"Didn't get along why?"

"Not sure. I just know there was bad blood there."

"Could Heflin have known about Oswald and his son?"

"Beats me. And I'm not sure how it's even relevant now."

I told him my theory that Ebersole came across evidence of Schmidt's affairs in the break-in, and then used them as a bargaining chip after his arrest. I explained what Darrell Weidner's widow had said about communication with Ebersole, supposedly after he died.

"What you're telling me is you have zero actual evidence of any of this." Stickdorn's tone, suddenly sharp as a lawyer on cross-examination, made me wonder if he knew more than he was letting on. It would make sense if he did. What interest would he, a lifer cop, have in discrediting Oswald? The blue code of silence and all. Maybe I had it wrong. Maybe Quinne wasn't the one I should be worried about. Then, as if to allay my fears, Stickdorn said, "I'll check with the college about this. See if it's even true. And we'll talk to the widow, just to be sure. I'll need her address."

I thought about stonewalling him and telling him to find it himself. But I didn't feel like testing the legendary temper of the cop nicknamed Dickstorm. I looked it up and read it out. He thanked me and hung up without further comment. I stared at the phone for a couple of seconds, wondering if I'd done the right thing. Then I texted Corey Robertson to give him a heads-up. A minute later, despite my reservations, I e-mailed Quinne the files on John Ebersole's death. Who knew what kind of allies I was going to need in the next few days?

I SURPASSED expectations and picked up Joe from school on time that afternoon. Instead of going home, we drove through Linworth and stopped at George's Diner for a burger. We were seated with our food and eating when Joe spoke up.

"Hey, Dad?"

I dipped a fry in ketchup. "Yeah."

"Has Mom said anything more about, you know."

"About what?"

"About me, like, coming to stay with you."

"Not since they left for Florida. Why?"

"No reason."

I studied my son carefully. "You sure?"

"Sort of."

"Sort of?"

He took an uncharacteristically small bite of his burger and chewed for much longer than usual. Several eons later, he swallowed and said, "You know that money I took from Bob?"

"What about it?"

"I'm sorry I did that."

"You've made that clear. It's OK."

"The thing is, that wasn't why Bob was mad."

"What do you mean?"

He balled up a napkin until it was scarcely bigger than a marble. "I didn't know where he was, when I went in his office. I thought he was outside or something."

I waited, saying nothing.

"His computer was on. I didn't mean to, but . . . I mean, it was hard not to—"

"Not to what?"

His voice dropped a decibel or three. "To see what was on it."

"Which was?"

He colored and looked away. "Porn."

My throat went dry. "Porn?"

"Yeah."

"What kind?"

"I don't know. Just, you know—"

"Were they kids? Children?" I blurted out. A man sitting at the counter looked over and stared at me.

"No," Joe said, shocked. Then, in a whisper: "They were, I mean, they were definitely grown-ups."

Not making eye contact, I asked him as tactfully as possible to tell me what he saw. Clearly embarrassed, he did so.

"OK," I said, struggling with the fact I was relieved that Joe had just told me he'd caught his stepdad watching porn, just not the kiddie kind.

"Let me guess—Bob saw you, at the computer."

"Yeah. He was really, really mad. That's why he yelled. That's why Mom came running."

"Does Crystal—does your mom know what you saw?"

He shook his head.

"Bob didn't tell her?"

"He told her I'd taken the money. He looked at me really funny when he did."

"Did he threaten you?"

"No. We just—it just happened, and then it was over. And then Mom—"

"And then your mom talked to me."

"Yeah."

"Is he still doing it? Watching porn, I mean?"

"I don't know. He used to spend a lot of time in his office. Afterward, not so much. But lately—the door's been shut again."

FORTY-FIVE minutes later we left the restaurant and headed to Mike's Friday night game, the cross-town rivalry matchup between Worthington-Kilbourne and Thomas Worthington. The car ride over was quiet. Joe slouched in the front seat, eyes glued to his phone as his fingers flew across the keyboard. Once we parked, I fought the urge to call Crystal on the spot, Orlando vacation be damned, and have it out. Bob watching porn in a house with kids around? What the hell. And could Crystal really not know? Was she just playing along at a charade involving Joe's loose-change larceny as a way of getting him out of the house so she could deal with the implosion of her marriage? Or, more to the point, the implosion of the carefully curated life she'd constructed for herself thanks to Bob and his plastic surgery riches? She didn't have a whole hell of a lot to fall back on if they divorced, I thought grimly. But the trade-off—trapped in a loveless marriage to a porn addict—didn't strike me as much of a consolation. Suddenly, her harried, unfit demeanor began to make more sense.

In the end, I decided against intervening. Joe probably wanted out of there as much as Bob wanted him gone. But a confrontation wasn't going to help anyone. Instead, I locked up the van and walked into the stadium, thinking about what it would take to convert my spare room into a teenage boy's bedroom.

Mike had a near-perfect game that evening, throwing for three touchdowns and running in a fourth, until he went down after a hard tackle with five minutes remaining and lay unmoving on the field. I rested a hand on Kym's shoulder, who sat one bleacher down with her husband, gripping his hand tightly. We were both rising to make our way down when Mike sat up, stood with the help of an opposing teammate's hand, and walked off the field to applause. Afterward he reported nothing worse than a bruised thigh, and no worries of a concussion. But Thomas Worthington took advantage of his absence, regained control of the field, and scored the winning touchdown in the final minute. No joy in Mudville that night.

Despite Mike's obvious preference to attend a party after the game, Kym told him in no uncertain terms that he was coming with me since Joe would be there as well. The fact she did it out of respect for Mike's and my relationship, and not to get him out of the house, as Crystal so often did with Joe, did not assuage his annoyance. I papered over the disappointment as best I could with pizza and unrestricted access to the Xbox I'd purchased for my place—much to Kym's own annoyance—for just such occasions. The boys both played for a while and then Joe got bored and turned to his iPad. The last I checked, he was Skyping with Amelia, Anne Cooper's daughter.

Both boys were sacked out when I woke up shortly after seven the next morning. If normal conditions prevailed, I'd start the wake-up process in earnest by eleven or so. I was back from

Schiller Park with Hopalong and on my third cup of coffee when the phone rang. It was Theresa.

"Hey, QB. You awake?"

"More or less."

"I think I found where Gina and Hailey were staying."

"Good for you."

"Don't get too excited. The thing is, they're missing, as far as I can tell."

I SHOOK JOE AWAKE, told him I had to run an errand, said I'd be back soon and not to answer the door under any conditions. He mumbled crossly that it was too early, rolled over, and went back to sleep. I left a note spelling out the exact same things I'd just said to my sleepy son, locked the house, and twenty minutes later pulled in behind Theresa's car. She was parked in front of a small, one-story brick house off Lockbourne Road with a decent lot but not much to write home about in terms of décor or yardwork.

"How'd you find this place?" I said, slipping into her passenger seat.

"There's a truck stop over on South High, down by 270. Not that far from Gina's house. I know some girls who used to work there, who know some girls who work there now."

"Work?"

"Like truckers ain't stopping there just for gas and food, QB. Use your imagination."

"I'd rather not. Keep going."

"One of them thought she knew this Freddy that Jeremy and Mae talked about. Said she hitched a ride to Indianapolis with him one time."

"He was a client?"

"Does it matter?"

"I'm not sure." I thought of Gina and her daughter. What price they might have paid to seek his help. How scared Gina must have been.

"Anyway, so I come down here—"

"How'd you know it was his house?"

"He called her a few days later. This girl. Said he wanted to see her. She came by. Job's a job."

She paused, collecting herself. "Door's locked, but you can see inside through the front window. I took a peek and saw a stuffed animal on the floor."

"The little girl's."

"What I was thinking. But there's no answer and no cars here."

"Be good if we could take a look inside."

"Also what I was thinking."

We waited while one car passed, then another. Assured the coast was clear, I returned to my van and retrieved an empty Donatos pizza box and ball cap I keep in the van for undercover work. I donned the cap, walked up to the front door with the box in hand, hoped for the sake of any nosy passersby that the pizza joint actually delivered this early, and knocked. After another few seconds I casually tried the knob, but it was locked. After another couple of moments I walked around to the back. The door there was also locked. But to the side, a window was opened a crack. I tried it, praying the neighbors were still asleep this early on a Sunday. It gave. I put the pizza box down and a second later was inside. I walked to the front and let Theresa in.

"Let's make this fast," I said.

We walked through the house, calling quietly for Gina or Hailey. No answer on any count. The home was sparsely furnished, as if rarely occupied. Unopened mail on an end table in the living room. All junk, addressed to Occupant. While Theresa investigated the bedrooms, I stepped into the kitchen and looked around. Sink clean, counter cluttered but not a mess, a coffee pot turned off with a few dregs in the bottom. I looked under the sink and examined the garbage can, remembering my find in Darlene Hunter's apartment. No luck on that front today. I replaced the bin and, on a whim, opened the refrigerator. The inside as sparse as the rest of the house, containing just a few jars, mostly ketchup and mustard, a gallon of milk well below half-mast, a package of American cheese slices, and what looked like a package of brats. I looked closer and read the label. Zweigle's. I'd never heard of it. I'd also never seen white brats before. I picked up the package and studied the fine print. And felt a rush of adrenaline. The meat wasn't brats: it was something called a white hot. And the company that manufactured them was located in Rochester, New York.

THIRTY MINUTES later, after a more thorough search of the house, Theresa and I were back in her car. We failed to turn up any additional signs of Gina or her daughter, but on the dining room table, beneath a pile of napkins, discovered a week-old copy of the *Rochester Democrat and Chronicle*. Next to that, a pile of gas receipts for stations along the New York State Thruway, in addition to one that appeared to be in Ohio, someplace off I-77 between Akron and Cambridge. Most paid in cash, but one with a credit card. F. Johnson.

"What's the deal with Rochester?" Theresa said.

I explained about the connection to Ebersole and his last sightings there and that it appeared Wayne was also from there originally.

"Looks like Freddy has ties there too," Theresa said. "Makes sense, if he's a friend of Wayne's. From way back or something?"

"I'm not sure." But her comment had me wondering a lot more about the connection between Ebersole and Wayne.

"Either way, where are they? Seems like they left fast, if Hailey dropped her bunny." Theresa had picked up the animal on the way out of the house.

"That's what has me worried." I resurrected an image of Ray Lambert atop me on my dining room floor, squeezing my throat as black specks thickened before my eyes. All the arrests that Stickdorn told me about—around Columbus and surrounding counties. Pickaway, Licking, Union. I shook the thought away and used my phone to look up info on Freddy Johnson, but the pickings were slim. A common name. Nothing that connected him to this address, but even in this digital age that didn't mean much. I tried the county auditor's office. The house was a rental, the owner something called Main Street Properties LLC, with an address in Newark, New Jersey. That wouldn't help much—such out-of-state rental agencies bloomed like crabgrass in Ohio after the 2008 housing crash. I tried calling but got only a persistent busy signal. I was debating what to do next when I noticed a woman across the street peering at us, a toddler perched on her hip. We crossed over and explained we were friends of Freddy looking for him.

"Sometimes he parks his truck cab out front," she said, a little warily. "He comes and goes a lot."

"You happen to see a woman and a girl recently, staying there?"

"What'd they look like?"

I realized I had no idea, then remembered that Otto had texted me the photo of Hailey he'd gotten from our good friend Javon. I was reaching for my phone when Theresa spoke up.

"Gina's sort of Goth-y. Black hair, black lipstick, a little bit heavy, big old lip stud"—she gestured at her bottom lip—"lot of tattoos on both arms. Hailey's blonde, ponytail, dinky and thin, wears a lot of pink."

"Yeah, I seen them," the woman said after a moment. "But not to talk to. Last couple of days."

"Any idea where they went?" Theresa said.

She shook her head.

I said, "It looks like they might have left in a hurry. Was Freddy here?"

She examined the house as if seeing it for the first time that day. "His cab was there yesterday, I think. Honestly, it's almost like you don't notice, because sometimes it's there, and sometimes it's not, and you sort of lose track."

After a couple more questions I handed her my card, thanked her, and we crossed back over to Freddy's driveway.

"How'd you know what they looked like?"

"Jeremy told me."

"Good job. I should have thought of that."

"You're the one always telling me to get as many details as possible on a case."

"Congratulations. You're the first woman in a long time to take my advice."

"Like that's a surprise. So what now?"

"Now we try to run down Freddy, I guess. And find out whether he's in Rochester, with Gina and Hailey. And if they are, why they left here in such a hurry." I looked at the bunny in Theresa's hands. "And do all that as fast as possible."

41

MIKE WAS STILL ASLEEP when I walked back into the house shortly after ten. Joe was at the kitchen table, a box of cereal propped in front of him, reading *The Secret Commonwealth* by Philip Pullman, earbuds in and connected to his iPad, which was silently pulsing with a Spotify playlist. Hopalong snoozed on the couch. I sat beside him and constructed a strategy for calling Quinne and telling her what Theresa and I had found. And along the way, casually asking her about the latex burns. Before I had the chance to execute my plan, a call came through. Matt Tigner.

"How's it going?" I asked.

"Been better, I guess. Sorry to bother you. Just wanted you to know we got a call from the prosecutor. Well, my dad did. The news is out, I guess."

"The prosecutor? Gene Sprague?"

"I think so. Hang on. Yeah, that's the guy. We're supposed to meet with him tomorrow."

"He called on a Sunday? Did he say what he wants?" This was a development I hadn't expected.

"Just wanted to know some things about Paul."

"Did he say how he knew? About Paul, I mean?"

"My dad's the one who took the call, but I don't think so."

I thought back to my conversation with Stickdorn. Who else would have tipped Sprague off but him? But why?

"I'm sorry about that. I know it's not what you wanted."

"It's probably for the best at this point. It's not like it could have stayed a secret anymore with everything going on. But that's not why I'm calling. I reread the last two weeks of Paul's diary. Between the break-in and Ebersole's arrest. Like we talked about."

"Anything there?"

"It's a little confusing. One thing I forgot to tell you is that Paul used lots of initials. Schmidt was always HS, for example. That tripped us up for a long time, but then a couple times he wrote 'Schmidt.' It was my aunt who eventually figured out that HS stood for 'Herr Schmidt.'"

"That's creepy," I said before I could stop myself. "Sorry."

"That was our reaction too, so no apologies necessary. There's lots of references to HS talking about how important it was to stay calm and keep quiet. And then a couple references to somebody named CO. I wish we knew who that was because it seemed like he was warning my uncle to keep quiet. Even more so than Schmidt."

"CO was probably someone named Carl Oswald. He was a classmate of your uncle's. And another one of Schmidt's victims."

"Another one? You mean there were more?"

I explained what I'd learned from Corey Robertson and Uschi Herschberger. The fact that Oswald was the son of the chief of police at the time. The line was silent for a few seconds.

"They never told us any of this."

"Who?"

"The college. When the deal was being negotiated."

"That reminds me. The person at the college who did the negotiating. Did you find out who it was?"

"Yeah. I asked my dad. It was a guy named Fulkerson. I think he was on the board."

I took a moment to process that. "You're talking to Sprague, the prosecutor, on Monday?"

"That's right."

"Don't hold back. Tell him everything—including the part about Carl Oswald."

"We will, I guess. Not sure what the point is hiding anything anymore."

"But until then, don't tell anyone else. No matter who asks. Refer anybody who contacts you to me or Sprague."

"Who would contact us?"

"Just promise me."

He said he would. I sat back after disconnecting and pondered the development. Fulkerson had lied to me—maybe to both Quinne and me. He'd brokered the deal that helped seal the family's silence about Schmidt's actions. Which meant he had to know what Ebersole had seen—likely passed down from his stepfather. Cold War secrets, my foot. Fulkerson wanted things kept quiet from those days, no doubt. Just not for the reasons he told us. But why, beyond the awkward publicity? Again, the big question: was any of this motive for murder? I thought of my conversation with George Huntington at the coroner's office about the missing autopsy report on Harvey Heflin. The police investigator who might have stumbled on all this and then suffered a freak accident. I shook my head. The whole thing seemed too implausible, as dingy as Fulkerson's real motives now appeared.

I took a break to check my e-mail. To my surprise, I had a message from Huntington. He'd forwarded me a response from the Office of the Medical Examiner in Monroe County in Rochester. It was succinct and to the point:

> No evidence of colostomy bag or injuries consistent with its use in decedent John J. Ebersole.

FEELING LIKE time was running out, I rose from the couch, went into the dining room, and dialed the number for the Monroe County Jail. I patiently worked my way through the gauntlet of extensions, was connected to a real human being, and to my surprise found myself speaking with Andrea a minute or so later.

"You draw the weekend short straw?" I said after reintroducing myself.

"It's called two kids in college, honey, so I'm a sucker for OT. What can I help you with? Little short-handed right now."

"The inmate whose name you looked up for me. John J. Ebersole?"

"What about him?"

"You said he had a colostomy bag."

"That's right."

"You're sure?"

"Sure I'm sure. I've looked that guy up like twice since you called. Popular dude."

Surprised, I asked her who else had requested information on him.

"Mainly our DA's office. Impression I got was they were asking on behalf of *your* DA."

"You get a name?"

"Nah. District attorney says jump, you jump."

"What'd they want?"

"Same as you—details of the arrest, etc. I told them what I told you."

"About the colostomy bag too?"

"That didn't come up. You're the lucky winner there. Too bad."

"How come?"

"Digging around so much, I found a record of the medical place he ordered from. He had to supply it just in case. Wasn't necessary, because like I told you, we weren't gonna keep that guy long."

I almost thanked her and hung up. Instead, I said, "Just curious—where is it? The supply place."

"Hang on."

A minute passed while I waited, more curious than ever about why the prosecutor's office here would be asking a favor from the district attorney's office there. What was Sprague up to? She was back on a few seconds later.

"Here it is. Some place down south."

"Down south where?" Spirits flagging, I pictured yet another unexplored angle to the investigation, entailing another, much longer trip hundreds of miles away.

"Hang on," she repeated. The line went quiet for a moment. "It's in Geneseo. Wadsworth Medical Supplies."

"Where's Geneseo?"

"South of here, I guess. Kind of in the boonies, I think."

"But how far?"

"Beats me. Thirty minutes? An hour? A long way from where I'm living, mister. That's all I can tell you."

REACHING GENE SPRAGUE ON a weekend on a non-emergency matter wasn't going to be an option, even assuming I could find his number. Instead I did the next best thing and texted Stickdorn.

> Why is Sprague making calls to Rochester about Ebersole?

Just as I sent the text Quinne called. I sent her once again to voice mail, but I knew that calling her back was inevitable. Before I did so, I made another effort to find Kenneth Oswald's whereabouts. After twenty minutes of searching I gave up and called Bonnie and asked as politely as I knew how if she could help.

"I'm not an invalid, you know. I'm just pregnant. My brain is fine. I think I could even manage to work a keyboard."

"Sorry. Didn't mean to imply anything. I just wasn't sure what you were, you know, up to right now."

"This morning I was up on the stepladder helping Troy paint the babies' room. Does that help?"

"Yes," I said, apologetically.

"So just this guy's whereabouts?"

"That's right—"

"Oops," Bonnie said. "Wait a sec."

"Everything all right?"

A few moments passed.

"Bonnie?"

"Sorry," she said, returning to the phone, her voice husky. "Contraction. That one hurt a little."

"Contraction? This can wait."

"Relax, Andy. It's one of the Braxton-Hicks ones. I've had them on and off the past couple of weeks. It's when—"

"False labor. I remember. Crystal had them with Joe."

"Not false, exactly," Bonnie said, sounding peeved. "More like preparatory, if you know what I mean."

"I won't insult you by saying I have the slightest idea what being pregnant means or feels like." I had never lived down telling Kym, Mike's mom, that I could empathize with labor because of doing late-summer two-a-day practices. "But are you really sure you want to do this?"

"I'm sure," she said, in a voice that brooked no further discussion of her condition. I thanked her, hung up, and called Quinne.

"We need to talk," I said.

"I've got time now."

"Let's do it in person."

"Suits me." A pause. "Would you like me to come to your place?"

I thought about using the boys as an excuse. Instead I said, "That's not going to work." I told her to meet me at German Village Coffee Shop.

"You're sure? I could bring lunch."

"I'm sure."

I promised the boys I'd be right back. Mike, barely awake by this point, didn't even look up from his phone, responding only with a grunt. I walked across the park and slid into a booth ten minutes later. Fifteen minutes after that Quinne joined me. She was obviously just out of the shower, wearing yoga pants, a sweater, and the slightest hint of perfume. I silenced a tiny voice at the back of my brain expressing frustration that my boys were home and my house unavailable for a meeting.

"So, what's the rush?" she said with a smile.

The server came with coffee. I ordered eggs and bacon. Quinne asked for toast and a fruit cup.

"To put it bluntly, either you or Fulkerson is lying. Or both."

Her face hardened. "What are you talking about?"

I told her about Paul Tigner and Gerhard Schmidt and the other students. About Fulkerson's stepfather's role in the cover-up. About Uschi's merry reaction when I explained the theory that Schmidt was a spy.

"Finding Ebersole has nothing to do with the Cold War, does it?" I said.

"I have no idea what you're talking about, Andy. I swear."

"How could you not know?"

"I'm telling you the truth. Grant's always been a straight shooter with me. I took him at his word."

It was hard to dispute that, given the look on her face. But I had more to say.

"Two nights ago, when you came over. After the attack. You said you thought I had latex burns on my neck. But I never told you that Lambert was wearing gloves. So why would you say that?"

For just a moment her face froze, as if I'd called her out as a liar in the middle of an important speech. A moment later, to my confusion, she turned red.

"Ugh," she said.

"What?"

She shook her head. "I can't. It's too embarrassing."

"What's too embarrassing?"

"How I knew to ask that. Maybe we could just change the subject?"

"I don't think so."

She looked down the narrow restaurant toward the front door.

"Hillary?"

She turned to face me again, her voice quiet. "A guy I dated once. He was into, you know, role-playing. His big thing was doctor-patient. I don't know why I went along with it. I'm so embarrassed by it now that it's hard to even talk about. But we, um, did it one time, and he had these latex gloves on and that's how, in a really unfortunate way, I found out I had a latex allergy. When I saw your neck, it just seemed obvious."

I took a drink of coffee without replying. The explanation seemed far-fetched at best. Not that I had a hard time believing Quinne could have her pick of almost any man she chose. But the idea of her and submission didn't add up.

"I hope you won't think badly of me, Andy. I've done a lot of stupid things I'm not proud of."

"Like porta potty stakeouts?"

She laughed, relaxing. "I'm not sure I'd want to relive that night. But I got the job done. Are we OK?"

"Maybe. But our work together is over."

The smile vanished. "What do you mean?"

"Regardless of what you did or didn't know, Fulkerson's been lying this entire time."

"I told you—"

"He's not worried about blowback from some Cold War scandal," I interrupted. "Who would even care at this point? But helping a college cover up a predatory professor whose actions led to a student taking his life? And how many other shattered lives down the road? That's another story altogether. Throw in Preston Campbell's murder and my attack, and his campaign's dead in the water once everything comes out."

"You still think what happened to Preston is related to all this?"

"I don't know what to think anymore. I'm not even sure I care if John Ebersole is alive. Frankly, it's moot at this point."

"He seems pretty dead, at least according to the Rochester fire department. And the medical examiner. Thanks for those by the way, even though our work together is 'over.'" She made a dismissive pair of air quotes.

"You're welcome." I made no move to mention the discrepancy about the corpse and the lack of a colostomy bag.

"So now what? You just walk away?"

I thought of what Theresa and I discovered on the South End in Freddy the trucker's rental house. The evidence that Gina and Hailey had hitched a ride to the Rochester area. But why? The uncomfortable truth that I couldn't relax until I knew they were safe. I'd promised Mae and Jeremy, after all, who I owed my life to.

"I pick my assignments more carefully, I guess."

"Is that so. And what about us?"

My phone buzzed with a text. Mike, in my group chat with my sons.

Where are you? The neighbors are here

Home soon

To Quinne, I said, "I'm not sure there is an us. Not right now."

"And not ever?"

The server arrived with our food. I picked up a piece of bacon and snapped off half. The direction of the conversation reminded me I'd forgotten to bring her apartment key fob by. I apologized for the oversight.

"Don't worry," she said dully. "It's a spare. And I changed the code anyway. Too bad. It could have come in handy, you having that."

"I didn't say it won't."

"Then what?"

My phone buzzed with another text from Mike. "Then I need to get going. Thanks for meeting with me. Maybe I'll call you when this is all over."

I stood, dropped a twenty on the table, registered the look of anger on her face with regret, and walked out of the restaurant.

43

THE SMELL OF FRYING sausage and onions and brewing coffee hit me as soon as I opened the door. I stepped inside and saw Kevin H. carefully setting a pane of glass into my dining room window, Joe by his side assisting him.

"Hey, Andy," Kevin said, without turning around. "You're missing all the fun."

"I can see that. I'm really sorry—I completely blanked."

"Not a problem. We're almost done, thanks to Joe here."

I stepped over the two Kevins' pugs, currently chasing Hopalong around the dining room table, and walked into the kitchen. Kevin's husband, Kevin M., was standing beside the stove, supervising Mike as he stood over my grandmother's cast-iron griddle. Mike looked oddly natural in an apron and holding a wooden spoon. At his age I would have fought like a tiger to ward off either.

"Boys said they were hungry," Kevin M. said. "Hope this is OK."

"You're better parents than me," I said, shaking my head.

"Maybe," he said with a grin. "But we get to go home afterward. Isn't that the difference?"

"How about I just send them with you?"

"They're welcome anytime."

After a late brunch and bidding the two Kevins goodbye, we packed up the boys' belongings. Mike wanted me to drop him off at his girlfriend's house to study instead of going home. I texted Kym to see what she thought.

That's fine

Really?

He's not a straight A student for nothing. Some guys actually study with their girlfriends

Will wonders never cease, I thought. Afterward, Joe was quiet as we headed north to Crystal and Bob's subdivision.

"You OK?"

"I don't really want to go home. Can't I stay with you?"

I thought of the long drive I'd have to make first thing in the morning. The repair job Joe had helped Kevin H. with just now, and the incident that led to the damage. The fact that Lambert was still out there, and Gina and Hailey were missing. The shit that was about to hit the fan once Matt Tigner and his family talked to the prosecutor.

Then I imagined the scene in Bob's home office as Joe, shy and bookish, stared in shock at the sight of a naked couple on Bob's computer screen banging the daylights out of each other for the low, low streaming price of $39.95 a month. My stomach shrank as I thought of Bob and Crystal's daughter Lyndsey growing up in that same environment, with no safe house to retreat to.

"How about we try it out for a few days. I just can't promise I won't be late from time to time."

"That'd be great."

I waited in Bob and Crystal's aircraft hangar–sized kitchen while Joe gathered some extra clothes and belongings. Bob was nowhere to be seen. Crystal sat at the island, a half-empty bottle of Bud Light in front of her. She didn't look like a woman who'd just enjoyed an Orlando getaway with her husband in a high-priced hotel. She looked like she'd driven straight there and back alone in a beater car with a muffler on the fritz.

"You need to get yourself together," I said.

"I'm trying, Andy. I really am."

"Try harder," I said.

Joe was settling himself in my living room later that afternoon, Hopalong on the couch beside him, when my phone rang with an unfamiliar number.

"Is this Hayes?" An old man's voice, weak and reedy.

"Yes?"

"It's Doug Fitzsimmons. Howie Campbell's partner. You called?"

I WALKED into the kitchen. Not only had Kevin M. made brunch, he and Mike had given the counters, sink, and stovetop a long-overdue cleaning. Another thing I owed him for.

"Thanks for getting back to me."

"Sorry it wasn't sooner. My wife's not well, and . . . not sure I really wanted to, tell you the truth. After what happened to Preston."

"I understand. I'm sorry to trouble you."

Treading carefully, I explained my efforts to find Ebersole and as casually as possible mentioned the fact Chief Oswald might have played a role in keeping things quiet.

A long pause.

"How much do you know about Howie?"

"I know he was never the same after what happened."

"That's putting it mildly. He was wound pretty tight beforehand. The shooting made it that much worse."

"I can imagine."

"Probably not." Yet another pause. "Thing is, we had an argument that night and he never forgave me."

"About what?"

"Stupid shit. We were taking a dinner break. He wanted to pick something up from the Huddle, by the campus bookstore. I wanted to go to Mama's Pasta and Brew."

Two campus-area institutions long gone by now, more fodder for the wood chipper of progress.

"We argued so much we never went to either. And then we saw the van, on Maynard, and well, that was that."

"Seems a petty thing to hold a grudge about."

"No argument there, except he got it into his head that if he'd eaten, he wouldn't have let Ebersole get the drop on him."

"Really?"

"That was Howie, trust me. We drifted apart, after everything happened. He just never wanted to talk to me."

"You think it had something to do with the case? The fact Ebersole disappeared?"

"Who knows. That was fishy, I'll grant you that. Why that son of a bitch was never charged and then just walked away."

"Could Oswald have, I don't know, intervened somehow?" I told him what Bruce Stickdorn had said about bad blood between the chief and Harvey Heflin, the detective who investigated the shooting, and died shortly thereafter.

"Hard to say. I know Oswald and Heflin butted heads over the whole thing."

"Did you talk to Heflin? About the shooting, I mean?"

"Gave him a statement. That was about it. He scheduled a follow-up, as I recall, but it never happened."

"Why not?"

A weak laugh. "You've got me going way back now."

"I know. I appreciate any help you can provide at this point."

"Seems to me Harvey told me he had more inquiries to do. He said he needed to talk to some people at the college."

"Which college?"

"McCulloh."

I took a breath. "Do you know why?"

"Supposedly he was following up on something to do with Ebersole. He wouldn't tip his hand, and why should he? I was just a patrol officer at the time."

"Do you know who he was going to talk to?"

"I don't. Somebody high up, I assume."

"Like the president?"

"Or maybe the head of the trustees. I'm sorry. That's all I can remember."

44

THE HEAD OF THE trustees. Jonathan Slagle. What was it that his stepson had said about his work on behalf of the college? Not a lot of people know this, but McCulloh was on the brink of bankruptcy when he joined the board in the seventies. He not only helped save it, he made it into one of the top small schools in the country. What if Heflin had stumbled across the revelations about Schmidt and the students, and confronted Slagle with that information? I could only imagine Slagle's reaction as he pondered the impact of that becoming public just as he was pulling the college back from the brink. Had Slagle put a call into Oswald to try to stop things in their tracks? To stop Heflin's inquiry—for good?

I was typing up my notes from Fitzsimmons's call later that evening, while trying to talk myself out of the notion that Oswald had engineered the death of a fellow police officer, when the judge phoned out of the blue. I decided to answer. She apologized up front for not telling me in person about her decision to run again for the Supreme Court. I told her I understood and that there were no hard feelings. Which was more than a white lie by a shade or two. Yet I was hardly in a position to complain to her about a lack of forthrightness after what happened between me and Quinne. She suggested lunch the following week. I told her I'd text her once I saw how the days ahead were shaping up.

I could tell she was miffed by my lack of enthusiasm, but I didn't have anything more to offer her. To be honest, I was still thinking about Quinne. *What about us?* It was a quandary. I couldn't possibly see us together after everything, yet I was somehow inclined to believe her explanation that Fulkerson had kept her out of the loop when it came to the real reason for chasing down the truth about Ebersole. Plus, the bigger and scarier question: was Ray Lambert working for Fulkerson? Was he that desperate to gain a Senate seat that he'd send someone to kill for information?

I made Joe turn off his light an hour later. Twenty minutes after that I lifted his iPad from the floor where it landed after he nodded off. Would that I could sleep so heavily. I was tossing and turning later on, trying to get comfortable, when a thought ripped me out of sleep for good.

Lambert.

I recalled my conversation with Quinne at the coffee shop.

But I never told you that Lambert was wearing gloves. So why would you ask me that?

It hadn't occurred to me then, but Quinne hadn't responded with the most obvious question of all: Lambert who? Instead, she confessed to a kinky encounter with an ex-boyfriend. An improbable story guaranteed to pull my mind elsewhere. To distract me from her slip-up?

I rolled over and turned on my nightlight. I listened to the sounds of the house. It was quiet except for the low growl of Hopalong's snoring in the next room, where he was sacked out beside Joe on the spare bed. I stumbled into the dining room, grabbed my laptop, and retreated to my bedroom. I pulled up the file I'd created on my attacker. The docket from his various arrests locally and in the surrounding counties. Pickaway, Licking, Union. I stopped on the last. Union County. I'd heard that mentioned recently, but not in the context of Mr. Ski Mask. Some other way. And not from Stickdorn, either. I'd only been there a couple times, once to track down a missing teenage girl who'd gone to ground with an older boyfriend in the county seat of Marysville, and once with Otto chasing a bail skip. The county the typical central Ohio exurban mix of farmland, manufacturing—both Honda and Scotts Miracle-Gro were headquartered there—and rapidly spreading subdivisions. Some of the new building was considered the most expensive and luxurious around, with fortunes being made every time a shovel hit the ground on a new construction site—

It came to me. Construction sites. One in particular, a magnet for thieves. A foreman who blamed the Mexican workers. But a stakeout proved differently. The story Fulkerson told over lunch at the Village Tavern. Quinne, holed up in a porta potty for hours. *Is that moxie or what?* A story whose telling in hindsight Quinne had blanched at. As if she really, really didn't want Fulkerson spilling those particular beans. I typed frantically, trying all the search words I could think of. A couple of minutes later I had it. A three-year-old article from the *Marysville Journal-Tribune.*

CONSTRUCTION FOREMAN CHARGED WITH THEFT, RECEIVING STOLEN PROPERTY

I skimmed the article quickly, looking for Lambert's name. It wasn't there. The foreman and another worker had been charged by grand jury indictment, but not him. I opened a new tab and called up the county clerk of court's website. Not two minutes later I found the indictment. Nothing there either. I scrolled down the list of filings, the usual blur of motions for discovery, the settings of hearings, the requests for continuances. I almost threw in the towel when I noticed a witness subpoena. For Quinne? I opened it and instead stared at a subpoena for an inmate who was then housed at the Tri-County Regional Jail, which held prisoners for Union and two neighboring counties. Booking No. 84378. Raymond Lambert, being held on an attempted assault charge from an arrest a month earlier. Subpoena from the prosecutor, which could only mean one thing. Jailhouse snitch. Lambert must have heard something after the arrests and was called to testify, helping convict the people stealing from Grant Fulkerson.

Kinky ex-boyfriend my ass. The reason Quinne asked about latex burns was because she knew the person who'd caused them, because she'd encountered him through the job she did for Fulkerson. Was that who she turned to when Fulkerson demanded quick action on Ebersole and the secrets he might spill if found? Secrets that Preston Campbell might have already stumbled on in his research, and then passed on to me? You scratch my back . . .

What a fool I'd been. I'd encountered discrepancy after discrepancy about Quinne, like a barrage of bird shit on my window, from how she and Fulkerson had known about Schmidt's burglary to her knowledge that Lambert had been wearing latex gloves. And yet I'd given her the benefit of the doubt again and again, no better than a sex-crazed teenager pining after the first girl who opened her legs to him.

I found Stickdorn's number and hit send, and disconnected immediately. What was I thinking? It was nearly 2 a.m. My son was asleep in the next room. This could wait until morning. Couldn't it?

Then I remembered the rest of my conversation with Quinne. Her thanking me for the fire department report and the autopsy results on Ebersole. Reports that included the fact that right before his death Ebersole had just been released from jail. I recalled my conversation the day before with Andrea, the jail guard. The medical supplies company in a town I'd never heard of, listed by Ebersole as his source for colostomy bags. A question she'd asked me previously: *Was he homeless?*

I thought further. Javon Martinez's costly tip that Gina said the money had come from New York. Carole Weidner's revelation to Quinne that she was certain she'd received money from Ebersole *after* his supposed fire death. Gina and Hailey's disappearance with Freddy, perhaps headed toward Rochester and . . . Ebersole? The person who'd helped out Wayne in their time in need, and maybe could help again by paying off the debt Martinez said she owed?

If Quinne put the same information together—if she made the same call to the jail to verify the information, suspecting that Ebersole could be around—what did that mean for the now frail old man?

And worse, for Gina and Hailey?

45

I MADE THE CALL I should have tried first. The phone rang five times before a sleepy voice answered.

"What the hell, Woody."

"I'm sorry," I said to Otto Mulligan. "I need your help."

"Now?"

I heard a muffled query in the background. Otto's wife. Never a big fan of mine, and this call was not going to help that situation.

I explained what I needed. Various sighs, thumps, and less muffled queries came down the line. Finally, just when I thought I'd lost him, Otto said, "Gimme half an hour. And you damn well better bring coffee."

The next call was even harder. The only thing that got me through it was the memory of Monica Mathers, Preston's sister, sobbing on the sidewalk the morning she discovered her brother, and the recollection of Lambert's hands around my throat.

"Andy?" Kevin H. said, answering his phone. "Is everything all right?"

"Remember when you said my boys were welcome anytime?"

TWENTY MINUTES later I was speeding east on 70, Joe and Hopalong safely ensconced in the two Kevins' own spare bedroom. For a teenager accustomed to the sleep of the dead, Joe had reacted fairly well to being awakened in the middle of the night and half-walked, half-carried to a neighbor's house with a promise that everything was going to be OK. I could only imagine what Mike's reaction would have been. Kevin M. said little as I met him at his door. I thanked him profusely and told him I would call as soon as I could. I stopped at an all-night Speedway on Main in Reynoldsburg two blocks from Otto's house, topped off my tank, and went inside to fill two thermoses. Otto was outside his split-level when I pulled up five minutes later, duffel bag in hand and looking for all the world like a guy accustomed to 3:00 a.m. jaunts launched on the merest of whims. I studied his waist as he climbed into the passenger seat.

"Don't worry, Woody," he said, touching a holster invisible through his windbreaker. "I'm locked and loaded."

"Let's hope we don't need it."

"Better safe than sorry, I always say."

We drove nearly without stopping, other than to trade driving duties. We hit the bypass around Cleveland by 5:30, roads already heavy with early morning commuting traffic. We made Erie by 7:15 and Buffalo by 9:00. An hour later we were exiting in Rochester.

The landscape was flatter here than central Ohio, the horizon to the north stretching far and wide, stopping only at a band of gray clouds that hugged the sky's edge over Lake Ontario like a rolled-up gym towel washed too many times.

As we headed south on the 390 Expressway, I once again recalled the unsavory memory related to Rochester that I'd tried to suppress. Which was: partying in a Buffalo hotel with a girl from a Rochester suburb called Webster. Grounded for the night by a snowstorm after a Browns-Bills game. Trying not to think about the engagement ring I'd placed on Kym's finger a week earlier. Grinning at the girl's flat Rust Belt "Oh my Gad!" cackles as we sat at the bar and, her hand on my knee, got drunker and drunker on Genny Cream Ale and vodka and tonics. Groping one another as we stumbled to my hotel room afterward . . .

I shook away the memory. One final peek was enough.

We'd passed the exit for a place called Lima and had just seen the first sign for Geneseo when my phone rang. *Anne Cooper.* I stared a moment too long at her photo ID, her green eyes and red hair and pretty smile, before answering.

"I just wanted to let you know—Bonnie's in labor."

"She is? Real labor, you mean, not—"

"The real deal. Started about an hour ago. Her water hasn't broken yet, so the nurse-midwives told her to take her time, pack up what she needs, walk around the block if it helps, before coming in."

"She's OK?"

"She's fine. Troy may have a coronary, but that's another story. Anyway, I need to pass along a message."

"From who?"

"From Bonnie. She wanted to tell you herself but I told her I'd take care of it."

"What is it?"

"It's an address for someone named Kenneth Oswald. You asked her to find it?"

"That's right. She said she was happy to do it," I added defensively.

She read out the address. I asked her to repeat it.

"You're sure that's it?"

"Yes. Why? What's the big deal?"

"It's nothing. Please tell her I said thanks."

"Where are you, by the way? There's a weird echo."

I peered out the window at the passing landscape, the gray double ribbon of 390 slicing through a ridge of rolling, forested hills. "Out of town. Won't be gone long."

"Everything OK?"

My thoughts were interrupted by the sound of Otto flipping the turn signal to exit.

"I'm fine. Give my best to Bonnie. I'll talk to you soon."

"Sure you're fine?"

"Never better," I said, and told her goodbye.

46

WADSWORTH MEDICAL SUPPLIES occupied the last space in a strip plaza on the outskirts of Geneseo, across the street from a Walmart and a Wegmans. I left Otto in the van and entered the supplies store alone. Inside, a man with thinning dark hair and glasses sat at a desk flipping through stapled packets of paper, a combination printer/scanner beside him. Walkers and wheelchairs lined the wall to his right like the senior citizen version of Harleys outside a biker bar.

"Help you?" he said, not looking up.

I handed him a card and explained the purpose of my visit.

"Popular guy," he said when I finished my spiel.

"I'm sorry?"

"Ebersole. People keep calling about him."

A moment of panic as I thought about Lambert. "People like who?"

"Somebody with a prosecutor's office, for starters." He examined my card. "Same as you—from Columbus. Buckeyes, right? You a fan?"

"In a manner of speaking. You were saying?"

"Wasn't really saying anything. Seems like a long way to come to find out about this guy, though. What's your interest in him, if you don't mind me asking?"

"Ebersole shot a Columbus cop forty years ago, and got away with it. The cop's son came across some evidence he might still be alive. He hired me to look for him. The trail led me here."

"Interesting. Lot more than the prosecutor said."

Hoping to maintain his goodwill, I explained about the fugitive's local ties, his one-time stay in the Rochester jail, the colostomy bag, and the reference to Wadsworth Medical Supplies.

"That was all before my time," he said, frowning. "I bought the business five years ago. I'd never even heard of this guy until the other day. He's not a customer now, I'll tell you that."

"But was he?"

"Listen." He pushed back his chair and stood and I found myself looking up at him; he had a good two inches on me. "You know how much business I've lost to online sales? There's lots of people who used to be my customers. Some of them even come in here, get a recommendation for a product, turn around, sit in their cars, and order it off their phones. I mean, I watch them do it. It's all I can do to break even these days. So I don't need any trouble, especially when it comes to selling something to a guy who shot a cop."

"But—"

His eyes unconsciously drifted to his desk. "I sent the guy what I had, because I'm a law-abiding citizen, and also because I need the warrant he was threatening like a hole in the head. I was willing to help them. And I was willing to help family. But an out-of-state private eye?" He shook his head and brushed back the remnants of his hair. "Sorry. There's only so much I can do. I've got a business to run."

"Family? What do you mean?"

"I mean Ebersole's daughter."

"His daughter?"

"I told you this guy was popular. She called first thing this morning. Said she was trying to find her dad. Said she knew all about the police, and she wanted to get ahold of him before they did."

Heart hammering, I said, "She didn't know where he lived?"

He shook his head. "Said they were estranged. I get it. I've been there."

"Did you tell her?"

He hesitated. "I gave her an address, yes. The only one I had. Just like I did the prosecutor."

"So what is it? The address?"

"Like I said, it's too much trouble at this point. Police and family are one thing, but . . ."

Our conversation was interrupted by an electronic bell signaling the opening of the door.

"Mrs. Jenks," the man said, turning to greet an older, white-haired woman.

"Hello, Tom."

"It's all set. We just had to recalibrate the motor."

Tom looked at me. "If you'll excuse me. Although I think we're probably done here."

He disappeared around the corner. I smiled at the woman. She smiled back.

"I'm from Ohio," I said.

"That's nice. My husband was from Cleveland."

"I know it well. You don't see birds like that, where I'm from."

"Birds?"

"The gulls, in the parking lots." I gestured out the window. "It's like you're at the ocean or someplace."

She peered outside to see for herself. I took a step toward Tom's desk, reached over, and pulled a single piece of paper off the corner. It was a copy of a ten-year-old invoice for a package of colostomy bags. I grabbed my phone and quickly snapped a picture of the address at the top. I replaced the phone in my pocket and set the paper back.

"Rats with wings," Mrs. Jenks said, still staring out the window. "I'd poison them all, give me half a chance."

"Real pests," I agreed as I dashed past her on the way out the door.

47

THE ADDRESS WAS ON York-Poplar Road in a town called West Avon. We were fifteen minutes away. I drove as Otto rattled off directions.

"Easy, Woody," Otto said as I blew through a light that had just turned red. "What's the rush at this point?"

"The rush is I've had it wrong all along. Quinne's been playing me the whole time. And Fulkerson's got resources. There's no telling what they could do." As I drove I had Otto try her number again, the third time since leaving the store. It went straight to voice mail once more.

The commerce hugging the edge of Geneseo soon disappeared as we plunged back into rural farmland. We exited off the main thoroughfare onto a country road and passed a pole barn the size of a medium-sized school standing beside several steel silos big enough to house missiles. We turned again onto a narrower road hardly wide enough for a tractor to pass, and after three long minutes turned again onto York-Poplar, a dirt-and-gravel road that dropped into a hollow surrounded on both sides by tall, thick-limbed oak trees starting to show their fall colors. We rode in silence, the only sound the crunch of tires on the rough surface, rooster tails of dust rising behind us.

"There," Otto said. "We just passed it."

"Shit." I braked so hard the van's back end fishtailed as its tires ground against gravel. The engine whined as we flew a hundred yards back in reverse. Reaching the mailbox, I roared up a long dirt driveway. A large Victorian farmhouse sat at the end of the drive, a pickup truck off to the side. The house was a riot of filigree and gables and chimneys but long past its prime. I would have thought it abandoned except for the power and phone wires running in taut lines from an upper corner and a satellite TV dish jutting from the roof, as incongruous as a mushroom growing from a sun-drenched slab of sidewalk.

As I stopped the van Otto opened his backpack, reached in, pulled out a gun, and handed it to me. I shook my head and instead grabbed my Louisville Slugger. He rolled his eyes, jammed the extra gun into his rear waistband, and took point. We reached the front door a moment later. I tried the bell but it wasn't working. I knocked loudly, waited a few seconds, and tried again. Nothing. I tried the handle but the door was locked. I knocked again. We listened in vain for sounds from inside.

We were debating next steps when we froze, each hearing it at the same time. Under different circumstances the noise might have been unremarkable, the kind of thing natural to hear outside an occupied house late on a sunny morning, no matter how deep in the country. Clear at the rear. A little girl's voice. One word: "Why?" followed by silence, as if she'd been cut off in midsentence.

We ran in that direction but saw nothing. But fifty feet back from the house stood an old outbuilding, half barn, half shed, listing to one side like a ship moored in the mud up on Lake Ontario. Weathered brown boards. Doors hanging open to reveal a jumble of wood and equipment inside. Plenty of places to hide. We headed in that direction, glancing back and sideways as we did, but seeing nothing. The back door of the house was closed. Had we imagined the voice? But no: without question a girl had spoken.

We crept into the outbuilding, which smelled of oil and dry rot and stale grass. Otto had his gun up as he looked to his left and his right and then above. The sky peeked through several large holes in the roof. Up or down, though, the building was empty except for ourselves. Otto shook his head and lowered his gun. He walked to the back of the building, past an old tractor covered in cobwebs. At the rear a lone window, pane broken in two places, provided partial light. He stood and looked out and signaled for me to approach. I walked over. A hundred yards farther back, behind a copse of pine trees, sat a trailer home set up on cinder blocks. A set of wooden steps led to the door, which as we watched slowly closed shut.

"Now we're talking," Otto whispered. "Trailer and a felon—old home week for me."

He told me his plan, which I disliked immediately. He explained that a guy bringing a baseball bat to a gunfight didn't get a vote. I acknowledged his point. A minute later, bat leaning against the old tractor's rear wheel, I walked weaponless and alone toward the trailer, feeling as exposed as a cottontail in a field after a January snowfall. I thought I saw a curtain in the trailer's window move. I swallowed and dropped my hands to my side and slowed my pace, taking each step with deliberation to show I posed no risk. The curtain moved again; now I was sure of it.

I reached the steps, a rough-cut assembly of pressure-treated two-by-eight treads warping after long exposure to the elements. I took the first step and the second, stopped, listened—heard nothing—and knocked.

48

"HELLO?"

No response. Thistles and goldenrod and long grasses in a surrounding field bent slightly in an autumn breeze. After a moment I heard movement inside the trailer, as if a chair was being moved from one side to the other, but no voices.

I knocked again. I said, "My name is Andy Hayes. I'm a friend of Jeremy and Mae's, from Columbus. I'm looking for Gina and Hailey. I just want to be sure they're safe. That's all." A second later I added, "I'm unarmed."

Still nothing. A count of nine and a half passed. Overhead a pair of sparrows carried on an aerial dogfight with a hawk against a backdrop of clouds like cotton candy lined with dryer lint. I wondered if Bonnie had delivered the twins. I knew from Kevin H. that Joe had made it to school just fine, but I pondered what the aftermath of that episode would entail and whether Joe would have second thoughts about moving in if it seemed likely to involve more such middle-of-the-night maneuvers. I thought about the lie I'd told Anne about everything being fine, and then I thought about her picture on my caller ID. I knocked again and repeated my explanation. I made it halfway through when the door was flung open. The sudden movement forced me off the stairs and onto the ground, where I nearly stumbled and fell.

"Get the hell off my property."

I looked up and found myself staring into the eyes of an old man. Age had hunched him, his hair had retreated far off his forehead, and a slight tremor shook his left hand, which left me all the more nervous about the shotgun he was cradling.

"John J. Ebersole?" I said, though the question was rhetorical. Based on all the photos I'd seen in Preston's file, it was him, forty years on and the ravages of age or not. Christ, I thought. Preston had been right all along, from the moment he cornered me at Plank's on Parsons.

"I said get the hell off my property. I don't care who you are or what you want."

I backed up a step. "I'll leave as soon as I see Gina and Hailey."

"You'll walk away now or they'll scrape what's left of you into a body bag. Your choice."

"Gerhard Schmidt," I said.

He narrowed his eyes but didn't speak, nor did he adjust the aim of his weapon in the slightest.

"I know all about him. And what you found in his house the night you broke in. Schmidt and the chief's son. I also know about the deal you struck with Oswald and the reason you're not rotting in some Ohio prison like you deserve. And I'm not the only one. Shoot me and that's one guy out of the way. But there's a whole army behind me." The last part half bluff, half wishful thinking. Ebersole had eluded authorities this long; was there any reason to believe his streak would be broken with me out of the way?

"Count of five," he said.

"Just show me Gina and Hailey."

"Four."

"One glimpse. Just to know they're safe."

"Three."

"I don't give a shit about you, Ebersole. I only care about them. Can you possibly think about someone else in your miserable life for a change?"

"Two," he said, raising the shotgun.

"One," Otto said from behind Ebersole, nudging the barrel of his gun into the back of his neck as I quickly moved aside.

WE SAT in the trailer's small living room. Ebersole glared at us from the couch, hands and feet zip-tied courtesy of Otto and his usual bag of tricks. Whether it was legal to detain the old man like this I had no idea. I was just happy he couldn't get near the shotgun. Or the arsenal of other weapons, a mix of handguns and long guns, we found in a cabinet inside the trailer. Gina sat in a chair on the opposite side, Hailey on her lap, the girl's eyes round as the knotholes in the dilapidated outbuilding across the field as she stared at me and Otto. A breeze blew in from the rear of the trailer from the bedroom window Otto had jimmied open.

"There's money in the house," Ebersole said.

"What?"

"Closet, second bedroom on the left. More than enough. Take it. Take them." A nod at Gina and Hailey. "You can just walk away. Leave me here, like this." He shifted and raised his bound hands. "You know damn well it'll take me a while to get free."

"And you know we can't do that," I said.

"You're a damn liar. You said all you wanted was to see them. Be sure they're OK."

"Not sure you're in a position to name call."

"Plenty of money," he said.

"What's our play here, Woody?" Otto interrupted. "Thinking we need a plan, if just to shut him up."

"Go to hell—"

"And see you there," Otto said cheerfully.

Otto was right, except I wasn't sure what to do first. Call the local authorities, tell them we'd found a fugitive from a forty-year-old Ohio crime? Call Stickdorn and inform him of our discovery? Or better yet, call Sprague, the prosecutor, who had the local jurisdiction in Columbus and whose feelers on Ebersole I'd been one step behind the whole time? Or the feds, on the chance Gina and Hailey hadn't come willingly with Freddy?

In the end I decided a combo meal was best; let Columbus authorities alert the locals, but not let Ebersole out of our control in the meantime. I recalled Quinne and the call she'd placed to Wadsworth Medical Supplies. And get the hell out of here while we were at it, I thought.

I stood. "The plan is I'm going to get the van and pull it around. While I do that I'm going to call some folks with badges back home. Once I'm back here, we're going to load everyone inside and drive into Geneseo to find a cop shop. Once I get the go-ahead, we'll take Mr. Happy Pants inside."

"Groovy," Otto said.

I looked around and satisfied myself that everything was all right. I never doubted that Otto's assault on the trailer's rear flank would work. I just had a bad moment or two wondering about the timing. As usual, Otto had come through.

"See you in a minute," I said.

I crossed the living room, entered the tiny kitchen, opened the door, and stepped out onto the porch steps. I made it down one step before stopping, frozen in place.

"Lucky you," Ray Lambert said for the second time in our short acquaintanceship.

49

"INSIDE," HE SAID, GESTURING at me with a gun.

I thought about the crowd in the trailer, including a little girl who shouldn't have to be seeing any of this. I recalled Monica sobbing at the discovery of her brother, and Lambert's cold, calculating orders to me to repeat the password to my laptop as a prologue to what should have been my own execution.

"No."

"I said, inside."

"And I said no." I took a step down. "If you're going to shoot me, just do it. Easier to clean it up out here."

Quick movement of his eyes to the side, as if looking for someone. "I will, believe me."

"I know you will. Just like you shot Preston Campbell. And almost killed me. Go ahead."

Although I should have been more scared, I felt oddly calm at that moment. I knew I wouldn't survive being shot by Lambert; it wasn't like in the movies or TV. You could see in his cold, flat eyes that he'd finish the job. No stealing-home moment this time. But I also knew Lambert wouldn't survive more than five or six seconds afterward with Otto inside the trailer. Once he heard the shots that would kill me, Otto would be out the door and take care of business in a heartbeat. Gina and Hailey would be OK. And that was my comfort now. I took another step closer.

"Do it or get out of my way," I said.

"I will," he said, and raised his gun.

I lifted my hands reflexively. But instead of firing, Lambert grunted and stumbled, clutching his right leg as a sound echoed behind us. I stared as blood bloomed from his calf, and then looked over him in the direction of the noise of gunfire. Lambert fell to the ground, rolled to his side, and sighted his weapon in the direction of the shot, but he wasn't fast enough. Two more cracks in the distance. Lambert flinched as if someone had jabbed him with a stick, and rolled onto his back. He groaned, staring up at me. I stared back, watching blood gush from wounds in his neck and chest. I crouched and looked across the field, toward the house and the outbuilding. Nothing moved. No car engine gunning, no squeal of tires. No sound other than the breath of the wind in the weeds. I rose, showing my hands. Nothing happened. I took a step back, then another, then reached the wooden stairs. Gripping the railing, I mounted the treads, reentered the trailer as fast as I could, and pulled out my phone.

AN HOUR or so later I was staring up—and up—at a New York State trooper looming over me, tall and straight as a Stetson-wearing utility pole.

"Let me get this right," he said. "If you didn't shoot that guy, and your bounty hunter pal didn't, who did?"

"Excellent question," I said.

I was in the back of a Livingston County Sheriff's cruiser with the window down. Otto was in the next cruiser over, with Ebersole occupying a third. Enough trooper and deputy vehicles lined the property to qualify for a car rally. Gina and Hailey had been taken away somewhere, out of sight, Hailey clutching the stuffed rabbit that I'd remembered to bring along. Lambert's body cooled in the grass, shielded by a portable white screen courtesy of the medical examiner. Crime scene technicians methodically examined him, the ground around him, and the trailer. I watched another team entering Ebersole's house, and closer to the road, plain-clothes officers searching the approximate area I said the shots came from.

The trooper said, "I take it you don't have an answer?"

I told him I didn't.

"Let's try another. We've got your van, the old man's truck, and the dead guy's Jeep. Meanwhile, we're in the middle of nowhere. Nearest farm's a quarter mile off. In that case, how'd the shooter get away?"

"Another excellent question."

"You being wise?"

"That's the last thing I'll ever be accused of."

They kept us two and a half days, which was at least one day short of what I expected. It took them that long to conduct the testing that confirmed what Otto and I told them from the start: the bullets that killed Lambert didn't come from either of Otto's legally registered weapons or any of those owned by Ebersole. Otto's bail bond licensing checked out, as did my private investigator credentials. Bruce Stickdorn vouched that I had never been a suspect in Preston Campbell's killing, and he verified the details of Lambert's attack on me at home. Gene Sprague confirmed the story of a cop-shooting fugitive named John J. Ebersole.

A warrant for a DNA swab to verify Ebersole's identity was placed before a New York State judge, though the fugitive's arrogance in never changing his name meant he'd lost half that battle. Otto and I split the cost of a hotel for Gina and Hailey, including calls home to Mae and Jeremy, and to Freddy, to let him know they were OK after he'd dropped them off at Ebersole's at the direction of Gina, who'd found the address in Wayne's belongings after the coroner released his body. After our midday dismissal Tuesday, we all piled in my van and drove straight to Columbus. I dropped Gina and Hailey off at midnight, took Otto home to Reynoldsburg a few minutes later, and was in my house and asleep by 1 a.m.

I set my alarm, though. Thanks to the address Bonnie found for me just before going into real labor—the address Anne Cooper passed along as we drove toward our rendezvous with Ebersole—I had to be up early and get to work. Despite everything that had transpired, I still had a lot to do.

THE THURBER HALL DINING hall was three-quarters full when I joined Mrs. Zimmerman at her table late the next morning. Residents' eyes collectively trained on me, as if she'd seated an orangutan beside her and not a lunkhead with his glory days—and less than glorious days—well behind him. Our conversation heavy on her grandchildren and my boys.

"The food's not bad if you like sauces," she said as our plates arrived. "Lots and lots of sauces."

I took a bite. "It's delicious—and the company is what matters anyway."

"You're very kind, Mr. Hayes."

"Please, call me Andy."

As she smiled and lifted a cup of coffee to her lips, I glanced discreetly around the hall. A wall of windows on the far side, overlooking the self-same glen, full of trees with rapidly changing colors. White cloth–covered tables occupied by trios and quartets of diners. Servers in black trousers and white dress shirts scurrying back and forth from the kitchen. And at the far end, sitting in a wheelchair at a table by himself, a man. The same man I'd seen in the library the day I met Mrs. Zimmerman.

"Could you excuse me, please?"

I stood, feeling a little bad about the look of surprise on her face, and crossed the room. I took a chair beside the man. Thin, hollowed-out face, watery blue eyes that were almost translucent. Skin pocked with liver spots. In appearance, not all that far from the shotgun-wielding man who'd greeted me at his New York State trailer a few days earlier.

"Mr. Oswald?"

He looked up at me blankly.

"*Chief* Oswald?"

Recognition flared in his eyes. I explained who I was and what I wanted.

"I know about Harvey Heflin. I know what you did to him. That wasn't an accident in his garage that day, was it?"

He stared at me, eyes now bright as reflecting pools.

"You killed him, to shut him up. To keep him from spilling what he knew about John Ebersole. About the cover-up. About the deal that let him go free."

His lips moved, shaping soundless words.

"I found Ebersole. He'll be back here, I promise. Whatever you hoped to accomplish is over. Do you understand?"

He was saying something now, but so quietly I couldn't hear.

"What?"

A multisyllabic whisper impossible to catch. I leaned in closer.

"Say it again."

A harsh whisper but clear as words shouted across a room.

"Fuck you, son."

I pulled back, keeping my eyes on his face. "That's your response?"

To my confusion, he shook his head, bright eyes filling with anger. He repeated the phrase.

"If you're sure."

A single tear rolled down his right cheek as he said it once more. I waited, but our moment was over. I looked Kenneth Oswald in the eyes, satisfying myself I saw nothing there. I didn't. It was like peering into an empty grave.

"Excuse me?"

I turned. A trim, younger version of Oswald stood before me. Mid- to late fifties, gray brushing his temples.

"Do you know my father?"

I stood and told him I didn't, that I was just visiting Mrs. Zimmerman and saw him sitting alone.

"That's kind of you. I'm Carl Oswald."

"His son," I said, before I could stop myself.

"That's right," he said, puzzled. Behind him a man about his age with about the same gray in his hair studied us. Each had a wedding ring on.

"I'm sorry if I intruded."

"It's all right. Interaction's helpful, even if he isn't always there."

I apologized again and walked awkwardly across the room.

"Everything all right?" Mrs. Zimmerman said as I retook my seat beside her.

"I'm not sure."

"Do you know Kenny?"

"Just in passing." The shock of seeing Carl, and the person I assumed to be his partner, had my mind racing. Something about the expletive Oswald directed at me.

"Sorry," I said. "You were telling me about your granddaughter in Des Moines?"

We resumed our conversation. We enjoyed a lunch that involved a lot of sauces. I tried my best to listen as I pondered Oswald's reaction to my question and periodically looked at him and his visitors. Tried to reconcile the juxtaposition of his defiant response with the anger in his eyes, seemingly born of frustration that I couldn't understand what he was saying.

It wasn't until I'd said goodbye to Mrs. Zimmerman and was walking to my van that it hit me. That I realized what Oswald was really trying to say. I leaned against the driver's-side door, head resting on my forearm, suddenly overwhelmed. Of course.

"Fuck you, son," Oswald said to my accusation.

But no. He'd been saying something different. Not a declaration. A name.

Fuck you, son.

Fulkerson.

51

I HAD TO ADMIT, the view from the condominium's window was spectacular. Directly below me, North Bank Park, perched on the banks of the Scioto. Popular for weddings and concerts. Just to the left, the Columbus skyline, modest but slowly expanding as the downtown residential building boom continued unabated. To the right, the opposite shore of the river, the cross-hatched iron lines of a railway trestle, and then the distant curling of interstate highways. Nature and the hand of man wedded into a single beautiful vista. I could only imagine what it looked like at night.

The click of a lock across the room as the door to the condo opened. I shifted in my chair, which I estimated cost at least what Preston Campbell gave me as a retainer. I cleared my throat, having had enough of unpleasant surprises for a while, receiving or giving.

"Jesus Christ," Hillary Quinne said, starting as she stared at me. "How the hell did you get in here?"

"Nice to see you too." I gestured out the window. "I can see why you picked this place."

She glanced unconsciously in the direction of the bedroom.

"Don't worry." I lifted the gun I'd found on her bedside table. "It's safe and sound." I set it onto the floor. I pulled the magazine and chambered round from my jacket pocket and showed them off before putting them away again.

"A little dangerous to leave it out in the open like that, but I get it. What's the point of self-defense if you can't reach it when you need it?"

"You need to leave. Now."

"Just to be clear, don't think I have any illusions this gun could be traced to what happened to Ray Lambert. I'm sure that weapon's far, far away by now."

She drew herself up. "I have no idea what you're talking about. And to repeat: how the hell did you get in here?"

I pointed at her glass-topped dining room table. Her apartment entry fob sat in the middle of a green beaded place mat.

"I'm calling the police."

"Go ahead."

She didn't move.

"Funny thing about Lambert, by the way. It only occurred to me afterward."

"Andy—"

"A shot to the head or torso ran the risk of the bullet hitting me too. Whoever it was, they took him to the ground with a calf shot before finishing him off. I thought that was a mistake at first, or an errant shot. Then I realized it was a way to change the angle in my favor. Not an easy shot to take. Which means the person who killed Lambert purposely saved my life in the process."

Her eyes were stones, flat and gray.

"Another funny thing. Cameras at the toll booths at the Pennsylvania line picked Lambert up in the Jeep. Buffalo and the Rochester exit too. One of the detectives out there showed me the pictures. You'd expect that, of course. Photo of the driver, I mean. But there's so much concern about human trafficking these days that they've installed cameras with extra-wide angles. They pick up stuff in the rear seats too. In Lambert's case, something big, covered in a blanket."

"Andy, I said—"

"What's odd, is that the blanket has shifted in each of the pictures." I stared at her until her eyes dropped. "Making you think the blanket might not be covering a what. But a who."

I stood. Slowly, so as not to alarm her. Alarm her more. I said, "This won't be easy. I know that. But I should be able to make a case. I can connect Lambert to you through the construction-site theft. And of course, that connects both of you to Fulkerson. By the way, I assume you sent Lambert to my house that night I went to see Carole Weidner?"

She stared at me, slowly shaking her head.

"The next part is trickier," I continued. "Connecting Fulkerson to the murder of Harvey Heflin. That's the part I had wrong. I thought Kenneth Oswald was responsible. He may have known about it; it explains his interest in the autopsy report. But it was Fulkerson who acted, probably on his stepfather's orders. Probably. That's why he was so eager to find Ebersole. Pull that thread and the whole thing starts to unravel. There's nothing like a murder in your past to screw up your run for the Senate."

Something like a smirk grew at the edge of Quinne's mouth.

"I know what you're thinking. Castles in the air. But lines can be drawn between dots. Dots that go a long way back between you and Grant, I'm guessing. New clients don't ask about kids quite so casually. Or is 'Madison' even real?"

"She's real," Quinne said. "She's just with her dad all the time."

"Now there's a surprise."

She folded her arms. "I repeat, I have no idea what you're talking about."

"I'm sure you don't."

"What's more, I know something you don't, not that that's a stretch."

"Which is?"

"Grant Fulkerson is dead. He committed suicide early this morning. His wife heard the sound of the gun and found him, poor thing. Been me, I would have just hired a lawyer. But there's no telling what pressure can do to a guy." She paused. "Now I've just got to figure out how to get paid."

Now it was my turn to stare, startled by the turn of events, not to mention Quinne's cold reaction to her boss's death. Trust her to turn the tables like that.

"You really don't have anything, do you?"

"I'll see about that," I said, realizing how lame it sounded as soon as I spoke the words.

"Good luck with that, Andy. Now I really need you to go."

"And here I thought we were more than just friends. At least according to you."

She laughed out loud. "Don't kid yourself. That was nothing. Do you understand? I didn't feel a thing. I was—"

"Too busy focusing on where you'd start looking for the flash drive afterward? Which is how I assume you dropped that?" I gestured at the apartment fob. "I don't think so."

"You don't?"

"I don't. Because now it's my turn to tell you something you don't know."

"Which is?"

"The number of women I've been with who faked it and thought I was fooled."

"I can only imagine."

"You can't, actually. Because I'm the king of understanding that I got something I wanted without fulfilling the other person. It's sad, how many of them thought I didn't know the difference. Sad for me and sad for them. But believe me, I can always tell."

"Get over yourself, Andy. I said I didn't feel a thing."

I crossed the room, forcing her to move aside as I passed, and opened the door. I turned and said, "The majority."

"What?"

"The majority of women faked it with me. That's why when it really happens, it's so special."

I held her eyes until she looked away, walked out, and shut the door behind me.

"HEY DAD?"

"Yeah."

"No offense, but—"

"Yes?"

"Do you actually know anything about art?"

The following Saturday. I'd watched Joe run on his home cross-country course, then taken him out for a late lunch or early supper, the distinction lost on a ravenous boy. Now I was driving him to a friend's for a sleepover.

"I know plenty," I said.

"Then who's your favorite artist?"

"Milton Caniff."

"Who?"

"Never mind. Anyway, knowledge of art isn't a prerequisite for the job."

"That seems weird."

"Life's weird, Joe."

The job in question was at the Columbus Museum of Art. I'd picked up the hours upon my return from Rochester, once it became clear Joe was ready to move out of Bob and Crystal's sooner rather than later regardless of my penchant for strange turns of events. The plan for now was a reverse of our previous arrangement—weekends at their house, weekdays with me. I'd hazard the long commute to his school each morning and evening, and pull dayside security shifts at the museum in an attempt at a more regular schedule. A hiatus from straying spouse and workers' comp fraud stakeouts, at least for now. Crystal hadn't blinked when I explained the deal. Understandably, since her eyes were red and swollen the day I made the proposal. Which indicated she might have come to terms with Bob's closed-door office sessions. It was almost enough to make me feel bad for her. Almost.

FALLOUT FROM the reopened case of John J. Ebersole continued. He'd found a lawyer who was fighting extradition to Ohio using the argument that he was too old for such a move. Gene Sprague wasn't having any of it. The investigation he'd quietly launched into the decades-old cover-up of the murder of Harvey Heflin was well underway, and he wasn't about to be deterred by a two-bit burglar. Local authorities in Rochester were pursuing an exhumation of the body burned in the fire presumed to have killed Ebersole. Best guess was—as Andrea at the jail had unknowingly suggested—a homeless man he'd met behind bars and then lured back to the house as part of a plan to disappear for good. The move possibly a reaction to word that Darrell Weidner had been running his mouth about him back in Columbus—a problem he may also have figured out how to solve, if Weidner's widow was to be believed.

Paul Tigner's family filed a lawsuit against McCulloh College, joined by several men—most of them John Does—who experienced similar treatment by Schmidt as undergraduates. The college president was said to be close to resigning, with trustees pledging a full and transparent investigation.

Monica Mathers hadn't replied to any of my recent texts or e-mails, and eventually I just wrote her a check for Preston's retainer and stuck it in the mail. It came back a week later with a Post-it Note from Monica.

Keep it. You're the only one who ever believed Preston.

As for Javon "Little J" Martinez, he had his own problems. He hadn't been back on the streets two days when he was caught moments after kicking in the door to Darlene Hunter's apartment, lured there by a text suggesting she was back home. He couldn't understand how the cops got there so fast, which remains a mystery—as does the identity of the person who sent the text from an unknown number.

AFTER DROPPING Joe off, I headed back to German Village. Anne had invited me for a drink that afternoon. To talk about the thing she wanted to discuss with me. She suggested Barcelona, her treat. I walked in at one minute after five. She was already at the bar. She wore a trim tan jacket over a light-green blouse and dark jeans. A headband held back her red hair. She smiled warmly as she spied me, raising a stemless glass of white wine in my direction.

"Thanks for coming."

"My pleasure."

I ordered a beer and settled onto the bar seat beside her.

"You OK?"

"I'm fine."

"You saved the day. Again."

"Stupid New Year's resolution. How's Bonnie doing?" I asked, eager to change the subject.

"Tired, as you can imagine. But she looks good. And the babies are doing great—they've latched on just fine."

"Latched onto what?"

She laughed and punched me lightly on the shoulder. "Onto Bonnie's breasts. They're a multipurpose body part, you know."

"Just testing you," I said, my face reddening.

My beer arrived. We clinked glass and I removed the top of the bottle's shoulders. I felt my phone buzz with a text as we replaced our drinks on the bar top.

"So, any agenda for this conference?" I said casually.

"Well, like I said, I had something I wanted to ask you."

"I'm all ears."

A commotion at the door as a pair of couples entered. As Anne looked up, I pulled my phone from my pocket. A text from the judge.

It's a little off our routine, but any interest in coming over for some takeout and then some dessert?

A winking-face emoji leaving little doubt about what she had in mind.

I looked up and studied Anne's profile. Recalled the hours we'd once spent together discussing books and movies. The meals we'd shared, at her place, mine, and out with our respective kids. The talks we'd had that skated around the possibility of a future together. The days and nights when I explored her multipurpose body parts.

"What?" she said.

"Nothing." I tapped out a quick response.

Sorry. Tied up at the moment. Rain check?

The judge's no-nonsense reply a few seconds later.

OK

I put the phone away. "You were saying."

"Well, the thing is. We've been through a lot together."

"True." My heart beating like a man climbing an out-of-order escalator. I thought briefly of the tidying I'd done earlier. The straightening up of my bedroom.

"I feel like you know me pretty well." Her eyes trained on my face.

"I think I do."

"And you've been very decent, given that it was me who walked away."

"For good reason," I said, studying the light emerald of her eyes as they studied me.

"What I was wondering, is . . ."

I waited.

She swallowed. "Would you be willing to be a reader on my new book?"

I blinked. "What?"

"The one I told you about. That day on campus. Dystopian science fiction? I've got the first draft done, but I could really use a second pair of eyes."

"That's what you wanted to ask me?"

"I know it's a big favor, Andy. But honestly, you're the first person I thought of. With how much you read? Plus, it's almost like you're a brother to me now. I'd really value your judgment."

Time slowed to a crawl. Make that a zombie-like shuffle. From a dystopian science fiction novel.

"Andy?"

"Yes," I said, rousing myself. I looked around. Time dusted itself off and went on its way. It was an ordinary, bustling late Saturday afternoon in a restaurant in German Village. Next to me sat my ex-girlfriend, concern in her eyes.

"I'm fine. Sorry. Yes. Your draft. Happy to read it."

"You're sure?"

"Of course. I'm excited for you. Anything I can do."

She smiled, squeezing my hand. "Thanks. I really appreciate it. I'll send it over in a day or two. And . . . one other favor?"

I took a long swig of beer. "Anything."

"How do I look?"

"How do you look?" Almost as surprising as the request to read a manuscript. Anne had never been one to solicit commentary on her appearance, despite what I considered her knockout features, scar or not.

"You look fantastic," I said, seeing no need to disguise my feelings at this point. "Pretty—no, beautiful. Plus, that's a great outfit."

"Thanks," she said. "I've got a date. I'm a little nervous."

"A date?" I said faintly.

"We met online. We've been e-mailing up until now. Don't worry, I've checked him out," she laughed, seeing the alarm on my face. "Turns out we're practically neighbors. He works at the library, actually. Isn't that funny?"

I told her it was funny.

She peeked at her watch. Minnie Mouse. She'd worn it as long as I'd known her. "Sorry—I've got to run. We're meeting at Little Palace, and you know parking over there."

"Indeed."

I left a twenty on the bar over her protests and walked her to her car. Before I knew what was happening, she wrapped her arms around me and hugged me.

"Thanks, Andy," she said, looking up at me. "I feel really good about this. I feel really good about life in general right now, if I'm being honest."

"That's great. Really, really great."

I stood on the sidewalk and watched her pull away, waving as she headed down Whittier. When she was gone, I pulled out my phone and stared at my text message exchange with the judge.

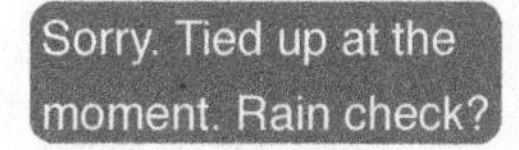

I replaced the phone in my pocket and walked toward home. It was a ten-minute stroll along the neighborhood's brick sidewalks, tops. The afternoon was mild. No need to tuck my hands into my pockets, though I did so anyway. As I walked, I remembered that I had a few chapters left in *Tigerland* and a new season of *Bosch* to catch up on. A fresh six of Black Label sat in my refrigerator. And of course, Hopalong, waiting as always for my entrance—and the possibility he could snag a treat or two. An evening to look forward to. Really, I could hardly wait.

Acknowledgments

As usual, it takes a village to keep a writer from screwing up. Thanks to Jen Del Carmen, Meredith Doench, Gerry Hudson, Todd Jacobson, Adam Nehman, Bill Parker, Chad Seeberg, Dawn Stock, Drew Wade, Martin Yant, and to the staff of Ohio University Press as always. A tip of the toothbrush to the real Dr. Debra Hurtt, superfan and dentist extraordinaire. A huge and special thanks to William McCulloh, Kenyon College classics professor emeritus, for lending his name to a fictional liberal arts college in Columbus. A special shout-out to Pam Welsh-Huggins for her ongoing love, support, and willingness to share cat-herding duties. This book is dedicated to Gillian Berchowitz, who greenlighted Andy's existence, leaned on him time and again to make him the best character he knows how to be, and was unceasingly generous with her encouragement and guidance. I appreciate her deeply, as does Andy. And Hopalong.